Donna Rae —

Someone to Love

WILD WIDOWS SERIES
BOOK THREE

Enjoy Adrian & Wynter!

MARIE FORCE

Someone to Love
Wild Widows Series, Book 3
By: Marie Force

Published by HTJB, Inc.
Copyright 2023. HTJB, Inc.
Cover Design by Kristina Brinton
Print Layout: E-book Formatting Fairies
ISBN: 978-1958035450

The Wild Widows Series—a Fatal Series Spin-Off

*"Listen—are you breathing just a little,
and calling it a life?"*
—Mary Oliver

One

Wynter

I knew I shouldn't have come here today. I hadn't planned to. So what if it's been one year since Jaden died? What makes this day any different from the three hundred and sixty-four that came before it? He's gone and coming to his gravesite doesn't ever make me feel better.

Why would it?

My twenty-two-year-old husband is buried six feet underground where I can never see him or touch him or talk to him again. What does it matter if I come here to stare at the stone marker with his name, JADEN MICHAEL HARTLEY, along with his lifespan in dates far too close together?

Officially changing my name from Wynter Snow, and yes, my mother thought that was a clever name that caused me no end of hell in school, to Wynter Hartley was one of the better days I've had as a widow.

Because I'm apparently an emotional cutter, I came. It's what's expected of me as his widow. I should visit him on the anniversary of his death. That means something to people.

It means nothing to me. It's just another day I have to get through without him to show me the way.

In the last year, I've learned that's something I have to figure out for myself. I'm no closer to knowing how to do that than I was the day he died. If anything, I feel further away from those answers than I did then.

With my Wild Widows friend Adrian's son, Xavier, strapped to my chest, I make my way up the steep hill to the spot Jaden's parents chose for his final resting place. I hate that I'm out of breath and sweating by the time I get to the top—every time. If Jaden is somehow still here, I hardly look my best showing up red-faced and out of breath. He used to tell me I had the prettiest face he'd ever seen. I doubt he'd say that now, with deep purple circles under my eyes that never seem to go away and new lines that bracket my mouth from frowning all the time.

What is there to smile about?

I feel like the best part of my life is behind me. How does someone go forward with that mindset?

Judging by the huge floral arrangements on either side of the headstone, Jaden's parents have already been here. Of course they brought gifts, and I came empty-handed. That about sums up my relationship with them—they do everything right and I don't. Or at least that's how they made me feel as Jaden slowly slipped away from us. As soon as I have that thought, I feel like a nasty, ungrateful bitch. They were always so good to me and never judged me. I was so busy judging myself during those brutal final weeks with Jaden that I barely had time to notice what they were doing.

Xavier lets out a soft coo to let me know I'm never alone when he's with me. Somehow I managed to convince Adrian to let me be his nanny, which has given my days the structure I badly needed. I had no idea how much I needed it until my life began to revolve around Xavier. Nothing takes your mind off your own problems quite like an infant with a diaper full of poop and an empty belly.

He's so sweet and happy. He's the one thing that can turn my frown upside down, as my always-cheerful mother likes to say. She drives me crazy with her peppy optimism and her this-too-shall-pass approach to my young widowhood.

What the hell does she know about it? She's never been married. To my knowledge, she's never been in a relationship that lasted more than six months. I was the result of a one-night stand with a man whose name she can't remember. Jaden and I were together for six years and would've been married the rest of our lives if it hadn't been for fucking bone cancer.

You might be asking how I could possibly know that, being as young as I am. When you know, you know. Jaden was it for me. He got me in a way that no one else ever has or ever will. From the day we met in ninth grade at a rave that neither of us was supposed to be at, we were soul mates. We crashed into each other in a mosh pit, and he grabbed me, keeping me from being trampled. He saved me then, and he saved me a hundred other times when I might've done something stupid to get myself killed. I had this weird desire to tempt fate back then, to do dangerous things, like riding on top of speeding cars and trying any drug that someone put in front of me. Doing that stuff made me feel alive because it didn't kill me.

Jaden was the one to tell me to cut that shit out and stop acting as if I didn't care if I lived or died. He cared, and that was enough to get me to stop risking my life.

And then he went and died on me. How is that fair?

"It's not fair, and you know it," I tell him as if he can hear me.

I kick the stone because that makes me feel a little better. For a second, anyway. And then I wonder if maybe he can feel me kicking him, which is ridiculous. Welcome to the madness that is my brain on grief.

Being here isn't doing a damned thing to help me, but at least the box is checked if Jaden is keeping score in heaven. I hate how early it gets dark this time of year. It's started to mist since I came up the hill, which will make my hair huge and the trip down that much more dangerous.

I used to love tempting fate, until I had someone else's baby strapped to my chest. Now there's nothing fun about danger. There've been days since I started working for Adrian that I honestly believe that my love for Xavier is the only thing keeping me alive.

No, I'm not being dramatic.

I didn't care about anything until I cared about him.

Funny how a person could change from being the biggest risk-taking daredevil to caring so much about a tiny boy that you'd give your own life if it meant saving him. He's the cutest little thing, with his pudgy brown cheeks and big dark eyes that look at me with so much love. Adrian keeps saying that Xavier needs a haircut, but I love his hair, which seems to get longer by the day. I even adore his tiny baby teeth and the way he drools when he smiles.

There's no way to overstate the impact this job has had on changing the trajectory of my widowhood. I've gone from total despair to having a spark of hope burning inside me. However, that spark is like a candle in a stiff breeze that could go out at any time.

If it does, I don't want to think about what would become of me.

Xavier has become tied to my survival.

It's that simple—and that complicated, because the longer I work for Adrian, the more I realize that I've developed one hell of a crush on my boss and friend. But who wouldn't crush on him? He's gorgeous, with brown skin, prominent cheekbones, the same dark eyes as his son and lips that have me thinking about kissing him far too often lately.

And what kind of an asshole am I to be dreaming about Adrian's lips when I'm visiting Jaden's grave? Widowhood is ridiculous in more ways than one.

I take one last look at Jaden's stone surrounded by the sunny yellow roses his mother insists on bringing for every occasion. "I'll be back. Not sure when, but I will. Don't go anywhere, okay?"

I chuckle at my own morbid joke as I begin the perilous trek down the hill.

One minute, I'm inching down the incline, and the next, I'm flying through the air with Xavier strapped to me.

We hit the ground hard. Thankfully, I land on my back, which knocks the wind out of me as I pitch forward again, rolling and turning and doing everything I can to protect the baby's fragile body from impact. This goes on for what feels like forever, and when it finally stops, I'm at the bottom of a weird ditch I've never noticed before. My left leg is bent at an awkward angle under me, and my back is screaming with a sharp pain that requires nearly all my attention just to keep breathing.

Xavier is so quiet that I immediately panic as the breath returns to my lungs in a great whoosh that makes me light-headed.

"Xavier! Sweetheart. Xavier!" With my hand on his back, I can tell he's still breathing, which is a huge relief. Maybe he slept through the calamity. That's possible, right?

I shift his weight on my chest and reach for my phone, which should be in my pocket.

Except it's not.

I feel all around us, hoping it's there, but the only thing I feel are damp leaves, rocks, sticks and cold water seeping through my clothes. My teeth begin to chatter as the skies open and the rain begins to fall in sheets.

What the hell am I going to do?

Adrian

EVERY MINUTE that passes with no word from Wynter takes a year off my life. Where in the hell is she with my child, and why isn't she answering her phone?

I made that a prerequisite to her employment: If I call you, you answer, no matter what else you might be doing.

Why the hell isn't she answering?

Gage and Iris are here, working the phones, but so far, they haven't gotten anywhere.

"Do you have a number for her mother?" Iris asks.

"I don't." I realize that was a major oversight on my part. I hired Wynter knowing she could be unpredictable. However, I never doubted her devotion to Xavier, which has been incredible since the day we met her, shortly after my wife died giving birth to him.

I was muddling through the swamp of grief and new parenthood until my mother-in-law died of a heart attack—or a broken heart if you ask me—leaving me without someone to care for Xavier while I'm working.

Wynter offered to help, our Wild Widows friends urged me to give her a chance, and here we are. I should call the cops, but I'm afraid to. Involving them is a last resort. Besides, the last freaking thing I need is child protective services breathing down my neck because my nanny was late getting home. A friend from high school went through a year-long nightmare with CPS after his daughter fell out of bed and broke her arm.

I'll give it another hour before I make that call.

"I think I have her mother's number at home somewhere."

Iris grabs her coat and heads for the door. "She reached out to me about Wynter joining the group."

My phone rings with a number I don't recognize.

As I pounce on it, Iris stops, waiting to hear if there's news before she leaves.

"Hello?"

"Is this Adrian?"

"Yes, it is. Who is this?"

"Wynter's mom, Ginger. Is she still there? I was expecting her home some time ago. We had dinner plans."

"No, and we can't find her or Xavier. I'm totally freaking out. Do you have a way to track her location?" That was another thing I should've insisted on with hindsight. What the hell do I know about being a single father to an infant?

"She stopped allowing me to track her after Jaden died."

My heart sinks. "Do you have any idea where she might be? I'm about to call the police."

"She didn't tell me her plans for the day, but it's the one-year anniversary of Jaden's death, so she may have gone to the cemetery, although she hates it there."

"Where's he buried?"

She tells me the location of a cemetery about four miles from my house. "He's at the top of a steep hill. You can't miss it."

"We'll take a look. If you hear anything from her—anything at all—please call me. I can't help but think the worst. She's got my son with her."

"She loves that baby with her whole heart and soul. She would never do anything to harm him."

"I know, but..."

"Let me know if you find her. I'll start calling her friends."

"Thank you."

I end the call as I run for the door with Iris and Gage following me.

"I'll drive," Gage says as Iris gets in the back seat. "You navigate."

I'm glad he gives me something to do since I feel like I'm coming out of my skin.

I use Waze to get us to the cemetery around the rush-hour traffic that's such a fact of life in Northern Virginia.

"Did we know today was Jaden's anniversary?" I ask them.

"No," Iris says with a grim note to her voice. "I should keep a list of these things."

She's the cofounder and de facto president of our Wild Widows group.

"You... You don't think she'd do something dramatic, do you?" The thought is so big and so overwhelming that I can barely wrap my head around it.

"Not with Xavier," Iris says emphatically. "No way."

The gates to the cemetery are closed when we arrive.

"There's her car!" Iris says, pointing to a vehicle inside the gates.

We park and get out of the car, going around the gates to run into the cemetery. I continue to call her phone, hoping it might lead me to her. What if she isn't here even though her car is? Where else will we look? I don't know much about her life beyond the things she's shared with our group, which isn't much.

"Wynter!" Gage calls out as he runs. "Wynter!"

I keep dialing the phone. Over and over and over again until I go mad listening to her voice mail message, which is quintessential Wynter: "Can't pick up. You know what to do."

"Wynter!" Iris yells.

In the distance, I hear the faint trill of a cell phone, or is that just wishful thinking?

"Do you hear a phone?" I ask Gage and Iris.

The three of us are puffing with exertion and shivering from the icy rain.

I dial it again.

We stop to listen.

"I hear it," Gage says. "This way."

We take off running again, calling for her as we go.

"Here! Help!"

Her voice is faint, but it's her.

I nearly collapse from the rush of relief that floods my system.

"Holy shit," Gage says. "She's at the bottom of a ditch. Call 911."

I dial the emergency number and detail the situation as best I can while watching Gage work his way down to them.

Wynter begins to cry as Gage reaches her.

"It's okay," he tells her. "We're here."

"Xavier…" I am almost afraid to ask.

"He's with her," Gage calls up to me. "He's breathing."

I start to cry, too. I'm shaking so hard, I can barely remain standing, and in that moment, I realize my fear is for both of them. At some point, she's become that important to me. I'm as worried for her as I am for my son.

Iris puts her arms around me. "They're going to be okay."

In the distance, I hear sirens, which means help is on the way.

I want to go down to them, but my legs won't cooperate. I drop to my knees and listen as Gage asks Wynter if she's hurt.

She says something about her knee and back.

I recall that I promised her mother I'd call if we found her. Somehow I manage to make that call.

"She fell at the cemetery. EMS is on the way."

"Oh my goodness. Is she all right? Is the baby?"

"She's hurt but okay. The baby seems fine. We don't know yet for sure." Would they tell me if Xavier wasn't fine? Why isn't he crying or making any noise? It's not possible for me to lose anyone else. I'd never survive it.

"Let me know where they're taking her?" Wynter's mother asks.

"I will."

"Thank God you found them."

"Yes, thank God."

Two

Wynter

I 've never been colder in my life. Despite heated blankets, I continue to shiver uncontrollably. The nurses say it's due to shock and that it'll stop when the medication they're giving me through an IV kicks in.

Any time now. Normally, medical stuff freaks me out more than just about anything, but after worrying that I might've killed Xavier, a few needles don't bother me.

"Have you heard how Xavier is?" I ask Iris, who rode with me in the ambulance and has stuck around even after my mother showed up to cry all over me.

"He's just fine," Iris tells me. "Adrian said he checked out with just a few bumps and bruises. You did a great job keeping him safe."

"No, I didn't." Tears spill down my cheeks. "He got hurt because of me."

"It was an accident, Wynter." Iris mops up my tears with a tissue. "All that matters is you're both safe."

Adrian will never trust me with his son again after this,

and how can I blame him? I had one job—keep his son safe—and now he's in the hospital with bumps and bruises on his fragile little body. It's unbearable to think of Xavier being hurt or cold or anything other than perfectly fine.

That little man has worked his way so deeply into my heart that he'll live there forever, even if Adrian never lets me see him again.

A deep sob erupts from my chest at the thought of never seeing that precious baby again. He's become my lifeline, my reason for being, the thing that gets me out of bed in the morning when it would be so much easier to pull the covers over my head and hide from the world. I did that for months before my mother forced me to attend a Wild Widows meeting. I did it for a while after that, too. Nothing happens quickly or easily in this grief journey. The widows did their best to build me up, but it didn't take right away.

Mostly because I was trying so hard to stay rooted in my life with Jaden.

Moving forward meant leaving him behind, which was too excruciating to imagine at first. But a funny thing happened over time. It became more exhausting to stay in bed than it was to get up and deal.

The doctor I saw in the ER comes in with the nurse who's been caring for me since they admitted me. I had numerous cuts and scrapes that they cleaned and bandaged after they sent me for X-rays of my knee and back.

"Good news," the doctor says. "Your knee is lightly strained, and your back is clear of any serious injuries. Nothing broken or torn in either place. You'll be sore for a few days, but you should bounce back quickly. We'll get you warmed up and rehydrated and have you out of here in the morning."

I should be thankful the news isn't worse, and I am. Of course I am.

It's just that I feel sick that it happened in the first place.

What was I doing taking Xavier with me to the cemetery of all places?

My mom strokes my arm and forehead, trying to get me to settle down, but how can I do that when all I can think about is how badly this could've ended?

It never occurred to me before we went that it might not be a good idea. I was just going to stop by to see Jaden on the anniversary of his death, which needed to be done during the day while I have Xavier. I wasn't about to go there at night.

Thinking about how Xavier might've been killed in the fall has me trembling harder than ever.

The nurse puts something into my IV that has an immediate effect. Whatever that was, give me more of it.

My eyes won't stay open, so I don't fight the need to sleep.

When I wake up, Adrian is there with Xavier asleep in his arms.

He seems relieved I'm awake, but with one look at his handsome face, I can see the strain of the stressful day in his puffy eyes and a pulse in his cheek that's new. "Hey. How're you feeling?"

I take a quick second to figure that out. "Okay, I guess." I'm not shivering wildly anymore, which is an improvement, but I'm aching all over. "How is he?"

"He's fine."

"What about you?"

"My nerves are a bit shot, but I'm okay if you guys are."

"I'm sorry, Adrian." My voice catches on another sob. "I'm so, so sorry."

"It was an accident. There's nothing to be sorry about."

"I shouldn't have taken him there. It's just... I... I never thought anything could happen." Tears slide down my cheeks. "I wanted to see Jaden. It started to rain..."

"Shhh." He pats my shoulder. "It's okay. Everything is okay."

13

"You must've been so scared when you couldn't find us. I'm sorry I put you through that."

"I was scared for both of you."

"I'm sure you thought I'd done something terrible—"

"I know how much you love Xavier. The doctor said you took the brunt of the fall to protect him."

I'm crying so hard, I can barely breathe, which makes me feel weak and stupid in front of Adrian. I want him to see me as a responsible adult whom he can trust with his precious son, and instead, I must look like a blathering idiot emotional girl child.

"You did everything right," Adrian insists. "You protected him and got hurt yourself so he wouldn't."

"I sh-shouldn't have taken him there."

"You wanted to see Jaden on his anniversary. I get it." He sits next to my bed with the baby on his chest. "I wish you'd told us it was his anniversary. We could've gone with you or done something so you wouldn't have been alone."

"I didn't want to deal with it at all. I can't believe it's been a year already. How is that even possible?"

"Time marches forward with a ruthlessness that's almost shocking when you've been through what we have."

"Yeah," I say softly, "it sure does."

I'm so tired I can barely keep my eyes open, but I don't want to stop talking to him. I'm relieved that he doesn't seem mad. I want to ask if he's still going to let me take care of Xavier. I'm not sure if this is the time to ask.

How can I make him understand how important Xavier has become to my own survival? If he decides not to let me watch him anymore... That can't happen. I don't know what I'd do without him to give me purpose. Taking care of Jaden was all-consuming for months before he passed. Even though our days in the hospital were full of nightmarish things I'll never forget, I had somewhere to be, someone who needed me, something to do. Without that after he died, my thoughts were like a balloon that had come untied, zipping all around with no point to anything.

Xavier has given me a reason.

That's the last thought I have before sleep—and whatever they put in that IV—drags me under.

Adrian

I HATE BEING A WIDOWER. I hate everything about it, especially days like this in which my whole life was briefly turned upside down and the only one I wanted by my side was the one person who'll never be there again. I yearn for Sadie, my wife, my love, my everything. She knew what to do in any situation, and without her, I'm like a top spinning out of control. At least that's how it feels.

I took a huge chance on Wynter, allowing her to care for my precious son while I'm at work, and until today, things had been going great. Xavier loves her, and vice versa. She's become a huge part of our daily lives, and I find myself looking forward to the time I get with her at the beginning and end of every day. She's fun, funny, playful with Xavier and hugely important to my ability to work without worrying every second I'm away from my son.

I'd begun to exhale ever so slightly since the one-two punch of losing Sadie and then her mom, who'd been such an incredible source of support to me always, but especially after Sadie died.

Alyssa and I had existed in a state of shock and despair lessened only by the presence of Xavier, who made it impossible for me or his grandmother to wallow in our loss. He needed us, and we needed him. And then Alyssa was gone, too, taken from us as suddenly as Sadie had been.

For a brief time today, I had to entertain the possibility that I could lose Xavier, too, and in that moment of darkness, I realized he's the one thing keeping me going. Without him... I just don't think I could go on. I know that must sound dramatic, but in the span of a few months, I lost my wife and the mother-in-law I loved deeply.

Alyssa showed me how to be part of a family, which was all new to me after a chaotic upbringing. Losing Alyssa had been an enormous blow on top of Sadie's death. They said a massive heart attack killed her, but I know she died of a broken heart.

Sadie and her sisters were her whole world, and when we lost Sadie, Alyssa struggled to go on. I witnessed that struggle every day as she showed up to care for me and Xavier. She got me through those first horrible weeks without Sadie as I tried to figure out how to be a single father to a baby who needed everything, especially a mother he would never know.

I can't even think about that time without wanting to wail at the sheer injustice of Sadie never getting to hold the baby she loved with all her heart from the first second we knew he was on the way.

My heart aches when I think of her missing everything with him. From the time she was a little girl, all she ever wanted was to be a mother. She used to say that sometimes she felt like she was setting back feminism by making motherhood her life's goal. When we first met and she told me that, I was a little freaked out. I won't lie. I mean, we'd only just started dating, and she was talking about how many babies she wanted?

The thing about Sadie, though, was that when she wanted something—really wanted it—she could make me want it, too. Her whole face would light up when she talked about our future children and how beautiful they would be because their parents were gorgeous. We'd laugh about that, at our own silliness, but when I say she wanted that baby like she'd never wanted anything else, I mean it.

She died of an amniotic fluid embolism, which occurs when the amniotic fluid enters the mother's bloodstream. Most of the time, that's not a problem, but in rare cases, the mother has a severe allergic reaction to it, which is what happened to Sadie. They said it comes on so quickly that the mother often dies before the doctor can react.

Alyssa and I spoke to several lawyers about whether we should sue. Each of them said the same thing. It would be a costly grind with no guarantee of ultimate success since what happened to Sadie is a known complication of childbirth. We'd been considering taking on the costly grind when Alyssa died, and all the fight went out of me. Sadie had life insurance through her work, which I've put away for future college tuition. I'm able to cover all our expenses on my salary, but it's tight, which is why I'm thinking about maybe adding a bartending shift once a week to the schedule. I tell myself that Xavier and I have what we need to survive.

But surviving without Sadie has been the hardest part.

For the first few months, I operated in a fog of grief and disbelief and fear. The fear was palpable. I was now solely responsible for the tiny infant we created together, which felt like a cosmic joke of epic proportions. That the parent least equipped to be alone with our child was the one left to raise him.

My sister and I grew up in and out of foster care as our mother battled a number of emotional issues that led to substance abuse. What do I know about raising a child? I have a niece and nephew I'm close to, but they've never been my responsibility. Loving them didn't prepare me for what was now expected of me.

Alyssa was there in the early, dark days to show me the way. As we united in profound grief over the loss of Sadie, she taught me how to feed him, change him, soothe him, play with him. I was just getting my legs back under me when she dropped dead.

Today I had a couple of hours to fear what I'd do if Xavier —and Wynter—were gone, too.

With the way things have gone for me this last year, I know now anything is possible. Even the unthinkable.

Iris comes into the room to check on Wynter, who's still sleeping.

"You ought to take him home to bed," Iris whispers to me. "I can stick around."

"Where did her mom go?"

"I think she left."

"Really?"

"She said something about having to work early and she'd check on her in the morning."

I may never be father of the year, but if my kid was in the hospital for any reason, there's only one place I'd be.

"Who's with your kids?" I ask her.

"My mom. It's all good. I can stay."

"I'll be back in the morning."

"Check in with me first. They'll probably release her."

"All right." I stand and readjust Xavier so I can carry him to the car. My guy is getting big. He'll be a year old soon, and he's starting to look more like a little boy than a baby.

"I know you're probably still in panic mode," Iris says, "but keep reminding yourself that everything and everyone is all right, okay?"

"Yeah, I will. Thanks for everything, Iris. Today and always."

I never would've survived losing Sadie and Alyssa without Iris and the rest of the Wild Widows. They've become my North Star in this journey, and I'd be lost without them.

"Love you," Iris says with the stark simplicity I've come to appreciate. If she loves you, she tells you.

"Love you, too." I'd never said those words to another living soul, except my sister and her family, until I said them to Sadie. Now I say them all the time to the friends who've become my second family. I know now how important it is to say the words, to tell the people you love how you feel because you never know when they'll be taken from you.

I hate thinking that way. I never used to be like that. I had no reason to. Sure, my childhood was a chaotic mess, but my sister and I survived. Our mother lives in Florida now with a guy she married five years ago who has, by all accounts, given her a nice life. She deserves that after overcoming so many challenges. We talk once in a while, but she's not really part of my daily life.

That's all right. Plenty of people in my life who love Xavier and me, and I'm thankful for every one of them.

In the waiting room, Gage looks up from his phone when he sees me. "Heading home?"

Nodding, I say, "I don't feel right about leaving her."

"Iris and I will be here. Xavier needs a good night's sleep, and so do you."

Who are these people willing to give up their own good night of sleep for a friend in need? They're the best friends I've ever had. "Thank you for staying."

"No worries."

"I'll see you tomorrow."

"Sounds good."

I walk out to the car and buckle Xavier into his seat.

He never stirs. From the beginning, he's been an excellent sleeper, which is such a blessing. At least I'm not intensely sleep-deprived on top of everything else.

At home, I change his diaper and dress him in a sleeper before putting him in his crib.

I stand over him, staring down at his perfect little face, thanking the heavens for his safety, for Wynter's safety, for the friends who sustain me.

Despite my losses, I'm blessed beyond measure, and I know it.

I miss Sadie with every fiber of my being, but over the last few months, I've tried to make peace with what happened, and I feel ready to move on with my life.

Today was yet another reminder that life is short and must be lived to the fullest.

It's time to get back to living rather than just existing.

I'm not sure what living entails anymore, but as soon as Wynter is back on her feet, I'm going to figure that out.

Three

Iris

My heart is broken for Wynter, who's worked so hard to gain Adrian's trust by diligently caring for Xavier. When they were missing earlier, a million scenarios went through my head, and I'm ashamed now to admit that some of them cast Wynter in a negative light. I love Wynter. I truly do, but she can be erratic and unpredictable at times, although never with Xavier. That I know of, anyway.

When Adrian asked our opinions of hiring her to be Xavier's nanny, I supported the idea. I would leave her with my kids. Is she young and sometimes outrageous and often sullen? Yes, but I've seen the way she's suffered over the loss of her young husband. I have no doubt she loved him with her whole heart and losing him sent her sideways.

I was in my thirties when I lost my husband. She was twenty when she lost hers.

Twenty.

When I was twenty, I was barely able to make it to work

on time, let alone mourn the loss of the person I'd loved the most.

She's become a very big part of my life since she joined the Wild Widows—against her will, I might add. Her mother made her come, but Wynter kept coming, and over time, her rough edges began to soften a bit as the first early days of gritty grief gave way to an acceptance of sorts.

It's been thrilling to see her thrive as Xavier's nanny. There's a sparkle to her in recent months that wasn't there before she had the new purpose that Xavier brought to her life. For so long, her days revolved around caring for her sick boyfriend, who became her husband shortly before he died. After he was gone, she floundered.

I certainly understood that. When my husband, Mike, died in a plane crash, leaving me with three young kids to care for, my life spun completely out of control for a while. The shock, the grief, the sheer madness of suddenly becoming a single parent... I'll never forget the raw agony of those early days and weeks.

That agony is what propelled me and my friends Tracy and Christy to start the Wild Widows in the first place. Being a young widow is a uniquely awful proposition, and having the support of others who get it makes all the difference. I know we've helped Wynter and so many others who've joined our ranks over the years. Our core group has become a family, and there's so much comfort in those friendships.

Wynter groans as she awakens, turning toward me and seeming surprised to see me there. "Hey."

"How're you feeling?"

"Sore and thirsty."

I help her take a sip of the ice water a nurse left on her table.

"Did Adrian leave?"

"He took Xavier home to bed. He said he'll be back to check on you in the morning."

"What about my mom?"

"She said she has to work early and will see you tomorrow."

Wynter closes her eyes. "You don't have to stay."

"Yes, I do."

"Really, Iris. I'm fine. Go home and get some sleep."

"I don't mind staying."

"Why do you do this stuff?" she asks, keeping her eyes closed.

"What stuff?"

"Spend a night in the hospital next to someone you barely know when you've got your own family to worry about."

The comment is so typically Wynter, it almost makes me laugh. She's the bluntest human being I've ever met. I place my hand on top of hers. "You're my family, too, Wynter. Don't you know that by now?"

I'm surprised when her response is a deep sob.

"Aw, sweetie." I sit on the edge of the bed and hold out my arms to her.

She sits up, slowly and painfully, and falls into my embrace. "I've never known anyone as kind as you are."

I hold her tightly, the way I would my own child, and let her cry it out. "I'm here for you. Always and forever. You're stuck with me and Gage and the rest of us."

"I was so scared that Xavier was hurt," she says between sobs. "I don't know what I would've done if he was."

"He's fine because you made sure of it." I smooth the hair back from her face. "You protected him."

"I keep reliving it in my mind, realizing I was falling with him in my arms and fearing I would crush him or something." Her entire body shudders. "I love him so much."

"I know you do. We all know that, especially Adrian."

23

"He won't let me take care of him anymore."

"Sure he will. He knows how much you love him."

"I do. I love him more than anything." She takes a deep breath that hitches with sobs. "After Jaden died, I thought I'd never love anyone or anything again because it was too painful to love someone that much."

"I understand that."

"And now I love Xavier that much, and I can't handle it. I just can't. If anything ever h-happened to him…"

"Shhh, Wynter, sweetheart, nothing is going to happen to him."

"How can you say that? We both know anything terrible can happen."

"Sure, but the likelihood is so incredibly low."

"Look at what happened today… It's not low. It can happen at any time. It's just easier not to care."

"Let me ask you something." I pull back so I can see her face. "If you didn't watch Xavier, would that mean you didn't love him anymore?"

As her chin quivers, she looks so achingly young. "N-no. I love him. I'll always love him."

"So wouldn't it be better to keep him in your life than to love him from a distance?"

She shakes her head. "It wouldn't be better. I'm not the right person to care for him."

"Did you think that yesterday? That you weren't the right person to care for him?"

"No, but…"

"No buts. Yesterday, you knew you were the best person to care for him because you love him like your own. What happened was an *accident*, Wynter."

"What if something like that happens again and he doesn't survive? What if I'm driving and someone hits us or hits him when we're out for a walk, or he drowns in your pool, or—"

"Stop. Sweetheart... Stop. You'll drive yourself mad with what-ifs."

"It's all I can think about. What if he'd died because of me?"

"He didn't."

"But he could have. I could've crushed him or broken his little neck or—"

"Stop. Kids are much stronger than we think they are. Did I ever tell you about the time I left Laney on my bed and went to take a shower? I came back, and she was gone. She'd rolled right off the bed onto the floor. I totally freaked out thinking she was dead, but she'd fallen asleep after she landed."

"And she wasn't hurt?"

"Nope. My mother told me kids are made of super elastic bubble plastic. Did you play with that when you were a kid?"

"Yeah," she says with the first hint of a smile.

"It's true. More often than not, they bounce. Do they get hurt sometimes? Sure, but everyone does. That's part of being alive. I fell on the pool deck last week chasing a raccoon out of my garbage cans. I have a massive bruise on my hip. At first, I thought my hip had to be broken, but it's not. I bounced." I tuck a strand of her dark hair behind her ear, which boasts multiple piercings along the edge. "Xavier bounced. You bounced. Everyone is fine."

"This time."

"Listen, I know you have good reason to anticipate disaster. You've already seen more of it than some people do in a lifetime. You're programmed now to expect the worst. But in reality, that's not what usually happens."

It occurs to me right in that moment that hanging out with a bunch of widows might be the worst possible thing for Wynter. Our very existence makes her point. Bad things happen all the time, and we have no control over them. Before

25

I can process that realization, Gage comes into the room to check on us.

"You're here, too?" Wynter asks. "You two need to get a life."

"Haha," I say, smiling. "We have a very nice life, and you're part of it whether you want to be or not."

"I do want to be. Of course I do. I just don't want to hurt anymore." She looks down at her fingers, which are linked. "I thought if I could get through the first year, everything would be better, but it's not. It's exactly the same, but it's been a year."

"The first anniversary is a kick in the teeth that way," Gage says.

He ought to know. He lost his wife and twin daughters to a drunk driver.

"It's like a beacon in the distance beckoning you forward, saying if you can just get to me, you'll be okay. And then you get there, somehow, someway, and it's the same thing, different day. They're still gone. You're still alone. What the hell difference does a year make?"

"None," Wynter says softly. "It makes no difference."

"Want to know something else?" Gage asks her.

"I guess."

"Same thing happens the second year and the third."

Wynter groans and puts her hands over her ears.

"Was that really necessary?" I ask him.

He grins. "When my girls found out about Santa at school, we told them the truth about the Easter Bunny and tooth fairy, too."

I stare at him in disbelief. "That's brutal!"

"One fell swoop, we said. Get it over with. No sense perpetuating myths." To Wynter, he adds, "The anniversaries suck. They'll continue to suck forever. The sooner you realize that, the less power they have over you."

"I suppose that's true," I say.

"It is true. And it's better to know these things than to be under some ridiculous illusion that things are going to suddenly get better at year one, two or three. The sharp edges soften over time, but they're still sharp."

"You guys are the wisest people I've ever known," Wynter says.

"That's nice of you to say," Gage says, "but wisdom is always hard-earned. Someday, you're going to be in a position to guide and counsel someone going through what you have, and you'll share the wisdom you've gained with them."

"I appreciate you sharing yours with me," she says.

"Any time," Gage says.

"I want you guys to go home. There's no need for you to stay. I promise I'm okay."

I exchange glances with Gage, and he shrugs, letting me know it's up to me.

"Go," Wynter says.

I put my hand on her arm. "Call me if you need me during the night?"

She nods. "I will, but I'm tired, so I won't need you."

"Still, if you do..." I don't feel right about leaving her alone.

"I know how to find you."

"I'll be back in the morning to drive you home," I tell her.

"I can Uber."

"I'll be back to drive you."

"Fine," Wynter says in the testy tone that's much more in keeping with her usual sassy self than the devastation that's broken my heart on her behalf.

"Fine." I lean in to kiss her cheek. "Love you."

"Love you, too. Both of you."

Gage kisses her forehead. "Love you, kiddo." He holds the door for me to go out ahead of him.

"I don't feel right about leaving her alone," I tell him when we're in the hallway.

"She's not alone. The nurses will check on her, and she said she's tired." He puts an arm around me as we walk to the elevator. "She'll get some sleep, and so will we."

"I couldn't believe her mother left," I say. "Where would I be if one of my kids was in the hospital, even if they're twenty-one?"

"You'd be with your kid, but not everyone is the kind of mother you are."

"I'm going to invite Wynter to stay with us for a while. I'm home during the day, so I can be there for her."

"You don't have to do that, Iris."

"I know, but I want to. I want her to have the support she needs right now."

We walk to the car, and he holds the passenger door for me, even though I've told him he doesn't have to. When I'm seated, he leans in to kiss me. "We're all lucky to have you in our lives, especially me."

I reach up to caress his face. "We're both lucky." After I lost Mike, the last thing I wanted was another relationship. Gage and I were friends for quite some time before things changed between us. Or, I should say, before I changed things between us by "accidentally" sneaking naked into his bed during a Wild Widows getaway at the beach.

Sorry not sorry. That was the best thing I've ever done for both of us. I'd forgotten what it felt like to be happy the way I am with him, and I know he feels the same way. After years of grief and pain, we've found a happy chapter two, and we're loving every minute of it, especially after a tumultuous first few months together. I found out Mike had been leading a double life and had another child, and Gage finally settled the case against the man who killed his family. We were working our way toward a new happily ever after when he found a lump in my breast that turned out to be stage zero cancer.

We're through all that now, on the other side of the insane few months that marked the beginning of our official relationship, and life is sweet. My kids love him, I love him, and he takes such good care of us. We're blessed—and we know it. Widowhood has taught us both to be thankful for every good day, every smile, every second of joy, because you never know when it will end.

My phone chimes with a text from Roni Connolly, another of our Wild Widows.

Heard about what happened with Wynter. Is she ok? Is Adrian? What can we do?

She's okay, resting in the hospital after taking the brunt of the fall to protect Xavier. Adrian is fine—now—but he was a mess earlier when he couldn't reach her. Poor Wynter had gone to the cemetery to visit Jaden on the first anniversary and fell down a hill with Xavier in her arms.

Oh no... I'm so glad they're safe. She must've been so upset.

She was, but she's doing better. She sent me and Gage home. I'll go back in the AM, and I'll invite her to stay with me for a while.

Where was her mother?

She came for a bit and then left bc she had to work in the AM.

Seriously?

Yep.

I don't want to judge her, and yet...

I was surprised when she left. Wynter didn't seem to be.

Hmmm. Is our meeting still on for tomorrow?

Let me make sure Wynter is up for it, and I'll let you know.

Sounds good. Hit me up if there's anything we can do. Give her our love.

I will!

Roni and her fiancé, Derek Kavanaugh, both lost their spouses to murder and later met in their Capitol Hill neighborhood. They work at the White House, he as deputy chief of staff to President Nick Cappuano, and she as communications director for First Lady Sam Cappuano.

It's been amazing to watch them fall in love and to blend their families. His daughter, Maeve, and Roni's son, Dylan, will grow up as siblings. They make me wish I could wave a magic wand and find a new happily ever after for each of my Wild Widows if that's what they want.

We arrive home to a quiet house with only a light on over the kitchen island.

"I'm starving," I tell Gage. "Are you?"

"I could eat something."

I make us sandwiches from leftover turkey that I made for Sunday dinner with my parents. We sit together at the breakfast nook that looks out over my backyard, where the pool is covered for the winter.

"Did I tell you this turkey is the best I've ever tasted?" Gage asks after he's eaten half of the sandwich he topped with stuffing and cranberry sauce.

"You might've mentioned that a time or two."

"It's so good."

"Thanks to the brining. That's the secret."

"I'm a convert."

I look over at him, so handsome in a rough-hewn sort of way that might not have appealed to me in an earlier life. Now I look at him and see everything I've ever wanted and things I never dared to dream of for myself. "This is nice."

"What is?"

"Having this little minute to ourselves after a stressful day. I'd forgotten what it was like to have someone to lean on during difficult times."

"Me, too. But I sort of thought we were through the difficult times."

We celebrated the end of my radiation treatments and have been on a high ever since. "We both know we're never totally out of the woods on the hard stuff."

"Makes me yearn for the days when I chose not to get involved with anyone."

"Stop," I tell him. "You don't yearn for that."

"Sometimes I do, like when I see Wynter and Adrian so upset. I want to run from that and hide."

"But you didn't, because you care too much about them to run away when they need you."

"Yeah, and that's the problem. Caring too much."

"I'd rather care too much than not at all. That's no kind of life."

"No, it isn't, which I've discovered since you forced me to fall in love with you and your kids."

"I forced you," I say with a laugh. "Sure."

"You did. I was minding my own business when you snuck into my bed all naked and sexy."

"That was an accident."

His bark of laughter is the best thing ever, because he didn't laugh for years after he lost his family. Now he laughs all the time, and every laugh is a victory to me. "Accident, my ass."

I send him a hooded glance. "Your ass is rather nice." Flirting with him is my favorite thing. I would've thought I'd forgotten how to flirt, but I've discovered a whole new level of skill since we've been together.

"Not as nice as yours."

"We can agree to disagree," I say as I gather our plates and take them to the sink.

He's right behind me, pressing his erection against my back.

"What's going on?" I ask, all innocence.

His low growl makes me laugh. With his hands on my hips, he directs me out of the kitchen and up the stairs to our room, the room I redecorated after I lost Mike and which has now become ours, since Gage moved in with us. My mother is asleep in the guest room. She's such a huge help to me any time I need her.

"I need to check on the kids."

"They're fine. Your mom checked on them before she went to bed."

That's true, and I know it, but I want to see them for myself. "I'll be quick."

His sigh is full of frustration and impatience. "Move it or lose it."

"It always comes back," I say over my shoulder as I head for Tyler's room.

As usual, the covers are more off than on my son. I recover him, kiss his sweaty head and whisper that I love him. Sophia and Laney are also uncovered, so I give them the same treatment. I love them so much, it's ridiculous. Since I was treated for early-stage breast cancer, I love them even more than I did before.

I'm so lucky it was caught early and treated effectively. My doctor says I shouldn't have to worry about it again, but it's made me extra grateful for my three beautiful, healthy kids. Being a single mom is a grind. There've been times in the years since I lost Mike that I wasn't as grateful as I should've been. Everything is different now that I know how truly lucky I am to have them and our good health.

The little things that used to bug me—the constant bickering, the mess, the nonstop demands, the endless laundry—seem different now. I'm all about the gratitude these days, and I want to pay that forward to anyone who needs it.

Gage is already in bed when I enter the bedroom, heading

for the bathroom to brush my teeth and apply the face cream that keeps the wrinkles away, or at least I hope it will.

I don't bother with clothes that'll come off the second I land in bed with him. We're still in that ravenous stage that comes with new love. I keep thinking it'll cool off eventually, but if anything, the opposite has been true. The more we have, the more we want.

It's funny because I didn't really miss sex that much after Mike died. I was too busy trying to care for three grieving little kids while keeping my own head above water. I had one quick fling shortly after Mike died to get the "first time" with someone else over with, and then nothing until years later with Gage.

But ever since the night I "accidentally" crawled into Gage's bed, sex has moved from the back burner to the front, and that burner is set to high.

Gage makes me feel like a teenager experiencing this for the first time, and I know he feels the same way. As much as I loved Mike and Gage loved Natasha, the fire between us burns hot. For a while, we both felt guilty about that, but we've gotten over it as time has gone on. We have no choice but to continue to live without the people we've lost. Our relationship brings us joy and a cautious kind of happiness, tinged now with the knowledge that it can be ripped away from us at any time.

He's ready for me when I get in bed and has me under him and wrapped up in him in a matter of seconds. His kisses are devouring, his hands setting me on fire and his hard cock pressing into me. The intensity with him is new to me. I loved sex with Mike, but it wasn't like this. It didn't make me feel possessed in the best way possible. It didn't wipe every other thought from my head, forcing me to focus only on him as we chase the highest of highs.

"Iris..."

"Hmm?"

"I want you to know..."

"What?"

"I love the way you love us all. The way you're so there for Wynter, as if she's your own kid."

"I love her."

"I know, and that makes me love you even more than I already do." He kisses me softly and then more intently, his tongue twisting with mine as he pushes into me, triggering the orgasm that's been building from the second he touched me.

"Yes," he whispers as he joins me, holding me so tightly, I can barely breathe, but who needs to breathe when the man you love is finding such pleasure in your arms? "God, Iris... What you do to me."

"You do the same to me."

We have this discussion almost every time. We're still amazed to have found this incredible second act with each other. Sometimes I have to remind myself that most of my closest friends are still grieving, still focused more on the past than the future. I have to be careful not to let my profound happiness with Gage make me inaccessible to them. Supporting my fellow widows has become a calling in this new life, and I have no intention of stepping away from them now that I've found a new love.

With my head resting on Gage's chest, I start to drop off into sleep, thinking of Adrian and Wynter and hoping they're able to get some rest after the traumatic day they had.

Four

Wynter

I dream of the wildest things. Jaden and I are at the top of a reservoir we used to visit with our high school friends. Our parents prohibited us from swimming there, fearing something awful would happen if we swam without lifeguards or a safety net. We didn't care. We were young and stupid and fearless.

Jaden used to jump from the highest-possible spot. I never told him how scared I was of him somehow killing himself. He didn't just jump. No, he had to do flips and other crazy things on the way down. It was okay if I did that stuff. I couldn't stand watching him do it.

The dream takes me right back there, as if it were only yesterday when he was able to climb to the highest part of the rock formation and launch himself into the air, spinning and flipping like it was no big deal before landing in a perfect dive.

Our friends are dazzled by him. We dare each other to try to do what he did, but none of us has the nerve. It's the summer before life as we know it changes forever, the summer before a lump on his shinbone threatened his survival in a way the reservoir dives never did.

I'm back in that small, airless room in a local hospital, where a doctor told us the lump was something called Ewing sarcoma. At first we didn't realize that meant he had cancer because the doctor never used that word. That realization came later when we googled Ewing sarcoma and found out just how bad it was.

The dreams carry me through surgeries, treatments that made him so sick, he could barely function, more appointments at which the news was never good, the amputation of the bottom half of his right leg, the despair that set in after that as he tried to come back from such a devastating loss.

It's so real, as if it's happening again. I can reach out and touch Jaden's blond hair, his handsome face, the chest that was once so well defined with muscles he'd developed playing football and soccer since he was a little kid.

I come out of it with a start, my eyes opening to my own hospital room, the nightmare of the previous day flooding me with memories I'd much rather forget. The incident at the cemetery with Xavier is mixed into the memories of Jaden's illness, his decline and death.

My heart races as tears fill my eyes and spill down my cheeks. How is it possible to hurt this much and still be alive? I've asked myself that question a lot in the year since Jaden died. We did everything together, often to the exclusion of our peers, which left me frighteningly alone when he died. I didn't have tons of other close friends. I had him. And he had me. We had what we needed.

People from both our lives showed up to his service. The funeral home told his parents that his was one of the biggest they'd ever handled. Part of me thinks people came because they were so freaked out that someone our age could actually die, especially someone like Jaden, who'd been so full of life.

They certainly didn't come for me. Half the girls hated me because he loved me. The boys resented me because he stopped hanging out with them after we started dating.

I was invisible to most of them. I haven't seen any of them since the funeral.

I'm fine with that. I don't need them. I didn't then, and I don't now.

I have new friends, people who understand my grief, who don't push me to get over him the way my mother does, who hold space for me in my time of need and don't try to fix the unfixable. They don't tell me I'm young and I'll fall in love a million times before I find "the one." I had "the one," and I lost him. And yes, it's possible to know at fourteen, fifteen, sixteen, seventeen, eighteen, nineteen, twenty that you've found the person you want to spend your life with. I'll fight anyone who says otherwise.

If I hear that one more time—you're young, you have so much time to find someone else—I'm apt to kill the person who says it. Especially if that person happens to be my mother, who says it as often as she possibly can. She doesn't want to hear that it hurts me every time she suggests that Jaden was my starter love. The real one is still to come, she says.

I've had the time to understand that's probably true, but I also know this to be true—if Jaden hadn't died, we would've been together the rest of our lives. Period. Full stop. The end. I can't stand when clueless people say that he was my "starter love." I really don't want to hear that bullshit. He was my whole heart, my soul, my happiness, my everything.

Part of me thinks my mother is jealous of what I had with him, because she's never come close to having that with the many men who've cycled through her life. And she knows it. That makes her bitter, I think. Imagine being jealous of your own kid who lost the love of her life at twenty. It's sick. She's sick. I love her, and I wouldn't have gotten through this last year without her, but sometimes I hate her, too.

She loves to remind me that she was twenty when she had me. I want to remind her that she made a mess of everything with me, that she was in no way ready to be a mother when I was born, and that it took me falling in love with Jaden and getting to know his amazing parents to see what'd been missing from my childhood. Things like stability, routine, common sense... The list goes on and on. I rarely made it to school on time. Jaden got the perfect attendance award when we graduated, which required him to be on time as well as present every day.

Even after he was diagnosed with cancer, he never missed a day of his senior year. He was so determined to keep his perfect attendance record going. On the other hand, it was a big deal if I got there before the first bell because no one at home was pushing me out the door the way they were at his house.

My mother simply didn't care if I made it to school on time. Even after the truant officer visited us, she still didn't care. I tried harder to be on time after that because I didn't want to have to go to summer school, which was the threat. I barely graduated from high school, while Jaden was a National Honor Society graduate with scholarship offers to multiple colleges.

He'd had to turn them all down, though. He was too sick by then to go to college, but I made sure his scholarship offers were listed in his obituary so people would know he'd been going places before cancer ruined everything.

A nurse comes into the room, moving so quietly, I almost don't hear her until she's right on top of me. "Oh, you're awake. Are you all right?"

Define *all right*. "Yeah. Just couldn't sleep."

"We could give you something for that."

"That's okay."

"Are you in any pain?"

"Nothing I can't handle."

"Can I get you anything?"

"I'm a little hungry."

"Let me see what I can find."

She returns a few minutes later with a bowl of chicken noodle soup and crackers. "This is the best I can do at three in the morning."

"It smells good."

She helps me sit up and turns on a soft light over the bed.

The movement to the sitting position reveals soreness I didn't notice before.

I gasp from the pain that radiates through me.

"I'll get you something for that," she says on her way out of the room.

The soup is delicious. The best chicken noodle I've ever had. I've eaten most of it by the time she returns with two pills that I take with the cup of ice water she hands me.

"Thank you so much."

"No problem." She arranges my blankets and fluffs my pillows. "Try to get some rest. I'll check on you again in a bit."

I wonder if I could take her home with me to tend to my every need.

That's something Jaden often said about the nurses who cared for him in the hospital. We became attached to them, thought of them as friends, as they guided us through a nightmare. I missed them almost as much as I missed him after he died.

When they came to his funeral, I wept at the sight of them. They were more my true friends than any of the people we went to high school with, who showed up to pay their respects after he was gone, but not while he was still alive. I heard later that they were scared to come to the hospital, to see him sick.

Poor babies. How difficult it must've been for them.

I'm still awake when the sun begins to peek through the blinds.

A new doctor comes by on rounds. I know it's called that because I've spent more time in hospitals than out of them in recent years.

"How're you feeling?" he asks me as his residents hover nearby, waiting to do his bidding.

"I'm fine. Can I go home?"

"That's the plan. You'll want to take ibuprofen every four hours for the next few days until the soreness improves. If you have any lingering concerns, check in with your primary care provider, okay?"

"I will. Thanks."

"I'll have the nurses process your discharge paperwork. You can leave as soon as your ride gets here."

He leaves me with his best wishes for my speedy recovery.

I text Iris. *Sorry to bug you, but I can leave whenever I have a ride.*

I'll be there as soon as I drop the kids at school. About an hour?

Ok, thanks.

Anything for you, kid.

The silliest things make me emotional, such as Iris saying she'd do anything for me. She's such a badass widow warrior, an amazing mother and a true friend. I feel so lucky to have her in my corner, pulling for me to succeed at widowhood and life. Seeing her and Gage find new love with each other has been truly inspirational to me and others in our group. If any two people deserve to be happy, they do.

My phone buzzes with a text from Adrian. *Hey, hope you*

slept ok and are feeling better today. Just wanted to check on you and see if you need anything. Let me know.

Thanks for checking. I'm going home shortly with Iris.

Glad to hear it. Hope to see you later.

He doesn't say anything about Xavier or what he's doing for childcare today since I'm not available, but I hope he's figured out something so he can work.

A different nurse comes in to help me get up and ready to leave. I'm so sore, I can barely move, but I shuffle to the bathroom to use the facilities and clean up before Iris arrives. They give me a toothbrush and a comb. I start to feel slightly presentable after I wash my face and brush my teeth.

I shuffle back to the bed and sit gingerly on the edge. Every muscle in my body is on fire, and sitting is painful, leading me to believe I must've smacked my ass on something in the fall.

I'm still there when Iris comes in with Xavier in her arms. She's so pretty with her light brown skin and curly hair that's almost always contained in a bun. Today, it's loose and makes her look younger than her mid-thirties.

Xavier lets out a happy cry when he sees me and struggles to get free of Iris so he can get to me.

"Be gentle with Wynter," Iris tells him.

I hold him close and breathe in the perfect scent of him, thankful to have him back in my arms as I try not to obsess about the bruise on his sweet face. "How'd you end up with him?"

"I volunteered since Adrian's nanny was out of commission."

"You're so good to us, Iris. What would we do without you?"

"No need to worry about that. I'm not going anywhere. Shall we get you out of here?"

"Yes, please."

I'm surprised when she takes me to her house rather than

41

my own. Does she even know where I live? I'm not sure. "Where're we going?"

"I thought I'd bring you to my house where I can take care of you until you feel better."

"You don't have to do that. You've got three kids to take care of."

"I want to do it." She glances over at me. "Will you let me?"

"Why do you want to take care of me?"

"Because you need someone, and I'm volunteering. This way, you can also be with Xavier. Win-win."

"You've got it all figured out." There's an edge to my tone that I didn't intend. "I'm sorry. You're being nice, and I'm a bitch."

"No, you're not," she says with a laugh. "You just want everyone to think you are."

"Quit knowing me so well. It's annoying."

She laughs even harder, which has my lips quivering. Iris has the most contagious laugh of anyone I've ever met. If she's laughing, it's hard not to join in. At first, I disliked that about her. I didn't want to be laughing when Jaden was dead. But Iris has a way of cutting through the grief bullshit to remind us we're still alive and have no choice but to move forward— and that we may as well do so joyfully.

God, that pissed me off to no end at first. I wanted to tell her to F off with her joy. She was like Cinderella with all the bluebirds chirping around her head. I wanted to shoot the birds out of the sky and go back to being furious at the hand I was dealt. How could she be so positive and optimistic when her dead husband left her with three little kids to raise on her own? And even when she found out how he'd deceived her, she didn't lose her overall sense of optimism.

I didn't get that. I'll be honest. I would be enraged if I found out that Jaden had a whole other family with someone else. And while we all saw Iris wobble a bit when she first learned of Mike's deceptions, she bounced back with a kind of resilience I'd never experienced quite so profoundly before.

Then, when she was diagnosed with early-stage breast cancer, and I had to imagine life without her, I realized how essential she'd become to my survival. I prayed—hard—for the first time since Jaden died. Losing Iris is not an option for any of us. Thankfully, she's doing well and is back to full health. The incident was a reminder of how quickly loved ones can be taken from us. Pretending Iris isn't a loved one to me would be foolish at this point.

You can't *not* love Iris. You just can't.

She has me settled on her sofa in a matter of minutes after we arrive at her spacious home.

Xavier plays with his toys on the floor next to me, and before I know it, Iris is serving me a lunch of grilled cheese and tomato soup on a tray—with a little sprig of flowers in a vase —and I never want to leave. Maybe I could move in with Iris, Gage and the kids. I could help her with the kids while she mothers me.

I realize that's a fantasy, but it's my fantasy, damn it, and I'm going to wallow in it for as long as I can.

Don't get me wrong. I love my own mother. I really do. But she's not... maternal. Not the way Iris is. Iris can't help but mother everyone. It's just who she is. My mother was all about raising me to be a fully independent woman who could stand on her own two feet, no matter what. I appreciate that upbringing, but it lacked some of the warm fuzzies that Iris puts out so effortlessly. I like the warm fuzzies, which still surprises me. Before I knew Iris, I would've said I didn't need that nonsense in my life. But now that I've experienced it first-hand, I can see how much I needed a soft place to land after Jaden died. Iris and the other widows have given me that.

They've saved my life. I have no doubt about that. I was

suicidal when I met them. I don't like to think about how low I fell after Jaden died. My mother was truly alarmed and had heard about the Wild Widows from a woman she worked with. She reached out to Iris and then made me go to the first few meetings. When I say she made me go, I mean she all but dragged me to Iris's house and stood outside the door to make sure I wouldn't try to leave.

She knew I needed help that she couldn't provide and that the therapist I began seeing when Jaden was sick wasn't enough.

I appreciate now that she connected me with Iris and the others, but at the time I hated her guts for thinking she knew better than I did about what I needed after losing my husband.

I'm not overstating anything by saying Iris and the others saved my life. They refused to accept bullshit from me and forced me to engage in the process of grieving when that was the last freaking thing I wanted to do. Grieving Jaden would mean accepting he was really gone, and that was unimaginable to me then.

The Wild Widows helped me see I had no other choice but to grieve and get on with it. Jaden was gone and not coming back, and the sooner I got on board with that, the sooner I could stop feeling like total shit twenty-four hours a day.

I still feel like shit a lot of the time, but not like I did in the beginning, and I'm thankful to them for getting me over that hump. And I'm thankful to my mom for making me join their group. I probably ought to tell her that at some point.

Speak of the devil... She texts to ask when I'm getting out of the hospital.

I'm out. Iris picked me up and brought me to her house. Gonna stay with her for a little bit.

That's great. Glad she is there for you.

What does it say about my mother that she's not even

jealous that I'm being mothered by someone else? It says that she has no idea what to do with me or my grief and would rather Iris deal with me until I'm back to "normal." The Wild Widows have taught me that's never going to happen. There is no going back to who I was before Jaden got sick and died. I'm still figuring out who New Wynter is and what her life will look like while my mother waits to get back the daughter she had before disaster struck.

It's comforting to know for sure that I'll never again be that girl. I might've spent years trying to get back to who I was before if my widows hadn't told me not to bother trying.

I remember Christy, who founded the group with Iris, saying nothing will ever be like it was before and we have to find a new normal for ourselves—and, in her case and Iris's, for their kids.

I'm not sure when I doze off on Iris's sofa, but I wake to the sound of kids trying to be quiet as they come into the house through the garage.

When I open my eyes, Laney is standing about three inches from me.

She scares the shit out of me, which makes her laugh.

Like her mother, if Laney laughs, you laugh. I give her a gentle poke to the belly. "You scared me."

"Laney! I told you not to bother Wynter."

"I didn't! She woked up."

I hook an arm around her waist and give her a squeeze that makes her giggle. "She's fine."

"She's not fine," Iris says with exasperation when she comes into the living room with Xavier in her arms. "I told them to leave you alone, and what's the first thing she does?"

"She didn't technically wake me up. I was already awake."

"Well, that's something," Iris says. To Laney, she says, "Go wash your hands and have a snack."

I hold out my arms for Xavier, who comes to me with what seems like relief.

"Wyn," he says.

"That's right. I'm here." I love that his shortened version of my name is one of the three words he says regularly, along with *Dada* and *no*. He loves to say no, which cracks me up. Adrian says I'm not allowed to find that funny, but damn if I can't help laughing every time he says it. "Did he nap?" I ask Iris.

"Not really. He dozed on the way to the school pickup, but that didn't last when my loud children got into the car."

"He's snuggling in like he does when he wants to sleep." I rub circles on his back as he cuddles up to me. "Maybe he'll take a quick one now."

"I'll try to keep the kids quiet."

"Don't worry about it. I play music when he naps, so he doesn't need total silence. I read that it makes them better sleepers to have a little noise."

She gives me an impressed look.

"What?"

"Look at you, reading about what helps babies sleep."

"I'm spending eight hours a day with a baby. Google is my best friend." It occurs to me that I still haven't heard whether Adrian is going to keep me on as Xavier's nanny. "Well, I *was* spending eight hours a day with him. Who knows what's going to happen now?"

Iris sits in one of the plush chairs that faces the sofa. "What do you mean?"

"We both know Adrian went out on a limb letting me be his nanny in the first place. I'd understand if he wanted someone else after what happened yesterday."

"It was an accident, Wynter. He's not going to replace you because of an accident."

"I wouldn't blame him if he did."

46

"He won't. Yes, he was upset when he couldn't reach you. We all were, but never once did any of us think that Xavier wasn't safe with you. We've seen how much you love him. He adores you, and vice versa. If I were Adrian, there would be nothing I could want more in a nanny."

"Still... I had to talk him into letting me do it—and I know the rest of you gave him a push in my direction."

"We gave him a push in the direction of the best person for the job—someone who already loved his son."

"Thank you for that. I've loved every second I've spent with him. He's given me a reason to get up in the morning again. I don't know what I'd do if I couldn't be with him every day anymore."

"That's not going to happen, so don't worry about it. Before I forget, I wanted to ask if you mind if the Wild Widows meet here tonight as scheduled."

"Of course I don't mind. Why would I?"

"I wasn't sure if you felt up to seeing everyone."

"I'm fine as long as Xavier is. I'd like to see them."

She pulls her phone from her back pocket and sends a text. "I let them know we're still on for tonight. Can I get you anything?"

"You don't have to wait on me, Iris."

"I don't mind."

"Do you have any ibuprofen?"

"Yep. Be right back."

She comes back with the pills and ice water that I juggle around Xavier, who's conked out. "Thanks."

"Rest with your buddy. All is well, my friend."

She makes me believe that's true simply because she does. I'm sure she's working behind the scenes to make sure Adrian doesn't dump me as his nanny. Whatever it takes to keep the job that's become a lifeline to me.

Five

Iris

I go into the kitchen to text Adrian. *Wynter is afraid she's not going to be your nanny anymore, and you can't let that happen. I know yesterday was upsetting, but look at them...*

I sneak into the living room to take a picture of Wynter and Xavier. Her arms are around the sleeping baby, and the expression on her face is nothing short of blissful.

She loves him so much.

Adrian replies with a heart for the photo. *Yesterday was a lot for me. My hands are still shaking.*

I know. It was awful, especially after everything you've been through. We've learned to expect the worst because that's what's happened in the past. But look at what she did to protect him. She's a mess of bruises and pulled muscles because every instinct in her was to protect him at her own expense.

I love Wynter. You know I do. And I know how much she loves Xavier.

But?

No buts. I'm just still trying to recover from the fear that I might've lost him. And her. I don't know. My emotions are all over the place like they were after Sadie and Alyssa died. I hate that feeling.

I get it. It's the worst. But everything is ok, and Xavier loves her as much as she loves him. I think they need each other—and you need her.

Would it be too much for me to ask if I can track her phone so if anything ever happened again, I could find her?

I don't think that's too much to ask at all.

I'm not sure she'll go for that. People are weird about being tracked. But I think that would be a deal breaker for me.

Understandable. Talk to her tonight. I'm sure she'll be fine with it. It's not like you're her mother wanting to know where she is at all times. It would only be for when she's with Xavier, and if you make it a safety thing, that's an even better argument.

I'll talk to her. Thanks, as always, for being there for me. For all of us.

Love you.

Love you too.

My widows and I are all about the love. We always say the words because we know how important it is to leave nothing unsaid. I love them. I want them to know it. Some of the best friends I've ever had are my widow friends. I spend more time with them than I do my friends from "before." They don't get my new life the way the wids do. I find myself relying on Gage, Christy, Lexi, Roni and the others in a way that I never did with my other friends. Sure, I enjoyed being with them, but I didn't *need* them like I do my widow friends. I've picked up on some resentment from my mom friends and other people who were important to me before Mike died.

One of them, Julia, accused me of blowing her off, which isn't the case at all, but I lack the energy to explain to her that she can't fill the needs I have for friends these days. She just simply can't, even if she wants to. I think she does want to, or at least she did. She was one of the first ones to arrive after word got out about Mike's accident, and she was there for me every day in those early weeks, when the influx of people and food and sympathy was so overwhelming as to nearly drown me. I'll never forget how she was there for me in those horrible days.

But as time went on, she went back to her happy marriage, and I forged ahead as a newly single mom. We didn't have as much in common anymore. I found myself checking in with her less and less often, until it got to the point where we spoke about once every six months. The conversations were awkward and strained and nothing like they used to be. I hate that it hurt her to lose me in her daily life, but I gravitated to people who could help me find my way through the darkness.

Speaking of those people, my phone chimes with a text from Christy, who was the first young widow I connected with after Mike died. She's become one of my closest friends. *So glad we're still on for tonight. I need it.*

What's going on?

The guy... He says he's done thinking about whether he can stand to be around my kids every day and wants to talk, but I'm not sure I care anymore. Did he really need THREE FREAKING WEEKS to decide he can stand my kids?

I sputter with laughter that I know she wouldn't appreciate. *It's a big deal to take on someone else's kids, especially when they're preteens and teenagers who witnessed the trauma of their father's death.* Christy's husband, Wes, died almost four years ago from an aortic dissection. He basically dropped dead in front of her and their kids, who were seven and nine.

I know it's a big deal, and I've told him he doesn't have to do anything he doesn't want to.

It seems like he might want to if he's come back looking to talk, right?

I guess, but now I'm pissed and not sure I care anymore.

Bring it tonight. We'll figure it out together.

Counting on that and a very large drink. Joy is picking me up so I can have two very large drinks.

LOL, texting Gage to get more wine.

I'll bring my own, girlfriend. Can't wait. How's our Wynter?

Better. Waiting to hear if Adrian is going to keep her on as his nanny...

Is he waffling? Come on! It was an accident.

He's rattled. They need to talk, which they will tonight.

Christy sends a sad emoji. *Poor guy. I see both sides for sure.*

Same. It's a tough one.

I am so, so, so on Team Wynter tho.

ME TOO. I love her, and I want all good things for her.

Yep. Let's help him see that he needs her as much as she needs him.

Sounds like a plan.

I feel a little sorry for him with us ganging up on him.

I respond with a row of laughter emojis.

I love these people, and I can't wait to see them all tonight. But first I have to get three kids through homework before I turn them over to my mom while I hang with my widows.

Adrian

I'm full of turmoil that has me on edge all day as I attempt to stay focused on work at my brother-in-law's insurance agency. After my last employer regretfully told me they couldn't keep me on any longer as I dealt with grief and new single fatherhood, Mick offered me a job at his agency. He's kept me employed through the difficult last year, and I try to pay him back by being one hundred percent attentive to our clients and the details while I'm on the clock.

But after yesterday, all I can think about is how disaster nearly struck again and whether I can really trust Wynter's judgment when it comes to Xavier.

I hate that I'm even having those thoughts, but she was right when she said she shouldn't have taken him to the cemetery. And yes, I get why she went when she did and the reason she felt the need to go there, but she could've dropped him with Iris or even brought him to me for the last hour of the workday rather than taking him with her.

I've told her before that he can come to the office if there's ever an emergency. That's the beauty of working for Xavier's uncle. Mick is always happy to see his little buddy. I try not to take advantage of his generosity, though.

I'm working through the last of the client calls I have to make by the end of the day when Iris's texts arrive about the meeting and Wynter. I had the idea about tracking her phone earlier and wondered if it would even be appropriate to ask that of her. Iris's endorsement has given me the courage to broach the topic with Wynter. I don't want her to think I don't trust her because I do. I have to trust her, or I'd never have a moment of peace while I'm away from Xavier. Yes, I could've put him in daycare, but I liked the idea of him having one person's undivided attention all day, and Wynter already loved him. It made me feel better to know he'd be in his own home during the day.

I took a big chance on her, and so far, it's paid off amazingly well. Yesterday was the first wrinkle we've had, but it was a big wrinkle. Not knowing where they were or if they were even still alive was more than I could bear. I wish I didn't jump right to worst-case scenarios, but can you blame me after what's happened to me in the last year?

Xavier's first birthday is coming up soon. That's also the day that Sadie died, but I'm determined to celebrate my son on that day while I try not to think about the catastrophe that befell us on the very same day. I'm not sure how that'll go, but all I can do is try to keep the focus on him.

That's what his mother would want me to do.

Sadie was all about positivity and finding the silver lining in any situation. Even she would be hard-pressed to find the silver lining in her dying before she ever got to hold her little boy. If she were still here, she'd be telling me "onward and upward." That was one of her favorite sayings whenever shit went sideways. She liked to say that we can't control what other people do. We can only control how we react to them. In our three years together, she taught me all the most important lessons about kindness, grace, forgiveness and love.

Other than my devoted older sister, I'd never been truly loved until Sadie loved me. Losing her and her love was the most devastating blow of my entire life. Sometimes I still wonder if I'll ever recover from it or learn how to go on without her. I've been in survival mode since she died. Care for the baby. Eat, shower, go to work, repeat. The drudgery of my routine has been critical to making it through this first year. That and my Wild Widows, who get most of the credit for seeing me through this hellish experience.

The bright light throughout has been Xavier. He saved me with his sweetness, his innocence and his infectious joy. He has no idea that two of the most important people in his life are missing. He's perfectly content with me, even if he shouldn't be, and the other people in his life, such as my sister and brother-in-law and their kids, as well as the Wild Widows, especially Iris and her kids. And Wynter, too, of course.

It's strange to realize that if Sadie hadn't died, I wouldn't know Iris, Wynter, Gage, Lexi, Christy, Roni, Derek or any of the other people who've become my closest circle of friends. A year ago, I'd never met any of them. Now I can't imagine life without them.

Mick comes by my desk as I'm packing up to leave. He's

starting to go gray at the temples, which my sister likes to tease him about. But we've been working out together for years, so I know he's as strong and fit as he was the day my sister first met him more than fifteen years ago. He's become one of my closest friends over the years, someone I turn to frequently for advice and counsel. "You sure you're okay, Adrian? You've been quiet today."

I haven't told him or my sister about what happened yesterday because I don't want them to lose confidence in Wynter or question my judgment when it comes to Xavier. Although they never said so, they took one look at Wynter with her pale skin, half-shaved head and piercings through her lip, nose and all the way up her ears and thought I was insane for hiring her to care for my son. But I know her heart, and they don't. That's why I hired her. I know how she loves deeply—so deeply that she'll be devastated over what happened yesterday. "I'm fine. Just getting close to Xavier's birthday, among other things."

"Nia and I were just talking about that last night. You're more than welcome to have the party at our place. She told you that, right?"

I hate how they worry about me. I should be used to it by now. "She did, and I appreciate it. I'm still trying to decide what I want to do."

"Let us know how we can help."

"Thanks, Mick, for everything."

"We wish we could do more."

"You do more than enough, and I appreciate you." We give each other a bro hug and say good night. I get into Sadie's Lexus SUV and head for Iris's house. The payments on the car are ridiculous, but I couldn't bring myself to part with the car she loved so much. She used a bonus she got in her job as a corporate recruiter for the down payment, saying we needed a "family" car with the baby coming.

After she died, I sold my Mustang and started driving her first baby, as she referred to it. I honestly can't afford it on one salary, but I'm getting by. Just barely. Wynter is a big reason why I'm keeping my head above water. The five hundred dollars a week I pay her to watch Xavier is three hundred less than the quote I got from the cheapest daycare. And who wants their kid at the cheapest daycare?

Wynter says five hundred is too much. I say it's not enough. We agreed to disagree at five hundred. The three hundred I'm saving on daycare is what makes it possible for me to keep the Lexus. My sister says I'm crazy to keep a car I can no longer afford, but she gets that it's tied to Sadie, one of the last things she ever bought, and neither of us will ever forget how excited she was the day she got it.

"It's *champagne*," she'd said of the color that looked tan to me.

I made the mistake of telling her that.

My eyes fill with tears as I recall her taking my head off for using the word *tan* to describe her *champagne* car. She got so mad over that.

I laugh even as tears slide down my cheeks. I had to seriously kiss her ass to get out of the doghouse on that one. The next day, I bought her a bottle of champagne to celebrate her champagne car, and that fixed everything.

That's how my Sadie was. Mad as a wet hen one minute and sweet as could be the next. She lacked the ability to stay mad with me for longer than a few hours, even when I insulted her new car by calling it something so basic as tan.

At a stoplight, I brush the tears from my face. God, I miss her sassiness, her outrageousness, her humor, her style, her way of cutting through bullshit to get at the truth and her friendship, which was the greatest gift of my life until she gave me Xavier. I never had a friend like Sadie, who was so fiercely loyal and protective of the people she loved.

With her came an extended family I also loved, including her mom and two sisters as well as their families. I got comfortable with her, with them, with my life. And then bam. It was all taken from me. Her younger sisters are still very much in my life, checking in regularly and offering to take Xavier for vacations, etc. But it's not like it was when Sadie and Alyssa were in the middle of everything, keeping us bonded the way they did so effortlessly.

I pull up to Iris's house a few minutes later and park behind Joy's car. Just seeing the cars and knowing my friends are already here gives me a lift I badly needed, not to mention knowing I'll see Xavier again in a few minutes. He always makes me feel better, no matter how low I get.

I walk into Iris's house because I know I'm always welcome to do so, which is something I treasure.

Xavier sees me and lets out a happy squeak as he speed-crawls to me.

Iris says he's going to walk at any minute, but he's not quite there yet.

I scoop him up and into a tight hug that has him squirming to break free almost immediately. "How's my big boy?" After peppering his pudgy face with kisses, I put him down to play with his toys. The noise from the kitchen tells me the rest of the group is in there.

My gaze connects with Wynter's. She's on the sofa, covered with a plush blanket, and I'm glad to see she looks much better than she did last night. "How're you feeling?"

"Fine."

Xavier brings his stuffed frog to Wynter and hands it to her.

"Thank you." She hugs the frog, which makes Xavier smile. "I'll take good care of him."

The frog is his favorite thing. Watching him give it to her is a good reminder of his love for her.

"Did he eat?" I ask Wynter.

"Yes, with Iris's kids."

"Great, thanks."

"Thank her, not me. She's the one who fed him."

"Are you pissed with me, Wynter?" I hate, *absolutely hate*, that I find her sexy. I've tried to tell myself nothing good will come of that, but what can I say? My nanny is sexy, and I'll never do a thing about it. I refuse to be that kind of cliché. She's seven years younger than me, and I desperately need her to care for my son. Hands off. End of story.

"What? No, why would I be?"

"I'm not sure."

"I'm not pissed with you. I'm pissed with myself for causing you so much stress."

"It's over and done with. Don't worry about it. As long as you're both safe, that's what matters."

"Are you going to fire me?"

I wasn't planning to get into this the second I arrived, but she's given me the opening I need. As I take a seat on the coffee table next to the sofa, I lift Xavier to sit on my lap. "I'm not going to fire you. I need you too much. But I do have a request."

"What request?"

"I'd like to be able to track your phone so I can find you if anything like this ever happens again. Before you can object, I'll reiterate that I'd only use the info in an emergency. I have no desire to invade your privacy."

"That's fine with me. I get it."

"Really?" I didn't expect her to agree so easily.

"Yes, really. I've got your kid with me. Of course you want to be able to find me if need be. Let's set it up." When she reaches for her phone, I notice the huge bruise on her arm and wince.

"That looks like it hurts."

"Everything hurts, but I'm fine as long as he is."

"I really appreciate you taking the brunt of the fall to protect him."

She looks up at me with vulnerability in her green eyes. "I'll always take the fall to protect him."

"Thank you for loving him so much."

"I do."

"I know."

She hands me her phone. "Do whatever you need to."

"To make it fair, I'll set you up to track me, too."

"Whatever helps you sleep at night."

I grin at her as I hand her phone back. "Thank you for understanding."

"I get it. He's your whole life. Believe it or not, he's mine, too." She reaches out to Xavier, who curls his hand around her index finger. "He gives me a reason."

"Same."

"Thank you for continuing to trust me with him. It means a lot to me."

"You got it. While we're talking business, I've been meaning to ask if you might consider doing Saturday nights with us for an extra hundred a week. I've got the opportunity to pick up a bartending shift at a friend's place that would give me some much-needed extra income."

"I can do that."

"And you can sleep over? I won't get home until after two."

"Sure."

"Thank you, Wynter."

"You're welcome, Adrian."

Iris comes into the room. "Thought I heard you talking to someone. Everything okay?"

"Everything is fine," Adrian says. "Wynter has agreed to let me track her phone, and she's going to do Saturday nights for me so I can pick up a bartending shift at a friend's bar."

"That sounds great," Iris says, smiling. "I'm happy for all of you."

As the others filter into the living room, Iris updates them on how things worked out for Wynter and me while I take Xavier and go get something to eat. I'm extremely relieved that she had no objection to me tracking her phone and that we'll continue an arrangement that's been working well for both of us.

Six

Wynter

I'm so relieved, I can barely function. He didn't fire me. He did the opposite and expanded my hours with Xavier to include Saturday nights.

"Hey," Iris says softly as she takes Adrian's seat on the coffee table. "Are you okay?"

"Yeah."

"Good news, right?"

"The best."

"I'm happy for you that it worked out this way."

"Me, too. I don't know what I would've done with myself if I couldn't watch Xavier anymore."

"Now you don't have to worry about that."

I exhale deeply. "Right."

"Adrian has chosen the very best person for the job. None of us have any doubt about that. We never did."

"Sure, you did," I say with a laugh.

"No, Wynter, we didn't. If we had, we never would've encouraged him to hire you. Xavier's health and safety are all that matter in that equation. We knew you'd be great with him."

I'm mortified when my eyes fill with tears. Her approval means so much to me, and when exactly did that happen, anyway? I use the back of my hand to wipe away the tears. "Thanks."

"You feel up to the meeting? You can hide out in my room upstairs if you need to."

"I'm fine."

"All right, then. Let's get this party started."

The others bring chairs into the living room and set up the circle to include me on the sofa.

Roni comes over to give me a light hug. "Glad to see you're doing okay."

"Thanks."

Christy, Brielle, Lexi, Gage, Derek and Joy also come over to hug me before taking their seats.

Adrian comes in with Xavier on his hip, juggling a plate.

I hold out my arms to them, and he hands Xavier to me so he can eat. "Thanks."

Xavier puts his thumb in his mouth and snuggles up to me.

I can't articulate the feelings that course through me when I hold him. It's the purest form of love I've ever experienced. Even loving Jaden wasn't like this. He liked to push my buttons, to piss me off just to get a rise out of me. I loved him even when he was poking at me. But with Xavier, there's none of that. There's only love.

I open my eyes and realize everyone is looking at me—and him. "Quit your staring."

They laugh, as they often do at my bitchiness.

"Who wants to go first?" Iris asks.

Christy raises her hand. "I need you people to tell me what to do."

"That's what we're here for," Derek says as he holds hands with Roni.

They're so damned cute together. I love seeing them so happy. They, along with Iris and Gage, give me hope that I might not always feel as shitty as I have this last year without Jaden.

"So it's like this," Christy says. "I've been seeing this guy, Trey, for a while now. We have a good time together, laugh frequently and like the same things. He loves Mexican food as much as I do, we love going to Virginia Tech games in Blacksburg—he went there, too—and I like his friends and family very much. They're good people. And for the first time since Wes died, I really feel a genuine connection to someone in bed and out."

"What's the problem?" Gage asks.

"A few weeks ago, he said he needed some time to think because he's not sure he can handle being the significant other to a mom with kids."

"Ouch," Roni says.

"Exactly. I didn't hear a word from him for three weeks while he did his thinking, and now he's come back around to say he wants to talk. Part of me wants to tell him to fuck off with his three weeks to think. But the other part missed him, and I hate that I missed him. So tell me what to do."

"It's a tough one," Brielle says. "It would be hard for me to get past that he needed three weeks to think about whether he can stomach my kids." Her husband, Mark, was killed in a skiing accident when she was expecting their son, Charlie. She's curvy and pretty with dark hair and eyes and is wearing her signature bright red lipstick.

"That's it exactly," Christy says. "From the start, he's known they come with the package. It felt sort of shitty for him to suddenly decide he couldn't deal."

"In his defense," Derek says, "he's never had to accommodate kids before, and when it was just the two of you, he still didn't have to accommodate them. Shit's getting real, and he's taking a pause to make sure he's capable before he goes forward. I don't think there's anything wrong with that."

"But *three weeks* of radio silence?" Christy asks. "It takes him that long to decide he can stand them? And if that's the case, do I want him in their lives?"

"What do they think of him?" Joy asks.

Before she can reply, Naomi comes in, bringing a blast of chilly air with her. "So sorry I'm late. Work is a disaster." She has red hair and a happy, sunny disposition that shines through despite the devastating loss of her fiancé, David, to lymphoma. She struggles with whether she belongs in a group of widows when she never got a chance to marry her love. We tell her all the time she's one of us, no matter what.

She grabs a plate and joins us in the circle. "What'd I miss?"

Roni brings her up to speed on what Christy has told us.

"To answer your question, Joy," Christy says, "my kids seem somewhat indifferent toward him. When I ask, they say he's nice or he's okay or something generic. There's no real connection there."

"Is that by design on Trey's part, do you think?" Iris asks gently.

"Probably," Christy says with a frown. "He isn't sure how he feels about taking on an insta-family, so why would he make an effort with them?"

"He sounds like a dick," I say.

The others look at me like I just uttered something outrageous. They do that a lot.

"What?" I ask, doubling down. "He does. He starts dating a widow with two kids, and a few months into it, he balks over the kids? That's bullshit."

63

"I hate to say that, in her own special way, Wynter has a point," Iris says.

"They're a handful right now," Christy says with a sigh. "I see that. Full of attitude and mouth and grief that hangs on despite the passage of time. I'm not sure *I'd* want them if they weren't mine."

Everyone laughs at that.

"Your kids are amazing," Joy says. "They've been through so much, and still they flourish. They're great students and athletes. They have awesome friends and so many interests. There's nothing not to love about them."

"Wow, you make them sound really good," Christy says.

"They *are* really good," Joy replies. "They're great kids, and anyone would be lucky to have them in their lives. If Trey doesn't see that, he's not the one for you. And PS, nothing says you have to go the distance with him. You can date him and have good sex with him and keep it all separate if that's what works."

"My sister said the same thing," Christy says with a frown. "It's just that I've never been wired for the transactional thing. I'm a relationship kinda girl. Always have been. Sometimes I still can't believe I have to go through all this again, you know? Like, where's Wes, and how did this happen to me?"

"We get that," Roni says. "It's still surreal to me that Patrick is gone, Derek is here, and everything has changed in the blink of an eye."

Christy sends her a grateful smile.

It always helps to know that other people get where you're coming from.

"Just because you've always been a relationship kind of girl doesn't mean you always have to be," I say. "There's nothing wrong with enjoying a guy on the side while you continue to raise your kids and do your thing with them."

"I know there's nothing wrong with it, but doesn't it need to be going somewhere?" Christy asks.

"Who says?" I ask. "Why does it have to go anywhere? Haven't we learned to enjoy the moment we're in without putting too much pressure on a future that isn't guaranteed to any of us?"

The others stare at me for so long I begin to fear that I either have something on my face or I said something stupid.

"That's so profound, Wynter," Joy says.

"It really is," Christy agrees, "and it was just what I needed to hear. Thank you for giving me that perspective, Wynter."

"No problem. I'm here all night."

That makes them laugh again, which fills me with a feeling of accomplishment.

"I could use some advice, too," Lexi says as she tucks a strand of her long dark hair behind her ear. She has light brown skin and gorgeous brown eyes. Her husband, Jim, died after a long battle with ALS, leaving her financially strapped because he didn't have life insurance, and she didn't work for years while he was sick. "My parents are driving me insane. They're constantly after me to figure out my life, to decide what's next, to move on. While I appreciate everything they did for us when Jim was sick and how they've been so there for me since he died, I can't live with them anymore. I just cannot."

"My place in the District hasn't been rented yet," Roni says. "The landlord told me today to ask around for him."

"That's so nice of you," Lexi says, "but there's no way I could afford it on my data entry salary." She applied for hundreds of jobs after Jim died and had to settle for the only one that was offered. "I ran into a friend from high school a couple of weeks ago. We grabbed a drink together, and I ended up spilling the whole sorry tale to him. He said he has an extra bedroom at his place that I'm welcome to for ridiculously low rent, but I don't know..."

"What don't you know, sweetie?" Joy asks. "Sounds like the answer to a prayer."

"It is, but it's just that I had the hugest crush on him in high school, and when I saw him, it was like no time had passed, like Jim had never happened... I felt sick with guilt about that afterward. And then he reached out with the offer of a room at his place and... Ugh, I want so badly to take it to get away from my parents, but, you guys... I was *crazy about him* for years, and he never knew I was alive."

"That is a dilemma," Iris says thoughtfully.

"Did you pick up on any vibes other than an offer of a place to live when you were with him?" Derek asks.

"Maybe a little," Lexi says. "He gave me his undivided attention and treated me like an old friend, even though I feel like he barely knew I was alive in high school."

"I think he's digging you, or he never would've reached out with the offer of a room," I say.

"Ugh, I have no idea what to think," Lexi says, "but since he made the offer, I can't stop fantasizing about getting away from my parents and having more time with him."

"Have you done your due diligence on this guy?" Joy asks.

"Uh, yeah," Lexi says almost sheepishly. "I tapped into my high school friends immediately to ask for an update. They said he's done really well as a contractor and has never been married. Was engaged once, a long time ago, but has no skeletons that they know of. And they'd know."

"I say go for it," Gage says. "What's the worst that could happen? You get there, realize it's not a good fit and you move back in with your parents."

"That would be a worst-case scenario," Lexi says.

"No, it wouldn't," Roni says. "There's much worse than that, and you know it."

"You're right," Lexi says, "and I'm sorry if I forgot myself for a second there."

"Don't be sorry," Roni says. "I only mean it as a reminder that we all know how much worse things can be than being stuck living with overly involved parents."

"Absolutely," Lexi says. "Sometimes the nightmare with Jim's illness seems so long ago, it's almost like it happened to someone else."

"I feel that," Kinsley says. She has flawless, creamy white skin that I'd kill for, light brown hair and pretty blue eyes. Her husband, Rory, died of pancreatic cancer forty-two days after his diagnosis. "The whole thing happened so fast for us that sometimes it feels like it was a bad dream. I wake up a lot of days and have to remind myself all over again that he really died."

"Same," I say, "even though Jaden's illness spanned years, it feels like another lifetime only a year after he died. And I want to thank you guys for all the messages yesterday for his anniversary. Other people didn't remember, but you guys did, and that means a lot."

"We're always here for you, kid," Gage says.

"Thanks."

"I've been struggling with when to start dating," Adrian says. "It'll be a year next month—and you're all invited to Xavier's birthday party. It's occurring to me that I'll have to celebrate the day Sadie died every year for the rest of my life, which is bizarre. But she would say that life is for the living, and I need to focus on Xavier."

"You're doing great, Adrian," Iris says. "And we can't wait to celebrate Xavier's birthday. Let us know how we can help. I'm a bit of a kid-birthday expert."

"I'll take you up on that."

"What are your thoughts on dating?" Gage asks him.

He spins the wedding ring around on his finger.

I want to tell him he probably ought to remove that before he starts dating, but I'm sure he knows.

"I've been looking at Tinder, Bumble, Hinge and some of the other sites."

"Have you set up profiles?" I ask him.

"Yeah, just so I could look. I kept mine private for now because I'm not sure I'm ready, but I figure you gotta start somewhere. It's just so weird to me that I'm even thinking about this. I still feel married." He puts his hand over his heart. "In here."

"That feeling never really goes away." Gage glances at Iris. "Even with things in my life moving in a whole new direction that I very much enjoy, I still feel Natasha with me."

"Was it ridiculously hard the first time you were with someone else?" Adrian asks him.

"I hope it was a little hard," I say to more laughter.

"Honestly, Wynter," Adrian says with a huff of exasperated laughter. "I'm trying to be serious here."

"My apologies. Please proceed."

He rolls his eyes at me. "As I was saying…"

"It was hard in every possible way," Gage says with a meaningful glance at me. "You feel like you're betraying the person you loved the most by touching someone else, even as you know on an intellectual level that your person is gone forever. Emotionally is a whole other story. That takes a while."

"It's good to know that it's normal to feel hesitant," Adrian says.

"It's *so* normal," Derek says. "It took a very long time after Vic died to stop feeling married." His wife was murdered, and his young daughter kidnapped as part of a hideous political conspiracy that still boggles my mind long after I first heard about it.

"You're doing everything right, Adrian," Iris says in the gentle tone we all rely on so much to get us through.

"You're taking good care of your son. You're working and living and moving forward. It's only natural you'd be starting to think about dating. But I want to say one thing…"

"What?" he asks.

"Often, the second year is harder than the first."

"How is that possible?" Adrian asks with a moan.

I'd like to know that, too.

"The first year is all shock and gritty grief and figuring out the new normal. The second year is about accepting that life as you know it is done and you have to start over. That can be harder than you expect."

"I can't imagine anything being harder than this last year has been," he says.

I point to him. "What he said."

"I don't want to stress you out," Iris says. "Just be aware that you may not be out of the woods yet."

"Great," Adrian says with a sour look.

"Iris is right," Gage says. "There's not a magic moment at year one where this suddenly gets easier. This is a multiyear process that in many ways never ends."

It's depressing to hear that, and I can tell Adrian feels the same way.

"If it's any consolation," Christy adds, "surviving the first year is a very big deal, and you should be proud of yourselves for that."

"I'm proud of myself," I say. "Are you, Adrian?"

"Hell yes. Worst year of my life. And the best, too." He fixes his gaze on Xavier, asleep in my arms. "Emotional whiplash. I'll never get over the fact that Sadie didn't even get to hold him. All she wanted was to be his mother."

"She will always be his mother, Adrian," Brielle says.

"I know, but…" He shrugs. "It sucks. And I hate myself for thinking it's time to get back out there and meet new people and start over. I don't want that. Not really. But again…"

"We understand," Gage says. "You've got a lot of years left to live. It's hard to imagine being alone for the rest of your life."

"Yeah," Adrian says with a sigh. "That. Exactly."

"I've found that keeping my relationship with Wes completely separate from what's come after him has allowed me to entertain new possibilities," Christy says.

"How do you do that?" Adrian asks.

"I try to imagine Wes inside a room in my brain that belongs only to him and us. Everything about our time together lives there. In another room are the new people I'm meeting. They never commingle with Wes. Does that make sense at all?"

"It does," Adrian says.

"It took a while for me to make this work for myself," Christy says, "but I felt better about moving on once I knew he was safe."

"I like that, making Sadie safe before I move on."

"I'm not sure if you've done any kind of visualization work before, but I can give you some links to things that have helped me," Christy says.

"I haven't done that," Adrian says, "so I'll take whatever you've got."

"Send it to the group," Derek says. "I'd love to check that out, too."

"Thanks for the support, guys," Adrian says. "It means so much to me. I don't know what I would've done this year without you all."

"Same," I say. "I didn't think I needed this. I was wrong."

"Wait," Iris says with a teasing grin, "did Wynter just admit that she likes us?"

I roll my eyes. "When did I say that?"

"I knew it was too good to be true," Iris says, laughing.

"In all seriousness." A sudden wave of emotion clogs my throat. I push through it because I want them to know how I truly feel. "My mother made me come because she didn't know what to do with me. I fought her every step of the way. But it turns out I needed to know there're other people who understand how I'm feeling. I'm not sure I would've made the effort to stay alive without the support you guys have offered. And I just wanted to say thanks for that."

"We love you, Wynter," Roni says. "Even if you don't want us to."

"Love you, too. All of you."

"I knew it!" Iris says with a fist pump.

"Don't ruin it," I say, making them laugh.

That's become my role in the group. To provide the comic relief.

A short time later, Adrian takes Xavier home to bed, and the others head out, too, leaving me with only Gage and Iris, who bring drinks to the living room before heading upstairs.

"I can set you up with a real bed," Iris says.

"I'm fine here. Most comfortable sofa ever."

"That's what Mike used to say, too," she says with a sad smile.

Since finding out he deceived her, she rarely mentions his name. I have so many questions about how she really feels, but I'd never ask. I don't want to open that wound when she seems so happy now with Gage.

"You guys don't have to hang with me. I'm totally fine, especially now that I know I'm not getting fired."

"I'm glad you two worked things out," Iris says. "I was hoping you wouldn't care if he tracked your phone."

"I would've cared a few years ago. I get it, though. I gave him a scare, and now he wants to be able to find me if need be. It's not unreasonable."

"I don't think so either," Iris says. "I'd want that if someone was watching my kids and going out with them."

"And he added Saturday nights to my schedule. He's going to pick up a bartending shift to make some extra money."

"That'll be good for him, to get out and be with people," Gage says.

"I hope so." I want nothing but the best for Adrian, and if that means having to watch him date other women, so be it. If that thought makes my stomach hurt, that's neither here nor there. It's not like I have some sort of claim on him or anything. He has every right to move on with his life, to find someone new to love and to build a new family for himself and Xavier.

It's just that the thought of being on the outside of that looking in breaks my heart.

But he doesn't need to know that.

No one does.

Seven

Adrian

I'm preparing for my first Saturday at the bar just over two weeks later when I hear Wynter use her key in the front door. She's right on time, which I appreciate. Xavier and I had a fun morning hiking on a local trail for a few hours with a stop at a playground on the way home. I'm getting more comfortable spending full days alone with him, which freaked me out at the beginning.

He's playing with his toys on the floor of my room while I get dressed in the white dress shirt and black pants uniform for the bar staff at my friend Brian's restaurant.

He and I went to high school together and worked side-by-side in bars for years. I reached out to him a few weeks ago to ask him if he had any need for a rusty bartender one night a week.

I was thrilled when he wrote right back and said hell yes, and perfect timing after one of his guys abruptly quit.

It was a relief to know I could add a few hundred dollars a week to the household pot, and it'll get me out of the house, too. I've become very one-dimensional since Sadie died and I became the single parent to a newborn. It's all Xavier all the time, which is how it needed to be at first. But I'm ready now for some outside stimulation beyond what I get from my amazing widow friends and others who've been in my life all along.

I'm not going to lie. I've been thinking a lot about sex again lately after it not crossing my mind for months after Sadie died.

I might be ready to do something about it. That's not to say it'll happen right away, but it'll never happen if I stay walled off at home with my young son every day for the rest of my life.

I see the way women look at me. I've always been aware that they see me as hot or attractive or whatever word is trending these days. Sadie used to tell me I was hotter than the sun, and I would joke that she had to say that because she was stuck with me. It used to drive her crazy that women would stare at me when she was with me. We had some wild fights about that, with me telling her it had nothing to do with us and her saying that I'd better never be tempted.

That used to piss me off. She knew full well that I never looked at anyone else from the day we first met. Her insecurities about me and other women used to make me crazy. I told her a million times she had nothing to worry about, but then some clueless woman would act inappropriately toward me when I was with my wife, and the whole thing would start up again, with me reminding her that I did nothing but stand in a room and breathe.

She hated when I said that.

I laugh to myself thinking about it. But it was true. How was it in any way my fault that other women found me attractive? I didn't lose my mind when I saw men looking at my gorgeous wife. I was complimented by it. She never was when the attention came my way.

Part of me loved that she was so possessive, that is until it led to screaming fights about stupid shit that didn't matter. Ironically, her pregnancy kept us home alone much more often than before. She was super tired, so we stayed home and fought a whole lot less than we did when we went out every weekend. Things were really good between us during that last year, which made it that much harder to suddenly lose her right after celebrating the birth of our son.

I can't even think of that day without spiraling, so I push those memories to the back of my mind the way Christy suggested.

Before I head downstairs, I quickly remove my wedding ring and put it in the top drawer of my dresser. I'm determined not to descend into an emotional basket case over something that needed to be done eventually, but it hurts, nonetheless. It feels like another step away from Sadie that I never wanted to take.

I collect Xavier from the floor and take him downstairs to greet his favorite person.

He loves Wynter more than ice cream, which is fine with me. He loves me, too, and if he loves her more, that's okay. The only thing that matters to me is his happiness and well-being.

As always, he lets out a happy squeal when he sees Wynter, who seems equally thrilled to see him.

She holds out her arms to him, and I make the transfer.

"I ordered pizza for you and pasta for him," I tell Wynter. "Should be here soon."

"Thank you."

"No problem. The guest room next to Xavier's room is all set for you. Make yourself at home."

"Will do."

"I might grab a drink after work with some friends. Is that okay?"

"Doesn't matter to me. I'll be out cold."

"Great, thanks. Call me if you need anything. I'll have my phone with me, and I told my friend I might have to take calls from my sitter during my shift."

"We'll be fine. Don't worry. We have a big night of *Toy Story* planned."

"Buzz!" Xavier says, stunning us both.

"Someone has a new word," Wynter says as Xavier gives us a gummy grin.

He's so damned cute. Every day, he seems to learn ten new things, and it's exciting to watch him blossom.

"I'm going to go before he realizes I'm leaving." I kiss my son on the forehead. "Be good for Wynter."

"Wyn, Wyn, Wyn."

"Look at that," she says, beaming with pride and love.

Any misgivings I might've had about her being his nanny —and I had a few at the outset, I can't lie about that—evaporate whenever I see her with him. I have no doubt whatsoever that she loves him as much as I do. That gives me tremendous peace of mind about leaving him with her, even after what happened on the day that shall not be mentioned.

She came back to work a few days after that happened, and it's been smooth sailing ever since. She texts me now whenever they go anywhere to tell me their plans. That's something she started doing on her own, and I deeply appreciate it.

I head out into a chilly spring night and jump in the car for the thirty-minute ride to the restaurant in Arlington. I've got Jay-Z turned up so loud, the car vibrates with the bass notes. I can only do that when Xavier and his young ears aren't in the car with me, so I take every chance I can get to put the music on blast.

I park in the garage that Brian has a deal with and hoof it

to 23rd Street, which is a hot spot of bars and restaurants in Crystal City.

Brian's place is called Luna, named for his baby daughter. It's a high-end steak house with a line out the door as I go around to the back and enter through the kitchen. I head straight for the bar, where Brian told me to meet him. He's working with two other bartenders when I duck under the mahogany-topped service area.

My friend grins when he sees me. "Not a minute too soon, my man."

"I'm here to help." I stash my coat under the cooler. "Tell me what you need."

He rattles off a list of drinks, and it takes off from there. A few times, I have to ask him to refresh my memory, but I do better than expected thanks to the time I spent studying up while Xavier napped earlier. It's been a few years since I tended bar, but the muscle memory is there. The night passes in a total blur of activity, which is actually a welcome relief. I have no time to think about anything other than what's right in front of me.

Brian shows me the basics with the computer system, an updated version of Square, which I've used before.

By nine thirty, the pace slows a bit from frantic to manageable. I wipe down the bar, cash out customers and greet two women who grab the first empty seats we've had in hours.

"Evening, ladies. I'm Adrian. I'll be your server. What can I get you to drink?" They're stunning and dressed to the nines. The one on the left gives me the once-over and smiles, apparently liking what she sees. I like what I see, too.

"I'll have an espresso martini," she says.

"Oh, me, too," her friend says.

"Coming right up." As I mix their drinks, I have to laugh. An espresso martini at this hour would have me awake for days. When I return with their drinks, I ask if they're planning to eat. "The kitchen is open until eleven."

"Depends on what's on the menu," the one on the left says suggestively as she gives me the eye.

I can hear Sadie saying, "See, I told you that you're a chick magnet."

I smile at her as I hand her a menu.

"I'm Kira," she says.

"Nice to meet you, Kira."

"It's very nice to meet you, too, Adrian."

Wynter

HOURS after I put Xavier to bed and long after I finish a movie on my laptop, I'm awakened from a deep sleep by the sound of moaning. I glance at the baby monitor that Adrian set up on the bedside table in my room and see Xavier is sleeping peacefully.

So who's moaning?

I get up and follow the noise, going downstairs as my heart pounds with fear. Is someone in the house? What's my plan if there is? I tiptoe toward Adrian's office, where the noise seems to be coming from, and hold my breath as I peek inside. A light from the bathroom provides just enough for me to see Adrian on top of a woman on the sofa in the office. His bare ass clenches as he fucks a woman who's moaning and clawing at his back.

I can't see anything but Adrian's muscular ass as he pumps into her like a jackhammer.

My mouth goes dry.

I need to go back upstairs, but I can't bring myself to move. In the moment, I'm well aware that I'm grossly invading his privacy. But ask me if I care about such things.

I'm mesmerized, as if I'm a virgin experiencing sex for the first time.

I've been having sex since I was fifteen.

However... Watching Adrian go at it has me aroused like I haven't been since Jaden got too sick for sex. It's been a long time since I gave sex a thought, and now a fire has been relit inside me, and all I want to do is go in there and ask if I can join them.

Oh my God, Wynter, you freaking perv.

Just as I have that thought, I hear Xavier cry out upstairs.

Adrian must hear it, too, because he stops short.

The woman under him lets out an annoyed sound at the interruption.

"That's my son."

"You have a *son*?"

He pulls out of her and gets up. "Yeah, I have a son."

Before I turn away, I get an excellent view of his very hard cock. Christ have mercy, the man is beautiful everywhere.

I'm halfway upstairs before my tongue makes it back into my mouth. I'm disgusted by my behavior, but not so disgusted that I wish I hadn't seen it.

Xavier is standing in his crib, crying his heart out.

I pick him up and am startled by the heat coming from him. "What's the matter, my sweet boy?"

Adrian appears next to me. "Is he okay?"

"I think he's got a fever." I glance at him and notice he's wearing nothing but a formfitting pair of white boxer briefs that highlight the huge erection he brought with him.

I look away, but I don't want to.

"Might be teething. He gets a fever whenever he gets a new tooth. I'll get the baby Tylenol."

While he's gone, I walk Xavier around the room, rubbing his back and trying to soothe him. I've never seen him like this, and it upsets me.

When I sit in the rocking chair in the corner of his room, I realize I'm still throbbing between my legs from seeing Adrian have sex. My nipples are tight, and every part of me is on fire in a way I haven't been in so long, I thought that might be over for me.

As I snuggle Xavier, I feel a little ashamed that I didn't immediately go back upstairs when I saw them. I should have.

I swallow hard when Adrian returns, now wearing a T-shirt and sweats.

He takes Xavier from me and administers the medicine that has the little guy smacking his lips. "Thankfully, he likes it."

"I can stay with him if you want to go back to bed."

See what I did there? I pretended that Xavier roused us both out of a sound sleep.

"That's okay. I'll stay with him."

The moaner must've left after learning he had a son upstairs.

That news would come as a shock to anyone getting screwed by a man she assumed was unencumbered. I wonder if she thought his wife might be upstairs, too, but it's not like I can come right out and ask him what he told the woman he was banging before he brought her home.

"Go get some sleep," Adrian says. "He'll be up early."

"If you're sure."

"I am. I've got him. Thanks for getting up with him."

"Of course. I'll get up with him in the morning if you want to sleep in a little."

"I wouldn't say no to that."

"Great. Good night." I bend to kiss Xavier's warm head and catch a hint of man and sex and cologne that makes me want to drool.

"Night, Wynter."

I'm back in bed before it dawns on me that Adrian just saw me dressed in nothing but a tank top and boy shorts.

These Saturday night sleepovers are going to be interesting.

Adrian

FUCK ME. That's all I can think of after Wynter walks away. I've gone hard all over again at the sight of her perfect ass in those tight shorts and her breasts nearly spilling out of the tank.

It's because I didn't get to finish with Kira.

Or so I tell myself.

It takes more than an hour to rock Xavier to sleep. After I put him in the crib, I stand over him for a few minutes to make sure he's okay. I worry all the time about him dying from crib death or some other thing I know nothing about. Per Alyssa's directions, I make sure there's nothing in the crib but the mattress covered by a sheet and him in the sleeper that also acts as a blanket.

At first, I thought it was odd not to cover him, but Alyssa showed me the stats on what causes crib deaths. That was all it took to make a believer out of me.

After I leave his room, I go downstairs to lock up and shut off the outside lights.

Upon hearing I had a son in the house, Kira bolted. I assume she got an Uber or Lyft and is long gone, but before I shut off the lights, I make sure she's not still outside. I see no sign of her. I don't have her number, so I can't text to make sure she got home okay. She strikes me as the kind of woman who can more than take care of herself.

I never would've invited her back to my place if Brian hadn't encouraged me to take what she was offering all night.

"Dude, if you're liking what she's putting out, don't let me stand in the way."

With those words, he gave me permission to take our flirtation to the next level with after-work cocktails that led to some foreplay under the table.

I feel a little sick that I picked someone up the first night I worked at the bar, but Brian didn't seem to care, so I suppose I shouldn't either. It's not like he doesn't see that every night in some form or another. Hell, we used to place bets about who would leave together when we were bartenders in college.

Kira was ripe for the picking, and when I asked if she wanted to come back to my place, she stood up so fast, she nearly knocked the glasses off the table. All the way home, she stroked me and played with me until I was on the verge of losing it in my pants. Somehow I managed to hold off, to get her inside, to get a condom on and to have sex for the first time since my wife died.

I expected to be upset, but I wasn't. I was thrilled to have a hot, sexy, enthusiastic woman under me, giving as good as she got.

But then Xavier started crying, and it was game over.

Kira was so shocked to hear there was a baby in the house that she bolted out of there two seconds after she got her dress back on. I'm sure she probably wonders if the baby's mother was there, too. I hope I get the chance to set her straight on that.

When I go back upstairs, I check Xavier and see that he's thrown his arms over his head, which means he's out. I cross the hall to my room and go into the bathroom to take a leak and brush my teeth. I wash the scent of Kira off my face and hands and then get into bed to pick over the details of this eventful evening.

I can't believe my dick is still mostly hard. The poor guy was finally getting some action that was interrupted before he could finish. I push a hand into my sweats and grip my rigid flesh, stroking myself as I try to put myself back where I was in the office with Kira. But as I stroke myself to completion, it's not Kira or even Sadie I'm thinking about.

No, it's freaking Wynter and those goddamned shorts that send me over the edge into release.

Eight

Wynter

By the time Adrian comes downstairs at ten thirty, I've made a huge stack of pancakes, fed Xavier and watched four episodes of *Paw Patrol*, which is his absolute favorite. He's in good spirts this morning, with no sign of fever or pain, which is a relief. Seeing him so upset rattled me, and it took me a long time to go back to sleep after our middle-of-the-night encounter.

I had a lot to unpack after seeing what I did and being turned on for the first time in so long, I'd nearly forgotten what that was like.

I thought about taking the edge off, but that felt so wrong and screwed up that I resisted the urge.

What kind of person watches her friend and employer have sex and then uses those visuals to get herself off? I mean, I know I'm a total mess, but that takes it to a whole other level, doesn't it?

And who can I even talk to about this without admitting that I perved on Adrian while he was having sex?

I'm disgusted with myself, but again, not so disgusted that I'm sorry I saw what I did.

I have to admit that if I'd gone down there knowing what I was going to see, I still would've looked. I hate myself for that, but it's the truth.

I cannot have feelings for him.

I cannot be attracted to him, even if he's the sexiest man I've ever met. And yes, even thinking that makes me feel like an asshole, because my late husband should be the sexiest man I've ever met. He was until I met Adrian.

From the first time I ever saw him, I've thought Adrian is ridiculously hot. I've heard Lexi and Brielle comment on his hotness, so I know I'm not the only one who sees it. You'd have to be completely blind not to see how beautiful he is. And now I know what his ass and cock look like and what he's like when he has sex, and I can't for the life of me process this information.

I don't blame him for bringing a woman home or having sex with her while Xavier and I were supposedly sleeping upstairs. Someone else might have an issue with that, but I don't. After having an up-close-and-personal view of his despair after losing his beloved wife, I'm happy for him to be getting back out there.

Adrian comes downstairs wearing the T-shirt and sweats he changed into after he appeared in his underwear in Xavier's room last night. Even first thing in the morning, the man looks too good to be true.

"Sorry I slept so late," he says as he reaches for Xavier on the sofa. "I haven't done that since before Sadie died."

I notice he's removed his wedding ring. I want to ask him about it, but I don't. "No problem. We had pancakes and watched *Paw Patrol* and played with trucks."

"He feels much cooler," Adrian says as he presses his lips to Xavier's forehead.

"He's been fine this morning."

"Glad to hear it."

"Well, I'd better get going."

"Thank you, Wynter. Not just for last night, but for this morning, too. I never get to sleep in anymore."

"You can do it every Sunday if I'm here the night before. I never have anywhere to be."

"I'll pay you extra."

"You don't have to. I'm offering. Friend to friend."

"You're the best. Thank you so much."

"No problem."

I hold out my arms to Xavier, and he comes to me so I can hug and kiss him. I'll miss him until I see him in the morning. "You boys have a good day," I say as I hand him back to his dad.

"You, too."

As I drive home, my emotions are all over the place. I didn't want to leave them. I wanted to stay with them and hang out and spend the day with them, even though I have no right to want those things. Taking care of Xavier is my job. Adrian is my friend, yes, but he's also my boss, and it would be wise to remember that.

The last place I want to be is home with my mother, who drives me crazy with questions about where my life is going and what my plans are. It's all I can do to get through the days without thinking too far ahead about where I might be and what I might be doing if Jaden had never gotten sick.

I feel like his life—and mine—came to a complete halt the minute we got the news about his dire diagnosis. I've been spinning like a top ever since he died and left me to figure out the rest on my own.

I'm not surprised when I find myself driving into Iris's neighborhood rather than my own.

Sometimes I feel guilty for the way I rely on her. Like she

doesn't have enough to contend with as the single mother to three little kids. Although she's not doing it alone anymore since Gage moved in with them.

A block from her house, I stop to send a text. *I'm nearby. R u home?*

She writes back a minute later. *We're here. Come on over.*

The relief is overwhelming. I'm not sure what I would've done if she hadn't told me to come over. I really need her, but as I pull into her driveway behind Derek's black Lexus SUV, I'm not sure what I'm going to tell her, if anything.

Derek, Roni, his daughter, Maeve, and her baby son, Dylan, are there when I enter Iris's house through the garage, which is open. She's told me before that I don't have to knock, but I still feel weird every time I go strolling in like I live there. But that's the atmosphere she's created. Everyone is always welcome, and I appreciate that so much, especially on days like this when I'm wound up.

They greet me like I'm a long-lost member of the family.

Iris and Roni hug me.

Maeve runs over to show me her new doll, and Iris's kids Tyler, Sophia and Laney drag me into the playroom so I can see the new Legos their uncle Rob brought them yesterday.

"Guys, let Wynter take her coat off and get a drink before you take off with her," Gage says from the door to the playroom. He holds out a hand to extricate me.

I take his hand and let him lead me from the playroom. "I'll be back, kiddos." To Gage, I say, "Thanks, Obi-Wan."

"You're a kid whisperer. They all want a piece of Wynter."

"What can I say? I'm still a kid myself."

"Wynter, make a plate," Roni says. "We brought all kinds of yummy stuff from the deli in town."

She and Derek live in the District, in a gorgeous townhome they bought together after they got engaged.

"I feel like I'm intruding on your get-together."

"You're not," Iris says. "We're not doing anything. Just eating and gabbing. You know you're always welcome here."

Does she have any idea what that means to me? To all of us? To have a place to go when we don't want to be alone or with people who don't understand the struggle of young widowhood? My mother will never understand, as much as she wishes she did. None of my friends from before get it. Even Jaden's family, who suffered the loss of the same person, didn't lose what I did. And I didn't lose what they did. It's such a mess.

"Are you okay?" Iris asks when she joins me at the big island that makes up the center of her kitchen.

I realize I've been holding an empty plate and staring off into space. "I could use some girl time if we can get it."

"I'll make that happen after we eat."

"Thank you, Iris."

She puts an arm around my waist and leans her head on my shoulder. "Always. You know that."

I'm appalled when her loving gesture brings tears to my eyes. "You have no idea what you and our group have come to mean to me." I'm rarely such an emotional sap, but the words are said before I take even a second to think about them.

"I do, love. I know."

That knowing. That understanding. It's priceless on this journey. They're all much older than me, but they don't treat me like a kid. They know I stopped being a kid a long time ago.

The stuff Roni and Derek brought from the District is indeed yummy. I don't even know what most of it is, but I try a little of everything.

Gage puts a glass of the iced tea I like in front of me. "Can I get you something stronger?"

"No, the tea is great," I tell him. "Thank you."

"Welcome."

Have I mentioned that I love these people and the way they take care of me and one another? None of them blinks an eye about me popping in uninvited to their get-together. When they say I'm welcome here, they mean it.

"How was the overnight with Xavier?" Iris asks.

"Fine," I answer between bites of tender chicken. "He's so easy that I feel bad getting paid to watch him."

"You shouldn't feel bad at all about getting paid," Roni says. "Knowing our kids are in good hands when we can't be with them is priceless."

"I agree," Derek says. "I've had a nanny since Vic died, and she's saved me. You're giving Adrian the peace to work and have a life separate from his son. That's huge."

My brain trips over the words *a life separate from his son* and *huge*. It's huge, all right, and it's all I can do not to dissolve into laughter at the direction my thoughts have gone.

Fortunately, they skip right along in their conversation.

"I bet Adrian made some good money on Saturday night," Gage says.

"I hope so," Iris says. "It's been hard for him without Sadie's income."

"Didn't she have life insurance?" Roni asks.

"She did, but he banked that for Xavier's college," Iris says. "He tries to forget he has it."

"That's so smart," Derek says. "He'll be glad later he did that. College is so ridiculously expensive."

"That's why I'm going back to work the minute Laney starts school," Iris says. "To save for college."

"I already told you that Daddy Gage is gonna pay for college," Gage says.

"Lalala, I can't hear you," Iris says.

"Why the hell not?" I ask her. "He wants to pay for their college. You should let him."

"Yeah," Gage says. "Listen to Wynter."

"He is not paying for my kids to go to college," Iris says.

"I assume he's going to help you raise them now that he's living here and they're calling him Daddy Gage and all that, right?" I ask her.

"Yes, but—"

"No buts, Iris. Let the man pay for their college if he wants to. I'd never say no to something like that if someone who loves them was offering."

"She does have a point," Derek says. "If some fairy godfather came along and offered to pay for my kids' college, I'd be all for it."

"The Collier College Fund is happy to include your kids, too," Gage says.

Derek stares at him. "No. I didn't mean that. Stop."

Gage shrugs. "Your kids, all your kids, are going to be mine, too, since I lost my girls. I should be able to do anything I want for the kids who are filling that terrible void for me."

"That's very manipulative of you," Derek says, smiling.

"Call it what you will. I love your kids. It would be my honor to put them through college."

"Gage, really..." Derek, who is one of the most articulate people I've ever met, is sputtering now.

"See what I'm saying?" Iris asks with exasperation. "It's all different when he's offering to pay for *your* kids, right?"

"Let me put it to you this way," Gage says. "You people saved my life. You gave me an all-new life that I've come to love very much. I sold my business for a ridiculous amount of money. Your kids bring me joy. Paying for their college would bring me joy. That's all there is to it."

"And we're all about chasing the joy," I add to help him make his case.

"That's right," Gage says. "Finding joy anywhere we can is our mantra."

"If it brings the man joy, what else can you say but 'thank you, Gage'?"

He points to me, gives me a thumbs-up and a grin.

"Thank you, Gage," Roni says softly. "I've never had friends like you guys. I hate that my Patrick had to die for me to find you all, but how blessed we are in this strange 'after.'"

"You're welcome," Gage says. "And I agree. How blessed we are. Who wants dessert?"

"I can't believe him," Derek says.

"I can hear you," Gage replies with a chuckle from the island where he's serving up treats from a bakery box.

"Good," Derek says. "I can't believe you. What a friend."

"I get way more than I give from this deal," Gage says. "I hadn't realized how much I missed having kids in my life until I got to be around yours. They can never take the place of my girls, but they bring me joy just the same."

He carries a platter full of cupcakes, brownies and cookies that smell as good as they look to the table and puts it in front of us. "Hurry and take what you want before the kids pick up the scent of sugar."

"You really are the best, Daddy Gage," Roni says softly.

"Love you all," he says. "To the moon and back."

"We love you, too," Derek says.

As we enjoy the desserts, Roni tells us about the upcoming state dinner at the White House for the German chancellor. "It got postponed after the chancellor's wife had heart surgery, but she's doing much better now."

"Have you got a dress yet?" Iris asks.

"Shelby, who's the social secretary, has tons of contacts with designers, and she's hooking me up."

"Oh, that's so exciting. I can't wait to see what you pick."

"I might need some help deciding," Roni says.

"Call us," Iris says, including me. "We've got you covered."

"It's so cool that you get to go to something like that as part of your job," I say.

"I still pinch myself every time I walk in the door to the White House to report to work."

"What will you do when President Cappuano isn't in office anymore?" I ask her. "Won't you both lose your jobs when they leave?"

She shrugs as if that's no big deal. "We'll figure out something. For now, we're enjoying the adventure."

"Do you guys want to see my crocuses?" Iris asks me and Roni. "They're poking up early."

"What the hell is a crocus?" I ask.

"It's a flower, silly," Iris says. "Come see."

I grab my coat and follow them out to Iris's backyard, where the pool is still covered.

"I was trying to get us a minute alone," Iris says.

"Wow," I say. "I totally missed that, but now I want to know what a crocus is."

They laugh.

"You're the funniest, Wynter." Roni links her arm through mine. "I'm so glad you came by."

These people. They always say or do something that puts a huge lump in my throat. Like someone said before, I've never had friends like them. Other than Jaden, most of the kids I grew up with seemed annoyed by my odd humor and treated me like I was weird, but these guys think I'm hilarious. Maybe what I've needed all along are older friends who understand me.

Iris walks us to the back fence and shows us where tiny purple blooms are pushing their way through the leftover mulch and leaves from last year. "That's a crocus. They're almost always the first sign of spring."

"Ah, I see. How do you find this stuff out? Is there a book

or something on adulting and the stuff you should just know? Like what the fuck a crocus is?"

They lose it laughing.

"There's no book, but we'd be happy to guide you through the stuff you need to know," Roni says.

"Tell me the truth. When did you find out what a crocus was?"

"My grandmother was an amazing gardener," Roni says. "I knew the names of all the flowers when I was very young."

"That's an unfair advantage."

"Granted, but I had no idea what a carburetor was until I married Patrick."

"What the heck is that?"

"Part of an engine," Iris says.

"See? How am I supposed to know all this crap?"

"You'll pick it up as you go," Roni says. "You'll leave here knowing two things you didn't know before."

"True."

"So what's going on with you?" Iris asks.

I feel my face go hot when the memories from last night suddenly return. "Something mortifying."

"We're here for that," Roni says.

"You guys can't ever tell anyone this. Not Gage or Derek or anyone."

"Promise," Iris says for both of them.

"I saw Adrian having sex last night."

"*Oh*, damn," Roni says. "How was it?"

"It looked pretty good for them, but left me feeling a little..."

"Aroused?" Iris asks.

"Yes! And I feel like such a creep!"

"You're not a creep," Roni says. "I assume you came upon them by accident, right?"

"I did, but I couldn't look away. I feel bad about that.

Kinda. I mean, he's so freaking hot, and watching him go to pound town was..."

They're crippled with laughter again.

"Honestly, Wynter," Iris says, gasping. "You kill me."

Roni wipes laughter tears from her eyes. "You didn't do anything wrong, Wynter. He's hot, and it's been a while for you."

"I saw the front of him, too, and now that's all I can think about."

"Whoa," Iris says. "It was impressive, then?"

"*Hell* yes. That's one word for it."

"Who was the woman?" Roni asks.

"No idea, and I can't exactly ask him. He has no idea I saw them. Xavier started crying, so I ran upstairs. That's where he found me when he showed up wearing only underwear that put the full package on display. I feel so guilty. I can't believe I stood there like a creeper and watched."

"I think that might've been the first time for him," Iris says. "Since Sadie."

"I don't think they got to finish. As soon as he heard Xavier crying, he stopped and said that was his son. She seemed surprised to hear he had a son. That was the last thing I heard before I got out of there."

"I can see why you might feel guilty," Iris says, "but you shouldn't. It happened. You saw what you saw. It doesn't change anything that matters."

"It's got me all..." I move my shoulders around. "Reawakened."

"*Ahhhh*," Roni says. "Maybe it's time for you to go to pound town." She starts laughing as soon as she says the words. "Sorry, that's still funny."

"I cannot *imagine* doing that with anyone other than Jaden." Before they can protest, I hold up my hands. "Yes, I know I am going to live most of my life without him, and there'll be others. I'm not in denial over that. I swear I'm not. It's just that I can't get my head to the point of *actually doing it* with someone else."

Iris puts her arm around me and leads me to sit on a bench under a tree.

Roni sits on the other side of me.

"You might not be ready yet," Iris says.

"My hooha is saying it's ready. There's a steady drumbeat of interest ever since I saw the Adrian porn show last night."

Roni rolls her lips together as if she's trying to hold back more laughter. "That's a good start, but maybe that's all it is. Just you waking up to the possibilities again."

"I agree," Iris says. "Think of it as an old furnace coming back to life. This might be how it begins."

"You guys... I don't want to do that with someone else. I just don't."

Iris puts her head on my shoulder. "I know, sweetie, but at some point, you're gonna have to."

I'm furious when tears roll down my cheeks. I'm so sick of tears. I brush them away with aggravation. "Sometimes I hate him for dying and forcing me to deal with this shit."

"I get that," Iris says. "That's perfectly normal."

"To hate the person you loved best?"

"Yeah," Iris says. "It's normal."

She has good reason to hate her late husband after learning he had another kid with someone else.

"Do you hate Patrick, Roni?"

"No, I don't. But I understand why someone would hate the situation we've been left in, which is what you really hate. Not him."

"No, I hate him for dying, for leaving me alone, for making it so I don't want to be with anyone but him."

"And you probably love him for all those reasons, too, right?" Iris asks gently.

"I guess."

"It's all normal, even if the situation is beyond screwed up," Roni says. "There're days when I still can't believe that my life is now Derek, Maeve and Dylan. Like, where in the hell is Patrick, I want to ask, you know?"

"You still think that?" I ask her. "Even though you're so happy with Derek?"

"Every day."

"I do, too," Iris says. "I wake up to Gage next to me in bed, and I blink a couple of times to remember how he got there and where Mike is and what's happened since he died. It's such a weird space to be in. Sometimes I think maybe I dreamed the whole thing, but there's Gage to remind me it's not a dream. It's real life, and we're doing it the best we can under the circumstances."

"You guys are all killing the widow game," I say.

"So are you, Wynter," Roni says. "You're so different than you were when we first met. You're still the funniest person I've ever known, but you've lost your sharp edges. You're not as bitter as you were then."

"I'm still bitter as fuck."

"Maybe so, but it's not as obvious to others as it was then."

Iris points to Roni. "I agree with everything she said. You're doing a lot better than you give yourself credit for."

"It's only thanks to you guys. You showed me the way through."

"And you'll do it for someone else someday," Iris says. "That's how this works."

"What do I do about Adrian?"

"What do you want to do about him?" Roni asks.

"Is pound town on the table?"

They laugh.

"It might be better to find someone other than your employer for that," Iris says.

"Everyone else is gonna look paltry next to him."

"Probably, but be careful playing with fire where he's concerned," Iris says. "You love taking care of Xavier. Don't do anything that'll mess that up for any of you. You need each other too much right now."

"I know," I say with a sigh. "You're right. But it's gonna take a while for me to scrub those images from my brain."

"No one says you have to scrub anything from your brain," Roni says. "If you have to relive it, you may as well enjoy it."

"Are you giving me permission to spank bank Adrian?"

They laugh harder than ever.

"Oh my God, Wynter," Roni says, gasping. "I never said anything like that!"

"Yes, you did. Tell her, Iris. She did."

"Kinda," Iris says with a grin for Roni.

"Well, that's not what I meant!"

The three of us laugh so hard, we can barely breathe, which was just what I needed.

"I love you guys so much," I tell them as soon as I can speak again.

"We love you, too," Iris says.

Wynter

The following Saturday night, I once again wake in the middle of the night to sounds coming from somewhere in the house. Rather than the moan of last week, this one is more of a squeal.

"Just stay in bed and mind your own business," I tell myself. "Remember that curiosity killed the cat." My grandmother used to tell me that when I was sticking my nose into everyone else's business when I was a kid. Alas, curiosity has me getting out of bed and sneaking downstairs to see what's going on.

Like last week, Adrian is in the office getting busy with someone under him. I don't think it's the same woman, because this one is making little mewling cat noises that almost make me giggle.

But who cares what she's doing when I can watch him and that perfect ass as he pumps that big old cock into a willing woman.

I wish it was me.

There.

I said it.

Every time I've looked at him over the last week, I've had that same thought. I want it to be me. I would spread my legs so wide for him and take that big thing. My entire body has gone liquid from wanting it, and the throb between my legs is more intense than it's been in longer than I can remember.

As Adrian picks up the pace to get them to the finish line, I turn to get out of there before I get caught being a creep. I feel sick over the invasion of his privacy, which was intentional this time. I can't deny that. Last time was an accident. This time, I knew exactly what I was going to see, and I went anyway.

I won't do that again.

Before I go back to bed, I look in on Xavier, who's flat on his back with his arms thrown over his head. He's so damned cute that I stand there for a few minutes watching him sleep while I try to calm my overheated body and mind.

I'm still there when I feel the air change behind me.

I turn to see Adrian in the doorway, wearing only those tight white boxer briefs that have starred in all my fantasies over the last week. "Is he okay?" he whispers.

"Yeah, I was just checking on him. Did you just get home?"

Hopefully, the nonchalant question indicates I have no idea what he's been up to downstairs.

He comes into the room and stands next to me at the crib, bringing an earthy, sexy scent with him that fills my senses and has me tingling from the urge to reach out and take what I want. "Little while ago."

"Did you have a good night?"

"Yeah, it was busy. Made about five hundred."

"Wow. That keeps me employed for another week."

"Yep."

"I guess I'll see you in the morning. I'll get up with him."

"I can't sleep in tomorrow. I've got to get ready for his party."

"Sleep until at least nine. I don't mind taking the six-to-nine shift. You never get a break. Take one while you can."

"In case I forget to tell you, you're awesome."

"Duh, I know."

I leave him with a saucy grin and catch him looking at my breasts. As I walk out of the room, I feel like he might be watching me go. He's just gotten lucky, and yet, he's still checking me out. Why does that fill me with this weird feeling of excitement and anticipation?

Because you're a freak who doesn't know how to mind her own business and stay out of trouble. Adrian would be trouble for me. I know that as much as I know that I loved Jaden and will miss him forever. Adrian is someone I could fall in love with, and that could be a disaster if it didn't work out. I wouldn't be able to see Xavier, and I'd probably have to quit the Wild Widows since he was there before me, so he could claim custody of the group.

I can barely get through a day without leaning on one of them for something, so I'd be wise to cut the shit when it comes to Adrian and my suddenly overactive libido.

Iris is right. If I want to go to pound town, I could find a guy to take me there. It would take about three minutes on Tinder to find someone with the needed equipment who'd be ready and willing. Men have been looking at me "that way" since the second my boobs showed up when I was in eighth grade. It used to drive my mother crazy that grown men would look at her thirteen-year-old daughter like I was an all-you-can-eat buffet or something.

She'd lash out at them in public. "Put your eyes away, you creep. She's *thirteen*."

That was mortifying.

I got so I never wanted to go anywhere with her because, no matter where we went, there were men with eyes that landed on me in a way that made us both feel uncomfortable, and she was always ready to put them in their place. That was when my "big shirt" phase started and spanned most of high school until Jaden convinced me to quit caring what any other guy thought of me or my body. He thought I was sexy, and he liked to look at me.

So I dressed for him and only him.

It wouldn't take much to find a new guy to scratch my itch.

Except...

When I think about doing *that*, I only want to do it with Adrian.

And we're right back to where we started with me knowing that's a bad idea and my brain refusing to look at anyone but him.

I haven't had self-destructive tendencies since Jaden broke me of that nonsense years ago. I had the most awesome boyfriend who made me feel like a queen, and I no longer had the need to do stupid things to sabotage my own life. Then he went and died on me, and now I don't give a crap about things like being proper with the hot-as-hell man who employs me to care for his son—who I love more than anyone on earth.

I don't care if I screw up everything by wanting Adrian. Side note: I do care. I care way too much, but that's not stopping these wildly inappropriate thoughts.

He doesn't seem to have any problem hooking up with randos, so maybe he wouldn't mind hooking up with me.

Could I come right out and ask him how he might feel about that?

Pre-widow Wynter never would've considered such a thing, but then again, she never had to. She had a boyfriend from the ninth grade on who satisfied every need she ever had.

He taught her about love and sex and orgasms and everything else that mattered. But he's gone now, and she's left to carry on by herself.

"Are you done thinking of yourself in the third person?" I say out loud.

Adrian appears in my doorway. "Did you say something?"

"Oh, um, I was kinda talking to myself. I do that."

"Ha, me, too. Does yourself ever answer?"

"All the time, and it tells me to do things that I shouldn't."

He puts his hands over his head to grip the door frame, which puts his incredible body on full display. "Like what?"

I'm so dazzled by his well-honed muscles, the toned abdomen and the big bulge in his boxer briefs that I'm momentary speechless. Add all that to his showstopper face, and it's a potent combination.

"Wynter?"

"Like, um, going downstairs to check on a noise and seeing you, you know..."

He cringes. "Shit. I'm sorry."

"Don't be. It looked hot."

He releases a deep sigh. "It was okay. I'm sorry you had to see that."

"I'm not." Look at post-widow Wynter go! She puts it all out there.

"You aren't?"

"Nope. And you may as well know... I saw you last week, too."

"Jesus, Wynter. Why didn't you say something?"

"What was I supposed to say? I thought there was a robber in the house, so I went downstairs and saw you banging someone in your office?"

"Well, yeah, that would've been a good place to start. I knew I shouldn't have brought them here. It felt wrong to me, but I couldn't exactly spring for a hotel room that would take half the money I just earned."

"You didn't do anything wrong."

"And yet, it feels wrong."

"Because it wasn't Sadie."

"Yeah, and because you and my son were sleeping upstairs, or so I thought. I should've at least given you a heads-up that I was bringing someone home. I'm sorry I didn't do that. I've lost all sense of decorum on these things. My sister would kick my ass if she knew I'd done that."

"It's all good. I'm sorry I invaded your privacy. I feel bad about that."

"It's okay."

"Could I tell you one other thing?"

"Sure."

"Ever since I saw you... Last week and then tonight... I've wondered what it might be like to, you know... Do that with you."

He lets his head fall back as he exhales loudly.

But the bulge in his shorts is suddenly much larger.

"We can't, Wynter. It would screw up everything."

I don't know what makes me do it, but I get up from the bed and go to him, placing my hands on his chest before he even knows I'm there. "Maybe it wouldn't."

He gasps when I touch him. "It would. I need you so badly right now with Xavier. I don't know what I'd do without you."

"I'm not going anywhere. You know how much I love him."

"I do, and I have to keep my focus on him, no matter how sexy I think you are."

"You think I'm sexy?"

"Wynter, any man with a pulse would think you're sexy."

"I'm not asking about any man. I'm asking about you."

He curls his hands around my wrists, and it's all I can do not to go up on tiptoes and kiss him. "Yes, I think you're sexy. I think you're funny and loving and sweet, even though you want everyone to think you're a nasty badass."

Then he removes my hands from his chest and takes a step back.

I look down and note that the crown of his cock is poking out of the waistband of his briefs. What would he do if I dropped to my knees in front of him?

"We *can't*, Wynter. We just can't. Sex screws up everything, and I can't do that after finally getting back on track after Sadie and Alyssa died. I just can't."

I hear what he's saying, and I even agree with him, but my heart aches, as if I've lost something I never had.

He kisses my forehead. "Get some sleep, okay?"

As if that's going to happen. "Sure."

"I'll see you in the morning."

"I'll be here."

I watch him walk away, noting the fine play of muscles and sleek skin, and it's all I can do not to drool.

The thing is, it's not just about his sexy body or perfect cock for me. I like *him*. I like how he is with Xavier, how he's stepped up to single parenthood after the worst possible loss and made it work—somehow. I like that he's a good friend to everyone and how he's right there to support any of us when we need it.

Adrian is the full package in more ways than one, and now I know something I didn't know before: He thinks I'm sexy, and he wants me, too.

I can work with that.

Adrian

How is it that I just had sex—and got to finish this time—and all I can think about is Wynter suggesting we get busy? The woman who came home with me tonight told me her name was Tulip. I'm not sure if that's her real name.

She made the weirdest noises when we were doing it, which was so distracting. Not so much that I couldn't get us both to the finish line, but it was odd.

Even with the noises, she'd be much safer to hang out with than Wynter, who's like a keg of dynamite. She's my nanny and my friend. We have a ton of mutual friends who'd be impacted if she and I were to make a mess of things.

The fact that she's my nanny is the most important thing. I need to put Xavier and his needs ahead of my own. He loves Wynter, and she loves him. Our arrangement is working out perfectly for all of us, and I'd be a complete fool to screw with that—literally.

But the truth is, it took every ounce of willpower I could muster to walk away from her just now. If she were anyone else, standing before me looking sweet and sexy and willing, I wouldn't have had the wherewithal to say no.

However, she's *Wynter*.

To my knowledge, she hasn't gone there since she lost Jaden. So despite how casual she made it sound, it would be anything but for her. Or for me. There would be feelings involved if it happened with her. I love her. Of course I do. We've been through hell together and are coming out the other side of early grief at the same time.

I lay facedown in bed, wishing my cock would get the message that fun and games are done for the night. All I can see when I close my eyes is Wynter in a tight black tank top and tight black-and-white polka-dotted shorts that left little to the imagination.

I can't believe she saw me getting busy last week and again

tonight. I should be concerned about that, but when I think about her watching us, I just get harder.

Groaning, I turn onto my back and push my underwear aside so I can tend to this situation, which needs to happen if I have a prayer of getting any sleep tonight. This time, when I take matters into my own hand, I don't feel guilty at all about letting Wynter be my inspiration. This persistent erection is her fault, after all.

Now that she's put the idea of us having sex in my head, how will I think about anything else?

True confession time. The first time I ever saw Wynter, I thought she was stunning. My immediate reaction to Wynter, shortly after I lost my beloved wife, shocked me. It also made me angry with myself. Like, how can I think she's stunning when I just lost my wife? For a while after that, I was chilly to Wynter, which I can now see was a dick move.

How was it her fault that I was immediately attracted to her when I had no business thinking that way about anyone with a newborn baby depending on me for everything? It wasn't her fault, and eventually, I got over being pissed with her for something she had nothing to do with.

However, I've never forgotten my first reaction to her.

If I could've pointed to any woman to be the first after my wife, I would've pointed to her.

She's too young for me.

She's too much for me.

She works for me.

There're a million reasons why she should be the last woman on earth who makes me hard, but as I stroke myself to an orgasm that makes the one I had earlier feel weak by comparison, there's no denying I want Wynter.

Ten

Wynter

Things are tense between Adrian and me as we prepare for the party. Expecting to spend the day there, I brought clothes to change into, and after I shower, I return to the kitchen, which is a beehive of activity as Sadie's sisters and our Wild Widows help get ready. Adrian told us he had no idea how to have a birthday party for a one-year-old, so we all pitched in to pull it off.

Lexi comes in carrying the firetruck cake she offered to pick up since the bakery is close to her house. She puts it on the kitchen table, and we gather around her as she removes the lid to the box.

"Oh wow," Adrian says. "That's a work of art. You were right, Iris. They're amazing."

"I had to pull some strings and use the widow card to sneak you into their always-booked schedule."

"Whatever you did to make it happen, thank you."

"They included a cupcake for the birthday boy," Lexi says of the second smaller box.

"What's that about?" Adrian asks.

"The tradition is for the one-year-old to serve himself his own cake," Iris says, "so there's always a smaller one for him or her to smash and eat."

"That sounds messy," Adrian says.

"That's the whole idea," Iris replies, grinning.

"Xavier will love the cake and smashing the cupcake," I say. "Well done, guys." I go to retrieve the bag I brought in from my car earlier and hand it to Adrian. "I got this at a party store. I didn't see any point to wrapping it. I hope he likes it."

As Adrian pulls the fireman costume out of the bag, the others ooh and aah over it. "Oh my God, Wynter. He'll go crazy for this. Where'd you find it in March?"

I love that the gift has made him smile. "The party stores are all Halloween all the time."

"How do people who don't have kids know that, and I don't?"

"Stick with me," I tell him. "I know everything."

"Does anyone doubt that she does?" Iris asks.

Lexi, Brielle, Joy and Christy laugh.

"I wouldn't argue with her," Christy says, smiling at me.

"I keep all you senior citizens hip," I tell them.

"Hey!" They all speak as one as I crack up.

"Who's she calling a senior citizen?" Gage asks as he carries in a cooler full of ice.

"All of us who are older than her," Iris tells him.

"Well, compared to her, we are seniors."

"That's right, Big Daddy," I say in a teasing tone. He and I once did the math and realized he could've been my father, not that he wanted to hear that.

"I love that nickname," Iris says, laughing.

"I do not," Gage says, which only makes us laugh harder.

"You guys are so fun," Adrian's high school friend Danielle says.

I tried not to hate her on sight. She's tall, Black, gorgeous, smart and just the kind of woman I can picture him with. I heard her telling Joy that she, too, is an attorney. In other words, she's everything I'm not.

"We try to keep it real," Iris says in response to Danielle's comment.

"When Adrian told me his Wild Widows were coming today, I wasn't sure what to expect," Danielle says.

"We can be an irreverent bunch," Brielle says. "It's how we cope."

"I think it's wonderful that you all have each other."

"We are pretty wonderful," Iris says, smiling, before she goes to tend to Laney in the bathroom.

I glance at Adrian, who seems to be having trouble making eye contact with me today. "I also got fire hats for the other kids, and I did some goody bags for them."

"You're the best, Wynter. Thank you so much."

"No problem."

Adrian's sister, Nia, arrives with her husband, Mick, and their kids, Chantelle and Malik, who are very polite as they shake my hand. I remember Adrian saying they're twelve and fourteen. They were here the night Alyssa died, but we didn't really get the chance to talk to each other.

"You're Adrian's nanny, right?" Nia asks, giving me a once-over. She shares her brother's prominent cheekbones and wears her hair in long braids.

"She is," Adrian says, "and don't do what you do, Nia."

"What do I do?"

"Critique my whole life. Wynter is awesome, Xavier loves her and we're all doing great. So butt out."

"I was just going to thank her for taking good care of my nephew," Nia says with sisterly exasperation. "I apologize for my brother. He's cranky."

I bite my lip so I won't laugh, sensing he wouldn't appreciate me finding her funny.

"Don't mind them," Mick says. "They're always bickering. You get used to it after a while."

"Good to know," I tell him. "Can I get you something to drink?"

"Is there beer?"

"In a cooler on the back deck."

"Thanks."

"Is that the brother-in-law you work with?" I ask Adrian when I join him at the counter to finish making the pizzas for the kids.

"Yep. We've been friends forever. He and Nia have been together since I was in middle school. I tell her all the time that I get custody of him in their eventual divorce."

I sputter with laughter. "That's rude."

"Just so she knows where she stands with me, and of course it's all in good fun. I never would've made it without both of them after Sadie and then Alyssa died. Nia practically raised me."

"Where were your parents?"

"Never knew my dad, and my mom had a lot of issues. Nia and I ended up in foster care a few times, and thankfully, we got to stay together."

"I'm glad you had her."

"I am, too, but now we love to bust each other's balls nonstop."

"Mom doesn't have balls, Uncle Adrian," Malik says as he steals a piece of pepperoni from the pile on the counter.

We crack up.

"Whoops." Adrian glances at me with a warm, affectionate look that makes my knees go weak. "Quit being so smart, mister."

"Can't help it. It's in my DNA."

After Malik takes another piece of pepperoni, he runs away.

"Is that what I'm in for in about twelve years?" Adrian asks.

"Might be even sooner. Xavier is the smartest boy I've ever met."

We get the older kids started with adding toppings to their pizzas, which was my idea when Adrian asked what he should do for food, while I make a plain cheese for myself. Xavier, dressed in the fireman costume he loved, is in his high chair, gnawing on crackers and little bits of cheese that I put on his tray.

He's all smiles as he watches the other kids make pizzas and then as he opens his presents while the pizzas bake.

It's so fun to watch his reaction to each new toy, book, game and even the outfit that Nia and Mick give him.

"He's styling like his daddy," Nia says. "From the time Adrian could afford to buy nice clothes, he was always the best dressed."

"What can I say?" Adrian replies. "Clothes make the man."

Today, he's wearing a pair of faded jeans and a light gray T-shirt that molds to his muscular body. I want to know if the shirt is as soft as it looks, but I don't dare go near him after last night's conversation. Even though nothing happened, it feels like everything has changed between us.

I'm at the sink, doing dishes after Xavier has smashed cake into his face and made a hellacious mess the way one-year-olds are supposed to, when Iris and Roni surround me.

"How's it going?" Iris asks.

"Fine."

"Nice party," Roni says. "Adrian said you were a huge help."

"That's nice of him. It was fun to help. Look at Xavier

111

with the red frosting all over his face."

"How are things?" Iris asks.

I glance at Adrian across the room, surrounded by friends and family as he watches Xavier add to the cupcake mess. I tip my head to tell them to follow me into the living room where we can speak privately.

"There was more sex last night, but not with me."

"Did you watch again?" Roni asks.

"Only for a second, and later I told him I saw him both times."

"What'd he say to that?" Iris asks.

"He seemed embarrassed. He said he was sorry, and it won't happen again. I told him I wasn't sorry because it was hot."

"Then what?" Roni asks.

I realize the two of them are hanging on my every word.

"I, um, sort of went over to him and tried to make something happen, but he said we can't for obvious reasons. But he wanted to. There was evidence..."

Iris fans her face. "Holy crap, that's hot."

"You guys, *what do I do*? It's all I think about now that I've given myself permission to do it with him—and only him."

"He's right," Roni says. "It could make a mess of things."

"It won't. I'm not going to suddenly stop caring about Xavier or Adrian just because my relationship with him changes."

"Speaking as a parent here and not as a woman," Roni says, "my daycare situation is critical to me being able to perform my job and make the money I need to support my son. I wouldn't do anything to mess with that. Ever. And that could be what Adrian is thinking, too."

"The kids come first—always," Iris says. "Someday, when you're a parent, you'll see what we mean. You can want something so badly, but if it's not in the best interest of your child, you won't do it."

"That's depressing as all fuck. Maybe I should quit as his nanny."

"Don't do that, Wynter," Iris says. "He needs you so much. You've saved him after Alyssa died so suddenly—and besides, you'd be despondent if you couldn't see Xavier every day."

"That's true. I miss him the minute I leave him."

"The arrangement is working out well for all of you, or it was until sex almost happened," Roni says.

"I hate being a cliché."

"How are you a cliché?" Iris asks.

"The younger nanny lusting after the single daddy."

"That doesn't make you a cliché since you're also his close friend," Roni says.

"Still, my emotions are a jumbled mess ever since I realized he wants me, too."

"Can I say something?" Iris asks.

I give her a confused look. "Since when do you ask for permission?"

"Only when what I say might cause pain for someone else."

"I'm sure whatever it is, I can take it after what I've been through."

"It just seems to me that you've turned a corner on your grief by wanting Adrian that way—and admitting it to us," Iris says carefully. "I hope you can see that as progress."

Even though they're said with the utmost care, Iris's words lacerate me. I feel disloyal to Jaden by even acknowledging the truth of what she said. "I'm... uh..." Tears fill my eyes. "Damn it."

The two of them embrace me.

"This is a *good* thing," Iris whispers, "even if it feels shitty when you first realize it's happened."

"I never wanted that to happen."

"I know, sweetie," Roni says, "but it happens because we're still here, still living and breathing and feeling and growing despite the worst kind of loss. From everything you've told us about Jaden, he loved you so much. He'd want you to find a way to be happy."

Tears fall unchecked down my cheeks.

"What's wrong, Wynter?" Adrian asks when he comes into the room and stops short when he sees me huddled with Iris and Roni. He's holding Xavier, who's been cleaned up after the caketastrophy.

"Nothing." I quickly wipe away the tears and force a smile for them. "How's my favorite one-year-old?"

Xavier reaches for me, and Adrian transfers him to me while continuing to look at me with concern that I can feel more than see.

"Why were you crying?" he asks.

"Jaden stuff. Nothing to worry about." I bounce Xavier on my hip. "Who wants to play with new toys?"

He lets out a squeal of excitement. "Toy."

"Another new word. Let's do it!"

I walk away, leaving Adrian alone with Iris and Roni. I hope they tell me later what he says.

Adrian

"Is she okay?"

"She will be," Iris says. "You know how it is."

"Yeah." I rub at the stubble on my face. "It's just that things took an odd turn between us last night."

"How so?" Roni asks.

"Uh, how to say this? We basically discovered we both

think the other is attractive." Never in my wildest dreams could I imagine sharing such a thing with anyone prior to being widowed. In the "after," I talk about everything with them because it helps to air it out with people who understand the challenges.

"Ohhhh," Iris says. "How do you feel about that?"

"Conflicted, for obvious reasons."

"You didn't ask our opinion, but you know we love you both," Iris says as Roni nods in agreement.

"I want your opinions, or I wouldn't have brought it up."

"You rely on her heavily," Roni says.

"Exactly, and she's so, so great with Xavier. He adores her."

"That's obvious to everyone," Iris says. "They have an amazing bond."

"I'd never want to do anything to threaten an arrangement that's working so well for all of us."

"But?" Roni asks.

"I look at her, and I want her. That's not new, by the way. And now I know she feels the same way. I don't know how to handle that information."

Iris fans her face.

"Stop," I say, laughing. "This is serious."

"I know it is," Iris says, "and we're taking it seriously. I swear we are, but it's just nice to see two people we love so much, who've suffered so deeply, starting to emerge from the fog to take a look at the world around them."

"I had sex with someone last week and with someone else this week," I confess after checking to make sure we aren't overheard.

"How was it?"

I shrug. "After I got over feeling like I was cheating on my wife, it was okay, I guess. Nothing earth-shattering. But I'm glad to have gotten it over with."

"That was how I felt, too," Iris says.

She's been open about having a random hookup shortly after her husband died because she didn't want to have to dread doing that with someone else. I've learned that everyone handles these things differently after being widowed, and our group is all about not judging the choices others make to get through such a huge loss.

"It's very difficult to move forward emotionally and physically, even if you love the person you're taking that step with," Roni says.

"It was hard for you with Derek?"

"Hell yes, and hard for him with me. Patrick and Victoria were right there in that room with us, where they'll always be. It's such a strange and painful and wonderful thing all at the same time. But I don't have any regrets about moving forward with him. It's nice to feel joy every day, even as I still mourn Patrick's loss."

"I feel like letting this happen with her would cross lines that can never be uncrossed."

"It would," Iris says, "but maybe you two would find new joy together."

"It's *Wynter*." I glance over my shoulder to make sure she hasn't come back. "She's so unpredictable and... well..."

"Sexy?" Iris asks with a grin.

"God *yes*. I noticed that right away, which made me feel so guilty."

"Guilt has no place in the after," Iris says. "Tell me you know that."

"I do, but I feel it anyway. She's also seven years younger than me."

"Wynter is an old soul," Iris says. "I have a feeling she always has been, but she's even more so after losing Jaden. I don't look at her and see a twenty-one-year-old. Well, except when she's being outrageous. Most of the time, I see a fully grown woman who's seen the worst life has to offer and still puts one foot in front of the other."

"I lost Patrick when I was twenty-nine, and it nearly killed me," Roni says. "I can't imagine going through what she did at twenty. When you consider your shared experience, the years between you hardly seem to matter."

"Are you guys enabling me to act on this attraction?" I ask them, eyebrow raised.

"Not at all," Iris says. "We're encouraging you to think very carefully before you allow a close friendship and employer-employee situation to become something more. You have to be prepared for your nanny situation to fall apart if the relationship doesn't work out, which would break a lot of hearts other than yours and hers."

Before I can respond to that painful truth, my sister and her family come to say goodbye.

"It was so great have the chance to get to know you all," Nia says as she hugs Iris and Roni. "Adrian has told us so much about his Wild Widows, and we're thankful for your support of him."

"We adore him and Xavier," Iris says.

"It was great to see you again," Roni adds.

I hug my sister. "Thanks for all the help with the party."

"Anything for you guys."

After Nia's family leaves, Brielle hugs me and then Christy does, too.

"Gotta pick up my kids from another party." Christy puts her hands on my shoulders. "Before I go, today isn't just Xavier's birthday. Are you doing okay?"

"The birthday has kept me too busy to think about anything else."

"If it catches up to you later, you know where we are."

"I do." I hug her again. "Thank you."

"We love you," Brielle says.

"Love you, too, and thank you so much for the gifts for Xavier. You guys are like his fairy godmothers."

"We love him, too," Christy says. "See you Wednesday?"

"I'll be there."

I wave them off and then return to the kitchen, where Iris, Roni, Derek and Gage are doing cleanup while Wynter plays with Iris's kids as well as Maeve and Xavier in my office-slash-playroom. Baby Dylan is snoozing in his car seat, which is positioned on the table where Roni and Derek can keep an eye on him.

"Cheers to a successful first birthday party," Iris says, raising a wineglass. "You only have seventeen more to go."

"Jesus," I mutter as I laugh.

"My mom still has a birthday party for me, and I'm almost thirty-nine," Derek says, grinning.

I stare at him, wide-eyed. "Shut up with that!"

They all laugh.

"It's true," Roni says. "Ruth called me last week to ask what we should do for Derek's birthday."

"Oh my God, you're such a mama's boy, Derek," Gage says in a teasing tone.

"Guilty as charged. She makes the best cake in the world, so I go along with the parties for the cake. And the presents, of course."

"Y'all are so lucky to have such amazing parents," Lexi says. "I love mine so much, but they smother me to the point of suffocation."

"You have a roommate offer on the table," Iris reminds her.

"I'm so tempted, it's not even funny."

"Do it!" Roni says. "What do you have to lose? You could always move home again if it doesn't work out."

"I think I might." Lexi brightens as she seems to decide right on the spot. "Would you guys help me move?"

"Of course we would," Gage says. "My dad has a big pickup truck that I could borrow."

"I'm in, too," Derek says. "Whatever you need."

"Same," I add. "Widow Moving Company, at your service."

The name of our fictional company sends us all into giggles.

"What's so funny?" Wynter asks as she comes into the kitchen with Xavier mostly sacked out in her arms.

I take him from her and catch her up on what we were talking about.

"I like that." She accepts the glass of Chardonnay that Iris poured for her. "Widow Moving Company. It has a morbid ring to it."

While Xavier sleeps on my chest, we enjoy the leftover pizza and snacks as we chat about Lexi's move, Tyler's upcoming baseball season and the book Gage has been working on, documenting his widower journey.

"Is it hard to revisit it all?" Roni asks him.

"The first few chapters were rough," he says. "When I had to write about what happened, how I found out, those first few days, the funeral and all that. But I'm through that part now and on to more about coping and rebuilding."

"I give you credit for being able to go back there," Derek says. "I couldn't do it."

"It was right about now, a year ago today, I was being told Sadie had hemorrhaged, that they couldn't stop the bleeding."

Everyone looks at me with sympathy and kindness. I look down at Xavier as the heat of his body seeps through my shirt. "He was three weeks early, so they took him right to the NICU. Sadie told me to go with him. I kissed her and said I'd be back to her as soon as I could. I didn't know I'd never see her alive again."

"God, Adrian," Iris says. "It must've been so shocking."

"I thought they were lying. Like, how could she be dead? I'd just seen her. She'd just given birth."

Lexi puts her arm around me and leans her head on my shoulder.

"I demanded they take me to her. They said it wasn't a good idea. I didn't care. I wanted to see her. Yeah, that was a mistake." After a long moment of silence, I continue. "For the longest time after that, when I thought of her, I only saw her how she looked then, just so... gone. I couldn't remember what she looked like when she was alive. I'd think of her, and I'd be right back in that room. I wish I had that to do over again, but I didn't believe them."

"I would've done the same thing, Adrian," Wynter says. "If it had gone down like that for us, I'd have wanted to see him, too."

"Same," Iris says as the others nod.

"It was a huge mistake in hindsight."

"As bad as it was," Gage said, "it's necessary. I saw Nat and the girls, too."

"You did?" Iris asks, seeming shocked.

"Yeah, I insisted on it."

Iris reaches for his hand. "I had no idea. My God, Gage."

"Like what Adrian said, I needed to see for myself that they were really gone."

"Did you feel like it was a mistake afterward?" Adrian asks.

"Huge mistake."

We wait to see if he might say more.

"But hey," he says, forcing a grim smile, "at least I knew they were really dead."

"Gage," Iris says softly as she curls her hands around his arm.

"It's okay," he tells her. "It was a long time ago now."

"How long did it take for you to not see them that way every time you thought of them?" I ask him.

"A while," he says. "Couple of years."

I nod, even as my heart sinks, knowing I've got a ways to go before I'll be able to replace the horror with better memories of my wife.

"Kick us out if you want to be alone, Adrian," Derek says.

"I most definitely do *not* want to be alone."

"We're here," Roni says. "For as long as you need us."

We feed the big kids, settle them with a movie in the living room and send out for Chinese food for the adults. I go upstairs to put Xavier down in his crib and nearly run into Wynter as she comes out of the guest room with her backpack on her shoulder.

"Are you leaving?" I ask her.

"Not yet. Just getting my bag so I don't forget it."

"Ah, I see. Thanks again for all the help today. I really appreciate it."

"It was fun. He had a blast."

"He's sleeping in his fireman costume because I didn't want to wake him up to change his clothes."

"You can change him when he wakes up hungry later."

"Yes, I guess he will be hungry since he only ate the cheese and crackers."

"And the cake," she says, grinning. "Don't forget the cake."

I want to kiss her. The feeling comes over me like a tsunami of want and need and affection for someone who's been such a big part of my journey this last year.

"Wynter..."

"Is that the doorbell? Food's here."

She escapes down the stairs before I can say or do something that'll change everything between us. I'm glad one of us is thinking clearly, because I'm not.

Eleven

Wynter

He was going to kiss me.

If I hadn't run off, he would have.

Why did I run off when that's what I want, too?

Because Iris and Roni are right. If we start something that ends badly, it'll screw up this thing we both rely on so completely. Today has been a reminder of how much we need our Wild Widows, and if Adrian and I are at odds, how do we both continue to be part of them? I love days like this when we come together as friends, not widows, to celebrate something.

I love how, after the dust settles, the ones still here are the ones we're closest to.

We're closer to one another than we are to our own families. Two of my cousins have been texting me for days wanting to get together, but I told them I couldn't until after Xavier's birthday. I'm sure they're puzzled as to why this kid they've never met is so important to me. I'll fill them in when I see them.

I hand over the cash Adrian gave me when he insisted on

paying for dinner to thank everyone for helping with the party.

"Thanks," the delivery guy says as he takes off.

I bring the food into the kitchen. "Dinner is served."

We descend on the food like locusts, a thought I share with them.

They laugh, as they always do. I love that they laugh at my jokes. I love that they get my jokes. I love that they love me, no matter what. Would they still love me if things went bad between me and Adrian? Would they choose sides? I don't know, and that's enough to give me pause on all the feelings I have for him.

I would say the feelings I "suddenly" have for him, but they're not sudden.

Not really.

I noticed him right away when I first joined the group, but I was in no place to have thoughts about anyone other than myself then. That was when it was all I could do to get out of bed as I stared down an entire lifetime without my love. It was impossible to conceive of life without Jaden, who'd been the most important person to me since I was fourteen.

That drove my mother crazy. Before I met him, it had been her and me against the world. After that, it was him and me, and she was so resentful. Her attitude caused my relationship with her to change dramatically. She didn't actively try to keep us apart, but she didn't encourage our relationship the way his parents did. They loved me, and vice versa. They were my first real exposure to a traditional two-parent, multiple-sibling family, and I soaked in their normalcy like a sponge.

My mother didn't like that either.

"Wynter."

Adrian's voice brings me back to the present.

"Where'd you go?"

I shake my head. "Down memory lane."

"Are you okay?"

"Sure." I force a smile. "As okay as I ever am these days. No. Wait. That's not true. I'm better than okay after celebrating Xavier today. He brings me joy."

Adrian's smile is a thing of beauty. "Me, too. Thank God for him."

"To Xavier," Gage says, raising his beer bottle.

"To Xavier," the rest of us say as we touch our glasses and bottles.

"He brings us all joy, Adrian," Iris says. "I'm so glad we'll get to watch him grow up and be part of his life."

"I'm glad, too. He and I need all the help we can get from you more experienced parents."

"You don't need any help," I tell him. "You're doing just fine."

He smiles at me again, and my insides melt even as I again review all the many, many reasons why I shouldn't be melting over this particular man.

"I do need help," he says. "Half the time, I feel like I have no idea what I'm doing."

"Welcome to parenthood," Gage says. "When we brought the twins home from the hospital, Nat and I used to say we couldn't believe they let us leave with them. We had no clue what we were doing, times two. It was madness."

"I can't imagine two of them at the same time," Adrian says.

"Neither could we," Gage says, "but we figured it out, just like you have. Think about what you knew about babies a year ago today and what you know now."

"That's true," Adrian says. "Alyssa was so great at teaching me what I needed to know. And my sister. They got me through that first insane month when I was in such a fog of disbelief and sleep deprivation. Seems like a long time ago now."

"It is," Roni says. "A whole year has gone by, and you survived. Here's to you, Adrian, Xavier's daddy. We're so proud of you."

We do another round of cheers to Adrian.

"I hope you all know how critical you and the others in our group have been to me surviving this year."

"We're glad you found us," Iris says.

"Me, too."

After dinner, everyone starts to leave to get kids home to bed, until only Adrian and I are left to finish cleaning up.

"I can do this," he says. "I'm sure you want to get home."

Not so much, I want to say. My mother texted me an hour ago to ask if I've moved out. I wrote back, *Haha, very funny. Be home soon.* She knew we had Xavier's birthday party today.

"Sadie's family is having a party for him next Sunday. Do you want to come with us?"

I have so many questions. Why is he asking me? What does it mean? Is this because of what happened last night? All of that goes through my mind in the span of a second.

"You don't have to," he adds when I don't reply right away. "I just thought you might want to."

"I'd love to go, but will that cause them to wonder if there's something going on between us?"

"They know you're Xavier's nanny, so it should be fine."

He'd know better than I would. "Sounds good."

"Thanks again for everything, Wynter."

"My pleasure. It was a great party, and you're a great dad. Xavier is lucky to have you."

"Thank you. We're both lucky to have you."

He hugs me before I have a second to realize he's going to.

I hug him back. The last thing I want to do is let go, but I have to. I absolutely have to. "See you tomorrow."

"See you then."

I get the hell out of there before I do something stupid like kiss him.

———

THE NEXT WEEK goes by in a blur of activity. I take Xavier to swimming lessons at the local YMCA and to a pediatrician appointment, so Adrian doesn't have to take time off. One of the hardest things I've ever done is hold Xavier still while he gets shots. He's so angry with me afterward, which breaks my heart.

He cries himself to sleep on the ride home, and I cry right along with him. "I'm so sorry, love. We're trying to keep you healthy."

What does a one-year-old care about being healthy when someone is sticking needles in him?

Adrian calls shortly after I get Xavier into his crib for a nap. His little body is still hiccupping with sobs, which breaks my heart all over again.

I take the call when I get downstairs.

"Saw you guys are home," he says. "How'd it go?"

"The shots were awful."

"That's the worst. Sorry you had to go through that."

"I feel like a monster."

"I know. I did, too."

I give him the full report of growth percentiles and other milestones. "In short, he is perfect and growing like a weed. He's up to twenty pounds!"

"I believe it. He's a load to carry around all of a sudden."

"For sure. They said we can move him to the next-size car seat. I'm going to miss that baby seat that snaps in and out of the car."

"I'll get two new seats on the way home."

I love that I get one, too. Duh, of course I do. I have him more than his father does during the week.

"Do we need anything from the store?"

"Running low on diapers, wipes and baby food."

"Got it. See you in a bit, and thanks again for taking one for the team."

"Ha, no problem."

After we end the call, it occurs to me that we are a team—he and I—a team devoted to the care of Xavier. That thought fills me with an incredible feeling of belonging to something bigger than myself. From the time I was very young, I looked forward to having kids, even though Jaden and I worried about what kind of screwed-up world we'd be bringing them into.

"The whole thing is gonna burn up in like thirty years anyway," Jaden used to say.

We talked a lot about global warming, which freaked us out until cancer gave us something much more urgent to worry about. I've always been squeamish about medical stuff, too, and since I saw him through his illness, I'm even more so.

Before he got sick, Jaden and I talked about being young parents who'd have their kids through college by the time we were fortysomething and could do whatever we wanted with the rest of our lives. We looked forward to raising a family and later having grandchildren.

Ever since Xavier came into my life, I've felt even more sad about the children I never got to have with Jaden. I'm not saying I want six of them, but one or two would be nice. I can hear Jaden saying, "Dude, are you really going to bring kids into the world so they can burn up before they're fifty?"

"We don't know for sure that's going to happen," I say out loud, as if he might hear me, "and besides, we can't live our lives waiting for catastrophe to strike."

Those words echo through my mind with yet another realization that I'm moving on from the catastrophe that took Jaden from me. I no longer want to dwell in that place of fear that governed my entire life for years before he died and for a long time afterward. Cancer was so freaking scary. I'll never forget the many appointments in which there was never any good news. The situation just got worse all the time, even when we were sure we'd seen the worst. We hadn't seen anything yet.

I hate thinking about that stuff, but those memories are indelibly burned into my soul, never to be forgotten.

I make a PB&J and take it to the cozy kitchen table to look out at the yard as I eat, zeroing in on a spot of color near Adrian's fence. Taking the sandwich with me, I grab my coat and go out to investigate.

"Fucking crocuses," I say with a laugh as I take a picture to send to Iris and Roni with that as the message.

Love it! Roni responds.

Me too! Iris says.

Will you teach me the other flowers?

Every one of them, Iris says.

I can't wait.

If the world is going to burn up someday, I plan to enjoy it while I can, starting with flower lessons. It's nice to have something to look forward to.

I WAKE up the next Sunday morning to realize I didn't hear anything funky last night. Does that mean Adrian came home from work alone? I really hope so. I understand the thousand and one reasons why he and I can't fool around, but I hate the idea of him doing that with other women.

And yes, I know that's insane, but there you have my mental state where he's concerned.

I've adopted a hands-off approach to him. That said, I wish I didn't have to. I wish I could give in to the desire, the need, the want, the affection, the attraction. All of it. I wish we could play house and raise Xavier as ours, rather than just his. If I could have anything I wanted for this new life of mine with no chance of negative consequences, that's what I'd choose.

Alas, the real world doesn't work that way. There're so many things to consider that the head spins. We've both worked hard to move forward on our widow journey, to get through that hellish first year without our beloveds, to get Xavier into a good routine, to process crushing grief, to make friends who understand our struggles, to find peace after the worst possible thing happened.

That peace is critical to our sanity. I know he feels the same way. I used to be a bit of a drama queen. Granted, I didn't like being part of the drama. I just liked knowing about it. Now that I know what real drama looks like, I stay as far away from that crap as I can. And a fling or relationship with Adrian would be dramatic in every possible way.

I go with Adrian and Xavier to the birthday party that Sadie's sisters, Sabrina and Selina, host at their late mother's home. I meet so many aunts, uncles and cousins that my head spins trying to remember all their names. Everyone is very nice and welcoming to me and they thank me for helping Adrian with Xavier.

"At some point, I suppose we need to clean out this place and get it on the market," Sabrina says as she walks us out after the party.

Adrian is hauling the huge bag of gifts that Xavier received. "I can help when you're ready."

"How do you know when you're ready?" Sabrina asks tearfully.

Adrian puts down the bag to hug her. "Thank you again for an amazing party."

"We love you guys," Sabrina says.

"Love you, too."

"Thank you for having me," I add.

"Great to meet you, Wynter."

Adrian is quiet on the way home.

"Are you all right?"

"I can't tell you how weird it was to be there without Sadie and Alyssa. I kept expecting them to arrive, full of explanations for being late."

I reach across the console for his hand and hold it all the way home, wishing there was more I could do make him feel better. But as we both know, there's nothing anyone can do to soothe this kind of ache.

WHEN XAVIER GETS UP from his nap on Wednesday afternoon, I change him and give him a snack.

Iris invited us over to play with the kids before our Wild Widows meeting later. I pack up the chocolate-chip cookie bars I made and grab the diaper bag with everything Xavier might need as I head out the door with him on my hip.

I'm slaying this nanny thing if I do say so myself. Sure, my confidence was severely impacted by the incident at the cemetery. That was almost a month ago now, and I rarely think of it. I don't think Adrian does either. It happened. We moved on. I appreciate that he gave me another chance, and I never take his trust for granted.

Whenever Xavier and I go anywhere now, I'm doubly aware of the many things that can go wrong, and I try to anticipate every disaster that could occur. If I'm a little more on edge than I was before the cemetery, that's a small price to pay to keep Xavier safe. That's my only goal. To keep him safe and happy.

He loves playing with Iris's kids. They're great with him, super gentle and sweet. He soaks up their attention like a hungry sponge while Iris and I enjoy a cup of hot chocolate in the kitchen, which has an open view into the kids' playroom. Tyler and Sophia know to stop him from putting anything in his mouth. Still, I keep a close eye on him just in case.

"How'd he do with the shots?" Iris asks.

"Better than I did. It was horrible."

"I used to hate that. I made Mike do it with Sophia and Laney. I couldn't handle it."

"It's the worst. You're basically holding them still so someone can hurt them. He was so betrayed. I could see it in his little face. Fortunately, he forgave me at some point while he was napping."

"They're good that way," Iris says, grinning over the top of her mug.

I get up to retrieve a couple of the chocolate-chip bars I made from under the foil and bring them back to the table, handing one to Iris.

"Mmmm," she says after taking a bite. "That's good."

"It's the one thing I know how to make."

"I thought pancakes were the one thing."

I recall making them at Adrian's after his wife's mother died suddenly. "Make it two things."

"I can show you how to cook, if you want."

"You've got enough to do without worrying about teaching me things."

"It's always easier to learn things when someone shows you how."

"You're like the nicest person I've ever met. Do you know that?"

"No way," she says, scoffing.

"Yes way. You're like what… twelve years older than me?"

She grimaces. "Almost fifteen."

"What does it say that I'd rather be with you than anyone my own age?"

"It says that you're mentally much older than your peers after having suffered through something no one should have to at your young age."

"Maybe it says that. It also says you're awesome, and I like being with you. I feel… at home with you."

She starts blinking, and I realize she's trying not to cry.

"What? Don't do that!"

Laughing, she brushes away a tear. "Can't help it. That's the sweetest thing for you to say."

"It's true." I fiddle with my mug handle. "When my mom told me about your group, I thought it was the stupidest thing I'd ever heard of. The Wild Widows? Whatever."

"Christy and I love the reactions people have to the name of our group."

"It's a great name, especially when you find out it comes from the Mary Oliver quote. I love her writing."

"Oh, I do, too. Sometimes I feel like she sees inside me."

"Same. And what's funny is I never used to be a reader, especially of stuff like that. I read *Twilight* to see what all the noise was about, but I couldn't get into the vampires-fighting-over-the-girl thing."

"That's because you were born without a suspension-of-disbelief button."

"What does that even mean?"

"In order to fully occupy a world like the one in *Twilight*, you have to suspend disbelief. Meaning, you have to allow yourself to believe that vampires are real, and they can fight over a girl and live forever or whatever else the author wants you to believe so the story makes sense."

"I can't do that. If I sniff bullshit, I'm out."

"Exactly," Iris says, laughing. "Your bullshit-o-meter is set to low, so you can't enjoy something that requires you to accept something that's bullshit."

"I couldn't do Harry Potter either."

"Not surprising. You'd need to accept that wizards are real and magic exists."

"Not gonna happen. It's interesting to know this condition has a name."

"Mike was like you. He couldn't enjoy something if he thought it was bullshit. Vampires, wizards, dragons and the like. I told him he had to shut up and let me have my Harry Potter. He nearly sprained his eyes from rolling them when I made him watch *Twilight*. It always made me laugh at how he'd suffer when it was my turn to decide what we were going to watch."

"I'm glad you have good memories of him."

"Oh, I have so many good memories of him."

"I wondered if they'd be overshadowed by what you've learned about him since."

"I try to keep the good stuff separate from the bad."

"How do you do that? How do you separate them?"

"I try to remember Mike, my husband, who I loved, who was the father of my kids, as someone separate from the guy who cheated on me and had a kid with someone else. It's like a mind game I play with myself."

"That requires suspension of disbelief."

Iris laughs. "Yes, it does, but it seems to be working. The two versions of him are like separate people to me."

I turn my hand up and rest my head on it as I study her. "How did you get to be so wise? I want to be like you when I grow up."

"Oh Lord, Wynter. Don't set your sights on me."

"Why not? You're the most together person I've ever met. You're kind, loving and welcoming to everyone you meet. Your kids are adorable and well-behaved. You have the best relationship with Gage. We're all envious of you two and what you have. And you know everything. How does that happen?"

"I'm incredibly flattered that you see me that way."

"*Everyone* sees you that way."

"Well, thank you. You're very kind."

"Not really, but you make me want to do better so I can make you proud."

"Sweetheart," she says on a long exhale as she places her hand on top of mine, "I'm *so* proud of you. The other day, I was talking to Tracy, who was one of the cofounders of the group, and I told her about you and how great you're doing compared to when we first met you. I said, 'Wynter makes me so proud of her and us and what we've built with this group.' I used you as an example."

"Wow. That's cool. Thank you. It means a lot to me that you're proud of me."

"I'm so, *so* proud. You're like a caterpillar about to become a butterfly. I watch you spreading your wings, and I'm so excited to see what happens next."

"I'd much rather spread my legs than my wings."

She laughs so hard there's no sound. "Honestly, Wynter!"

"I need to make that a drinking game. Every time one of you guys says, 'Honestly, Wynter,' we take a shot."

"We'd be drunk in no time."

"Exactly!"

After Iris's kids leave for the night with her mother, Hallie is the first to come through the front door for the group meeting. At some point, we stopped bothering to move the meeting to other people's homes. Iris's house is our base, and it's where we all feel at home. Thankfully, she doesn't mind having us.

Hallie hugs us both. "It's good to see you."

"You, too," Iris says. "We missed you last week."

"I missed you, too."

I admire Iris's restraint. She wants to ask what's going on with Hallie, who rarely misses a meeting, but she doesn't. If Hallie wants to talk about it, she knows she's come to the right place.

Twelve

Wynter

The others trickle in, bringing main dishes, sides and desserts. Somehow we always have a perfect combination of food without any real coordination. And some of us are amazing cooks. Hallie brought a chicken dish that melts in my mouth, and Joy's jambalaya is a favorite among the group.

They rave about my chocolate-chip bars and ask for the recipe, which makes me feel legit. They know my culinary talents are extremely limited.

I put Xavier in Laney's high chair and feed him tiny bites of chicken, cut-up green beans and a roll that he pulverizes before he eats a little of it.

Adrian is the last to arrive, apologizing for being late. "The freaking traffic is getting worse all the time."

"I don't miss commuting," Gage says. "In fact, I don't miss working."

"Don't rub it in," Adrian says with a good-natured grin as he comes to find Xavier.

And me.

Or at least I'd like to think he's looking for both of us.

Xavier lets out a happy shriek at the sight of his daddy.

Adrian is so sexy in his work clothes. I think that every day when he comes home wearing one of those tight dress shirts that mold to his muscular body.

Yum.

He bends to kiss Xavier's chubby cheek, bringing the scent of spicy, citrusy cologne that makes my mouth water. "How's my buddy doing?"

"He had a great day."

Xavier raises his arms to his daddy, wanting out of the chair.

I remove the tray to free him and hand Adrian a wet paper towel to clean him up. "Watch out. His hands are dirty."

"That's okay," Adrian says, eyes closed as he snuggles his little boy.

Watching them together makes my heart do weird flip-flops in my chest.

As we follow the other widows into the living room, Adrian puts Xavier on a blanket in the middle of the circle. When I bring some of his toys, he rewards me with his big spitty smile that reveals six adorable little baby teeth.

"Welcome, everyone," Iris says. "How are things?"

"Can I go?" Hallie asks.

"Of course."

"So I met someone."

That announcement is met with wild applause that has Xavier looking up to see what's going on.

Hallie holds up her hands to quiet us. "Don't get too excited. It's complicated."

"It's always complicated for us," Gage reminds her.

"This is unusually so," Hallie says. "She's fresh out of a

fifteen-year marriage to a man, for one thing. For another, she has two kids, twelve and nine, and I'm the first woman she's ever considered dating. So yeah... Not sure how I feel about that."

"Oh, so you'd be her first," I say. "That's kinda cool."

"And awkward," Hallie says. "I like her. I really do, but I'm not sure I have the energy to help someone experiment with their sexual identity."

"Did you tell her about Gwen?" Iris asks.

"No details. Just that I was married, and she died. We're still kind of feeling out whether this is going to be a thing or not. She'd like it to be. I'm not so sure."

"What does she say about her feelings toward dating a woman?" Roni asks.

"That she's always had intense feelings toward other women but tried to fit into the expected mold of a relationship with a man. She said she knew the day they got married that she'd probably made a mistake."

"Wow," Brielle says. "I can't imagine feeling that way on my wedding day."

"She said it was terrible," Hallie says. "Like she was going through the motions rather than celebrating something that felt so right. She spent fifteen years trying to make it work, mostly for the sake of her kids, but then she just couldn't do it any longer."

"That must've been rough," Derek says, "being married to someone for that long when it wasn't what she wanted."

"I guess it was. They didn't fight, per se. She said it was apathy more than anything. He was a good guy, a wonderful father and all that, but their relationship was platonic for the last seven years."

"I have some concerns," Iris says tentatively.

We all look to her as our fearless leader.

"After everything you've been through, I don't love the idea of you being involved with someone who could, several months in, decide that maybe you're not what she wants either."

"I know," Hallie says with a sigh. "I agree, and I've had that same thought, believe me. It's just that there's a connection I've only had one other time." She gives a helpless shrug. "I feel that thing. You know what I mean?"

"Yeah," Gage says. "I do know, and it sort of makes the risk worth it, right?"

"Exactly," Hallie says. "She's the first person I've met since Gwen died who makes me want to try again."

"Then you should," Iris says, "as long as you go into it with your eyes wide open. No one wants to see you hurt."

"I don't want that either," Hallie says, "but what is it we're always saying? We gotta get back out there and start living again, right? That doesn't happen without some risks."

"That's right, baby," Joy says. "Just make sure the risks aren't too great. If she makes you happy, then we already love her."

"Thank you, Joy," Hallie says softly. "That means everything to me." She waves her hand. "Enough about me. Tell me what's up with the rest of you."

"I went on a date," Joy says.

All eyes shift to her.

"And?" Roni asks.

"It was okay. I spent most of the time comparing him to Craig and finding him lacking." Her thirtysomething husband died in his sleep, of "natural causes," whatever that means.

"Don't do that," Lexi says gently. "No one will ever measure up to him. You have to try to meet each new person where they are and not where you were."

"That's very well said, Lex," Brielle says.

139

"It was," Kinsley says, "because I've found myself comparing new people to Rory. It's not fair to them or to him. I mean, nothing will ever be like it was with him, so I've realized I need to stop trying to find Rory two-point-oh and find Paul one-point-oh or Dan one-point-oh. Names inserted to make a point, not because there's a Paul or a Dan. There isn't."

"Your point is well taken, Kinsley," Gage says. "When Iris and I were first together, I thought it would be like I remembered with Natasha, and in some ways it is. There's a fundamental similarity in the feelings that I recognize. But everything about Iris is different from Nat, which is to be expected. No two people are exactly the same, and no two relationships are either."

"I've had the same experience with Roni." Derek smiles at his fiancée. "In all the ways that matter most, Roni is similar to Victoria, but our relationships are totally different. I feel guilty sometimes because Roni is getting a much better version of me than Vic got. It took losing her the way I did to wake me up and to make some badly needed changes in my life."

"This helps," Joy says. "Thank you for sharing."

"Are you going to see him again, Joy?" Christy asks.

"Haven't decided yet. He's reached out, said he enjoyed our date and would like to do it again. But I don't know. I might not be ready."

"Only you can know if you're ready," Iris says, "but don't avoid him because he didn't remind you of Craig."

"I'm trying to reconcile that in my mind before I decide one way or the other," Joy says. "Such a weird conundrum, right?"

"The weirdest," Kinsley says. "You gotta love the widow life."

"Do we, though?" Lexi asks, and we all laugh.

"Worst club we never wanted to join," Brielle says.

"I've felt myself starting to tune back in to things I thought I'd never care about again," I say, keeping my gaze diverted from Adrian.

"Like what?" Iris asks, even though she already knows.

"Physical things. Sex. Desire. That kind of stuff."

"Tell me you know that's normal, sweetheart," Lexi says.

"I do. It's just strange to feel it again and to have to figure out what it means and what to do about it."

"You don't have to do anything until you're ready to," Christy says.

"I know. I'm starting to feel ready, which is exciting and sad at the same time. I never wanted that with anyone but Jaden, so I have no idea how to want it with someone else."

"You'll know when the time is right," Roni says. "And when the person is right. There's no rush."

"The problem we all have is the last time we did that, it was with someone special," Adrian says without looking up from watching Xavier playing on the floor. "We're all looking to find that again. When it's just transactional, it makes you feel worse, if that's possible."

It's interesting to hear him basically admit that his one-night stands didn't do it for him.

"It's always better when it's special," Christy says gently. "But it doesn't have to be special every time. Sometimes it can just be to scratch an itch."

"Maybe so." He pauses, and we give him a second because it's obvious he has more he wants to say. "I've been having a hard time this week with realizing Xavier's birthday will never be just that, you know? It's also the day his mom died."

The sadness in his voice kills me. I want to wrap my arms around him and make everything better for him and Xavier. I no sooner have that thought than it sends me reeling from the intensity of my feelings toward them.

I love them. Of course I do. How could I not after what

we've been through together over this last year? But as we all know far too well, there's love and then there's *love*. I fear I'm starting to venture into the latter category with Adrian. That scares and excites me at the same time.

I can't have feelings for the man who employs me to care for his son.

Or can I?

It's all so confusing. It's also a relief to know I can still feel this way. Even if it's the worst possible guy I could have feelings for. I'd laugh if it wasn't so ridiculous. I tune back in to the others giving Adrian advice to feel all the feels around Sadie's deathiversary, a word I'd never heard until I joined this group. Why would I know about such things when I was off living my life with no idea that cancer would take the most important person in that life from me?

"I've sort of wallowed in every one of the three anniversaries," Gage says. "I give myself one day to feel all the bad shit, and then I try to put it away for another year. You were so busy with Xavier's birthday, you didn't give yourself that chance to be in the moment for Sadie, too."

"You need a new tradition," Christy adds. "You celebrate Xavier's birthday, and the next day is for you and Sadie. You can do whatever you want that day, but you allow yourself to experience all the memories, especially the good ones."

"That's a great idea, Christy," Iris says. "That way, you could separate the two events. What do you think, Adrian?"

"It is a good idea. Maybe I'll take a personal day this week and go for a long hike on our favorite trail or something."

"That's a perfect way to honor her," Lexi says.

"Thanks, guys," Adrian says. "This has really helped. I'm going to take Xavier home to bed, but I want the rest of you to reach out if there's anything I can do for you."

"Focus on you during this tough time," Iris says. "We're here if we can help."

"I know we say this frequently," Adrian says, "but I mean it when I tell you I never would've survived this year without you guys, and, well... I love you all. Very much."

After he collects Xavier from the floor, the rest of us stand to hug them both.

"See you in the morning," he says to me when he hugs me.

"I'll be there."

"I feel for him," Joy says after Adrian and Xavier leave. "The best and worst things to ever happen to him were on the same day."

"It's a tough one for sure," Brielle says, "but he seems to be doing well."

They look to me as if wanting me to confirm that.

I'm like a deer in headlights for a second as I try to think of something to say. "He's doing the best he can. Like the rest of us."

"He appreciates you so much," Iris says. "I hope you know that."

"I do, and I love taking care of Xavier. It's given me a purpose that I didn't know I needed. It's all good."

"We're so glad it's working out well for both of you," Derek says.

Thankfully, they move on to other topics, such as Roni and Derek's wedding, which will happen sometime in the next year. They aren't sure yet of when. Christy hasn't returned the texts from that guy Trey, even though he's reaching out every day to tell her he misses her, and he wants to talk. She's not sure yet if she's going to bother.

We make plans to help Lexi move into her new place on Sunday. Gage reminds her that he offered up his dad's truck, which brings Lexi to tears because she wasn't sure how she was going to get all her stuff to the new place.

"We've got you," Gage says with a warm smile that makes Lexi cry even harder.

Lexi wipes the tears from her face with a tissue Iris hands her. "What Adrian said before about this group... I agree with every word. I don't know what I'd do without you."

"You're stuck with us," Roni says, smiling.

After the others leave, I hang back to help Iris clean up, and then I gather Xavier's toys into the backpack I use as a diaper bag because I wouldn't be caught dead with one of those silly-looking bags they sell at the baby stores. Someone gave one to Sadie for her shower that has baby animals on it, but it's still in the closet in Xavier's room.

Iris walks me to the door. "Are you okay, Wynter? You were quiet tonight."

"I'm fine."

Iris hugs me. "Love you."

"Love you, too."

How does she do that? How does she reduce me nearly to tears by being nice to me, by telling me she loves me? As I drive home, I wipe away tears that piss me off. What in the world am I crying about? I hate being an emotional basket case. I never was before I lost Jaden. My mom says I hardly cried as a baby. It was never my thing. Now I cry every day. It's like someone has put all my nerves on the outside of my body or something, forcing me to feel everything, even when I don't want to.

My phone rings, which gives me a reprieve from my thoughts.

Until I see it's Adrian calling.

"Hey, what's up?"

I can hear Xavier wailing in the background.

"Is he okay?"

"That's why I'm calling. He's asking for you. Nothing I do is working. I think he's teething."

"I'll come by."

"I hate to ask you so late."

"It's fine. See you in a few."

"Thanks, Wynter."

The first chance I get, I do a U-turn and head for Adrian's. I can't wait to see them both.

Thirteen

Adrian

I hate having to call Wynter to come back to work when she already spends more time at my home than she does at her own. I get the feeling that she likes it here better than there, but she doesn't say much about herself other than when we discuss our common widow journey.

And why is it that I want to know everything about her? I ask myself as I walk Xavier back and forth in the living room, patting his back, hoping he'll calm down.

"Wyn, Wyn, Wyn," he says between sobs.

"She's coming, buddy."

I should be dealing with this on my own rather than asking her to help me.

But when I hear her key in the door, the only thing I feel is relief that she's come to help us both.

"What's wrong with my baby?" she asks as she takes Xavier from me.

He immediately stops crying. "Wyn."

"I'm here," she says, cuddling him close as her gaze collides with mine.

She's so ridiculously pretty, it's not even funny. Before I lost Sadie, I had a whole other definition of what I found attractive. Now it's Wynter who does it for me like only one other woman ever has.

I want her.

I need her.

I can't have her.

I must keep telling myself that.

Xavier loves her. We'd be lost without her. Romantic entanglements ruin everything when they go bad. But what if it didn't go bad? What if it was good, so good that it gave us both a second chance to be happy?

As I watch her calm and soothe my son, the push-pull of what I want versus the risk rages inside me.

In what seems like no time at all, Xavier is asleep in her arms.

"You have the magic touch."

"I love him so much."

"He loves you, too."

And so do I, I want to add, but I can't say that. She'll think I mean it as a friend, a grateful employer, a fellow widow. I love her for all those reasons. However, I suspect I love her for other reasons, too. I can't ever admit that when I was with those two women the last couple of weeks, all I thought about was how I wished I was with her.

Then to find out she'd seen me... God, every time I think about her watching, I get hard as a rock.

Don't think about that now, Adrian, unless you want her to see what she does to you.

"I'll put him down."

I follow her upstairs, keeping my gaze on her shoulders and not her ass.

Think about the risks, Adrian. Think about Xavier, who loves her. Think about something other than what it would be like to have sex with Wynter. Think about anything other than that.

I'm so absorbed in the lecture I'm giving myself that I nearly crash into her as she bends to put Xavier in his crib.

That wouldn't have been good.

Or maybe it would be.

I wait for her to get Xavier settled, and then I follow her from the room.

"Thanks for coming."

"Any time."

"Do you want a drink?"

"I'd love a drink."

As I lead the way downstairs, I'm so glad she's staying. I'm less lonely when she's around, which is something I realized a while ago.

I make us each a vodka and soda cocktail that we take into the living room.

We sit at opposite ends of the sofa, but she turns toward me.

"He was so fussy tonight," I tell her. "I've never seen him so worked up."

"It's the teeth. I joined an online forum and read about it. People say teething changes their entire personality, but luckily, it only lasts a few weeks. They also say we're lucky we can't remember how painful it is."

I'm blown away that she did research on our behalf. "Thank you for looking into that."

"No problem. I figured I ought to know what makes him cranky."

"There's so much to know about him," I say with a sigh. "I feel like I'm flying blind a lot of the time."

"You love him, and he knows it. He lights up when he sees you."

"And when he sees you."

"Being with him makes me happy. Thank you for giving me another chance."

"You don't have to thank me. I'm the one who should be grateful. It's a huge relief to know he's with someone who loves him when I'm at work—and that he gets to be in his own house. Not that I have anything against daycare, but I like that he has your full attention."

"He definitely has my full attention. We have so much fun together."

I've never seen her smile quite like she does when she talks about Xavier.

She takes a couple of sips from her drink and then puts it on the coffee table.

"Is the drink okay?"

"Yeah, I just have to drive."

"You could stay if you wanted to. It's getting late."

"Oh. Um. Yeah, maybe I will. Thanks."

"Any time."

She picks up the drink and downs a big mouthful.

"When Sadie and I bought this place, we imagined the third bedroom would be for our second kid. We were going to have another one right away so they'd grow up close, and we could get all the baby stuff out of the way quickly." I release a nervous laugh. "Not sure why I'm telling you this."

"I'm sorry your plans didn't work out the way they should have. What happened to Sadie—and to you and Xavier—is heartbreaking."

"Yeah, it is. We were so naïve, you know?"

"How so?"

"We had no idea it was possible she could die."

"That's not something expectant parents want to think about."

"No, but we should've been told it was possible, you know? Every doctor we saw assured us that she was healthy, the baby was healthy, everything was fine. Even the childbirth classes didn't cover potential complications." I glance at her. "They said it was an amniotic fluid embolism."

"What is that?"

"It's when some of the baby's amniotic fluid enters the mother's bloodstream, which happens frequently. It's just that in some cases, like Sadie's, the mother has like an allergic reaction that leads to system-wide issues. They said it comes on very quickly and is often fatal. The doctor has expressed grief and regret. He says he thinks of her every day. I wonder if he says that so I won't sue him."

"Do you want to?"

"Sometimes."

"Have you talked to a lawyer?"

"Yeah, but they said it would be tough because it's the sort of complication that does happen, even if it's rare. But who expects their perfectly healthy wife to die giving birth, you know?"

"It's terrifying. Medical stuff is so scary to me, especially after what I saw Jaden go through."

"From what we were told in the childbirth classes, you forget about it pretty quickly after the baby arrives. You're so excited to have the baby that you barely give the birth a thought."

"We're not talking about me. We're talking about you. What are your thoughts about suing?"

"They'd probably settle to make me go away. The money would come in handy."

"But it wouldn't give you any more information than you already have, right?"

"Probably not."

"I'd worry that it would reopen a healing wound," she says. "I get wanting to understand what happened. I have a lot of questions about Jaden's last few weeks that I'll probably never get answers to. But then I think that it's probably easier to let it go than it is to revisit such an awful time. I mean, what will the answers get us? Sadie and Jaden will still be dead."

"What answers do you want?" I ask her.

"I want to know why they never told us that he was going to die until that became obvious. Like, why didn't they just tell us the truth so we could prepare ourselves?"

"Maybe because they didn't want you to give up hope?"

"Probably, but I'm sorry. That's bullshit. Why give us hope when there isn't any?"

"I don't know, but I've heard Kinsley and Naomi say the same thing. The doctors were full of hope that gave them a false sense of confidence about the outcome."

"It's not fair that they do that to us."

"No, it isn't."

"Like why would I think my twenty-two-year-old husband was actually going to *die* if the doctors weren't saying that could happen? Afterward, so many people said, 'Well, at least it wasn't sudden. You had warning that he was going to die.' No, I didn't! I had like six days to process that."

As she speaks, I find myself moving closer to her, wanting to offer comfort. I reach for her, and she hesitates, but only for a second before she tentatively moves close enough for me to put my arms around her.

"You don't have to do that," she says.

"I know, but it seemed like you needed it."

She releases a long exhale and relaxes against me. "You smell good."

I laugh. "Okay."

"I mean, you always smell good."

"So do you." I take full advantage of her closeness to breathe in the fragrance of her hair.

"We, uh, probably shouldn't, you know..."

It helps to realize she's as undone by this as I am. "No, we really shouldn't."

Wynter

HE AGREES WITH ME, but he doesn't let go. My whole body is on fire as he holds me close to him. I want to touch him and kiss him and—

I can't!

He's my boss! He's Xavier's dad.

I start to pull back out of sheer self-preservation.

"Don't go," he says. "Not yet."

I'm burning up with desire. And guilt. That's part of the mix now that I want someone who isn't my beloved Jaden. I can't deny it, though. I want Adrian. I have for a while, since long before I saw things I shouldn't have, things I haven't been able to stop thinking about.

My heart beats wildly. I can barely breathe, and every part of me wants to take this to the logical next step. If it wasn't for Xavier, I'd be all over him. It's Xavier that has me pulling back. It's Xavier that has me standing on shaky legs. It's Xavier that has me grabbing my coat and getting the hell out of there before I do something that can't be undone.

"Wynter. Wait."

"I can't. I have to go."

"No."

"Yes, Adrian. I have to go."

His hand on my shoulder stops me, and the heat of his touch is nearly enough to make me forget why I was so certain that leaving is the right thing to do. "Don't go."

"I have to."

"Why?"

"Because."

"That's not a reason."

I force myself to turn to face him, to look up at him. "This... All of it... You as my friend, Xavier, who I love, it's too important to me to mess it up."

"We won't mess it up."

"You can't possibly know that."

"I do know that. You're important to us, too. You've become the most important person to both of us."

I shake my head. "Don't say what you think I want to hear."

His fingers on my chin force me to meet his intense gaze. "I'm telling you the truth. At some point in all the madness, you've become the most important person to both of us."

I shake my head. "Adrian, please..."

He leans in slowly.

I should turn away, but I can't. I'm completely frozen in place as his lips brush lightly over mine.

"Don't go," he whispers.

This reminds me, all of a sudden, of the time I nearly drowned as a teenager at the beach in Ocean City with Jaden and some friends. As I fought an intense rip current, I was so sure I was going to die that I almost gave in to the tremendous pull of the water before a lifeguard saved me.

"I think I would die if I couldn't see Xavier anymore."

That stops him cold. "What? Why wouldn't you be able to see him anymore?"

"If we did something that couldn't be undone, and it turned into a disaster."

"It won't. I won't let it, and I'd never stop you from seeing him. He loves you as much as you love him."

He's offering me everything I want—him and Xavier and

the possibility of new love and a future with them. So why do I still feel like I need to go?

"I... Um... I'm not ready for this, Adrian. I thought I was, but I'm not."

His hands move from my shoulders down my arms to clasp my hands. "I'm not going anywhere, and neither is Xavier. When you're ready, let me know. I'll be here."

"What if I'm never ready?"

"You will be. Eventually. And when you are, I want you to come to me. No one else but me."

"You're crazy."

"I'm crazy about you, and I have been for almost as long as I've known you. That caused me a lot of grief at first, because how could I be having feelings for you when I was still mourning my wife? Over time, I came to see it as yet another sign that life goes on even when we think it won't."

I tip my forehead to his chest.

He runs his hands over my back in soothing circles.

I've forgotten what it's like to be touched by a man, to be wanted by a man and to want him right back.

"I'm worried about us making a mess of things for ourselves, for Xavier, for our friends."

"Then let's not do that, okay?"

I raise my head to look up at him again. "Is it that simple?"

"It can be if we want it to be. We both know what it's like to be in a relationship that works. Why can't we have that with each other, too?"

"I... I guess we could. What about your other friends?"

"What friends?"

"The women you brought home." I hate the note of insecurity I hear in my own voice, but I'm not willing to be part of a harem, and he may as well know that now.

"That was just sex, Wynter. What I want with you is much more than that."

"Why me? What makes you want that with me?"

"Why you? Have you met you? You're amazing. You're strong and resilient and courageous." He tucks a strand of hair behind my ear. "You're the funniest person ever. You're loyal to your friends, and you don't suffer bullshit. If you think it, you say it. No one ever has to wonder where they stand with you because you tell us. And, last but certainly not least, you're sexy as fuck. Any questions?"

He's rendered me speechless, which amuses him.

"*Our* Wynter with nothing to say? When does that ever happen?"

"Not very often. I think you're pretty awesome, too. You're an amazing dad to Xavier, and despite what happened with Sadie and Alyssa, you still find a way to be joyful with him and with your friends."

"Joy is not always easy to find in the after, as you know all too well. But I feel joyful around you. Do you remember the night Alyssa died and you were the first of the Wild Widows to arrive?"

"What about it?"

"I'll never forget what you said to me."

"What did I say?" I have no recollection.

"You said that this latest kick in the teeth sucked as bad as anything had ever sucked, but that you and the others would be there for me the way you had been from the start of this nightmare, and I would never be alone with Xavier. It was exactly what I most needed to hear when everyone else was telling me that things happen for a reason and God has a plan."

"I hate when people say that stuff."

"Right? You knew what I needed to hear, and you put it right out there."

"I'm glad it helped you. I still can't believe you lost both of them."

"On many a day, I can't either, but having you and the others in my life has made all the difference in me surviving it."

"Is it possible that this... thing... between us is a result of proximity more than anything?"

"I thought of that, and I can see why you would, too. I mean, there's such comfort in spending time with people who truly understand what I'm going through."

"For me, too."

"But I don't feel this way for Iris or Brielle or Lexi or Christy, as much as I adore them all. What I feel for you is different."

"This is a lot for me to process." After a pause, I ask the one question I most want the answer to. "If you felt this way about me for a while now, why'd you sleep with those other women?"

He exhales a long deep breath. "Because I was trying to resist what I feel for you for all the reasons you stated. I thought if maybe I tried with someone else, I could get past this thing I have for you and not rock the boat of our arrangement with Xavier. But being with them just made it worse. I wanted to enjoy it, but I couldn't because they're not you."

I fan my face as I laugh. "Whoever's writing your material, they're doing a great job."

He laughs. "All original content, and I mean it, Wynter. I'm sorry you saw what you did. I never should've brought them here when you were in the house. That was wrong, but I figured you'd be long asleep by then."

"Sleep is a challenge for me."

"I get that."

"You've given me a lot to think about."

"Can you stay here and do your thinking?"

As much as it pains me, I shake my head. "I can't think clearly when you're in the room. That's been a problem for me for a while now, too."

His smile is a thing of beauty, and it lights up his entire face.

"Don't smile at me. It scrambles my brain."

"Good to know."

"I'm going to leave and go home and take a breath. You should do the same, and soon, we should talk again."

"I'm here whenever you want to talk." He leans in to kiss my neck, and this must be what it's like to be struck by lightning. I feel that kiss everywhere. "I'm here for you, Wynter. I want you in my life and in Xavier's, but not until you're ready."

"Thank you for understanding."

"Always. Will you be okay driving home?"

"I'll be fine."

"Text me when you get home, so I won't worry."

"Okay."

He kisses my cheek. "I'm glad we finally talked about this. I feel much better now that you know."

"I'm glad we talked, too. I'll see you in the morning?"

"See you then. Can't wait."

I walk out the door and down the stairs like I'm floating on air. I'm not sure if anything will come of this thing between us, but I already know that for the rest of my life, I'll never forget the things he said.

Fourteen

Adrian

After Wynter leaves, I'm so keyed up, there's no chance I'll sleep. So I take the baby monitor down to my gym in the basement for a workout, hoping to burn off some of the excess energy buzzing through me.

An hour later, it's clear that all the weightlifting in the world isn't going to clear my mind and body of the desire she's stirred in me.

I feel myself coming back to life when she's around. Did I want that so soon after losing Sadie? Absolutely not. But what I've learned and seen is that you can't plan these things. They just happen, and when they do, you have the choice to either go for it or run away from things that have the power to hurt you.

Wynter could hurt me—and my son—but I can't imagine her ever doing that. Not intentionally, anyway.

I remember Gage's reaction to finding a lump in Iris's breast and how he ran away for a brief time, as he was unable to face the possibility of losing someone else he loved. Thankfully, his exile didn't last long, and they powered through her surgery and treatment until she was cancer-free. Thank God for that, because we all need her to be healthy for many years to come.

The incident was a reminder of how much is at stake for people who've already suffered staggering losses.

Wynter is young and healthy and full of life. There's no reason to believe she won't be in our lives for decades to come. However, I thought the same of Sadie—and Alyssa, for that matter. You just never know what's coming around the next bend, and having seen the worst of the worst, it takes tremendous courage to start over with someone else.

I appreciate that Wynter said she isn't ready. I wouldn't want to press her for more than she's got to give. It's just been a year for her with Jaden and me with Sadie. In many ways, we're still in the earliest stages of widowhood. Like Gage said, the second year can be harder than the first, as the early fog of disbelief lifts to reveal the gritty reality. If that's the case, I'd rather go through that with Wynter than by myself, and I'd want that for her, too.

After the workout, I go upstairs to shower, checking my phone before I turn on the water.

I have a text from Wynter: *Home.*

Thanks for letting me know. Sleep well.

Yeah, not likely. You've given me a lot to think about.

It'll keep. Get some rest.

You too.

I stand under the hot water for a long time, letting it wash over me and beat down on muscles twitching from the workout. When I get out, I stand with a towel wrapped around my waist to shave so I won't have to do it in the morning. Before I go to bed, I check on Xavier. I love to watch him sleep, always with his arms thrown over his head like his daddy. I wake up that way most days.

It makes me so sad, every day, that Sadie never even got to hold him. She would've been such a wonderful mother. I wonder whether we'd already be expecting a second child if she was still here. If I could have anything I wanted, it would be her back here with us where she belongs.

Since I can't ever have that again, I'm taking steps to figure out the rest of my life without her. I really hope Wynter will be part of that life.

Wynter

I'M anxious as I arrive at Adrian's the next morning. Will everything between us be weird or different after last night? I really hope not, because that would totally suck. I have no stomach for any kind of drama after enduring Jaden's illness and death. That was enough drama for one lifetime.

Today, I'm taking Xavier with me to have lunch with Jaden's mother. I haven't seen her in a while, and she's invited me a few times. I don't want her to think I don't care about their family anymore, so I agreed to come for lunch as long as I could bring Xavier. She'd said of course he could come, and she's looking forward to meeting him.

Eileen and her family were always so good to me and made me feel like part of them from the time Jaden and I were first together. They were a huge source of support to both of us through the worst of his illness.

I'll admit that I've avoided them a bit in the last year. It's just too painful to be with them without Jaden. I want to keep them in my life, though, so that's why I agreed to see her at a time when the rest of the family will be at work or school.

Small doses to start with. That's my plan, anyway.

I go upstairs to Xavier's room, eager to see him. I love him first thing in the morning when he's all smiley and excited to start another day.

"Wyn!"

Jaden was the only one who ever called me that until Xavier did. When Xavier said it as one of his first words, it was like a knife to the heart. I got used to it over time, and now I love that Xavier calls me that. I retrieve him from his crib and take him to the changing table to remove the heavy overnight diaper. Then I clean him up with the fresh-smelling baby wipes and change him into a onesie for breakfast. I've learned not to dress him for the day until after he eats.

We're about to head downstairs when Adrian comes into the room, wearing a light blue shirt and matching tie. He looks so handsome that all I can do is stare for a hot second.

"Morning," he says, smiling.

"Morning."

"I heard my little man chirping."

I hand him over to his daddy.

Adrian kisses him until he squeals with laughter.

"That belly laugh is everything," I say.

"I'll do anything to make it happen because I love it so much."

I was hoping it wouldn't be weird or awkward between us after our intense conversation last night. As we go downstairs with him carrying Xavier, I enjoy the view of his snug dress pants against his backside. Jaden had a flat ass that I used to tease him about constantly. Adrian's is muscular. I try not to think about seeing it in all its naked glory. That's easier said than done.

While I make a bowl of baby cereal, Adrian deposits Xavier into his high chair and gives him more kisses. "Be a good boy for Wynter today."

"Wyn, Wyn, Wyn."

"You're his favorite," Adrian says, smiling at me over his shoulder.

"No way. You are. You always will be."

"I'm not so sure about that. My son has good taste in women."

And now I'm flustered. Awesome.

"What's up for you guys today?" Adrian asks as he pours coffee that he made the night before and put on a timer.

"We're having lunch with Jaden's mother, Eileen."

He stops what he's doing and turns to me. "Are you okay with that?"

"Yeah, it's fine. She's great. We've been trying to get together for a while."

"Still… It's apt to be hard, no?"

I shrug. "Maybe a little. Everything is hard in the after, right?"

"For sure." He takes a good long look at me that has my skin feeling like it's gotten too close to something hot. "Did you sleep okay?"

"Define 'okay.' Like I said, sleep is a challenge for me. I do fine all day, but when I go to bed, it's like every negative and upsetting thing that's ever happened runs through my mind like a movie I can't shut off."

That's way more than I intended to say, so I keep my focus on feeding Xavier. He's always hungry first thing.

"I know that movie. I hate it."

"It's the worst. And the best sometimes. You were in it last night as one of the good things to come out of the worst thing. You and the other widows show up a lot these days."

"I'm glad to hear that. You're in mine, too. I find myself thinking of you more often than I do Sadie, which makes me feel guilty."

I have no idea how to respond to that.

"I suppose that's 'normal,' right?" he asks. "Or whatever passes for normal these days."

"I guess so. Remember what Gage said about guilt being an unproductive emotion. There's nothing you can do to change what happened to Sadie. All you can do is live the life you have left the best way you can."

"Thanks for that reminder. I needed it after our conversation last night."

"You didn't do anything wrong," I tell him. "You've been nothing but respectful of Sadie and her memory."

"Until lately."

"You haven't done anything wrong, Adrian. Despite how it might feel sometimes, you're not married anymore. You can do what you want."

"Keep reminding me, okay?"

"Any time you need reminding."

"Do you feel guilty?"

"I wasn't married that long."

"You were with him for years, though."

"When I think of him, it's hard to remember anything other than him being sick. The last month was brutal. Those are the memories I wish I could forget."

He comes over to where I'm seated at the table as I feed Xavier and squeezes my shoulder. "I'm sorry. That has to be awful."

"It's all awful and beautiful and painful and every other thing." I glance at the clock on the stove. "You'd better get going."

He tries to never be late to work. He doesn't want to take advantage of his brother-in-law.

"You guys have a good day."

I look up at him with a smile. "You, too."

He stares at my face for a long moment before he seems to

pull himself out of it. He keeps his hand on my shoulder as he bends over to kiss Xavier again. "Call if you need anything."

"I will." I can barely breathe after having him so close.

I don't exhale until he goes through the door to the garage, leaving his fresh, clean scent all over me and Xavier.

"Your daddy smells good," I tell him.

"Good."

Smiling, I clap in response to another new word.

"Wyn."

"That's me, buddy. I'm your Wyn."

After I get him dressed, we play for a while before he goes down for a morning nap. From what I've read, he'll be giving up the early nap any time now. He still seems to need it, though. When he starts frantically rubbing his eyes, I can tell he's ready. While he naps, I throw in a load of his laundry and then pop onto Instagram to read Gage's daily post.

My sweet Ivy and Hazel would've been twelve today. I try to imagine them at twelve and wonder what they'd be excited about. Would I be scrambling to get tickets to Taylor Swift? Would they be ready for sleep-away camp this summer? Would they still be dancing? I'll never know the answers to those and so many other questions. I'm sure their mom is throwing them a huge party in heaven. I wish they were still here with me. Please don't drink and drive.

With tears in my eyes, I scroll through the photos of his twin girls from the time they were infants through their first day of kindergarten to their last-ever first day in fourth grade. They were so beautiful and full of life. As was their mother, who also died in the accident. Sometimes I wonder how Gage could've survived such a momentous loss and still be such an amazing source of support to the rest of us.

I send him a text. *Happy birthday to your Ivy and Hazel. They were lucky to have you as their dad, and I'm lucky to have you as my friend. Please reach out if you need anything today. We're always here.*

I reread the text before I send it, marveling at how far I've come in my own journey to be able to write a text like that. Before I lost Jaden, I didn't have much experience with grief or how to manage it. I'd still be flailing at the starting line if it wasn't for Gage and the others who helped me find a way through it. Before grief, it wouldn't have occurred to me to tell a friend to reach out if he needed support. Now I do that without even thinking. That's what we do for one another. We step up during the hard days, and we celebrate the victories, however small they might be.

I text Iris. *Can you talk for a min?*

Yep!

She always says yes, even when she doesn't have time.

"Hey," she says. "How's it going?"

"Good. I guess. How's Gage? I read his post. It's so heartbreaking."

"It is," she says with a sigh. "He seems to be doing okay. The kids asked if we could get a cake for his girls later, so we're doing that."

"Ah, that's so sweet. I love that."

"He did, too. So what's up?"

"Adrian and I talked last night."

"Oh! How'd that go?"

"He said he wants us to, you know, be more than friends or employee-employer or whatever we are."

"Wow. How do you feel about that?"

"Conflicted. If it wasn't for Xavier, I'd be all for it. But it scares me that something could happen between us that would remove them both from my life somehow. I couldn't handle that."

"It's good to think about the possible implications before you leap."

"I also think about our entire group and how messy it could get if things went bad between us. Did you and Gage worry about that, too?"

"Definitely. It was a big concern for us. We rely so heavily on our group to get through the days."

"Same, and I never thought I'd say that."

Iris laughs. "Trust me, I know. You were the most reluctant new member we ever had."

"I'm sorry if I was a brat."

"You weren't. You were hurting. We could all see that. I'm thankful every day that you stuck with us."

"I am, too. I have no idea where I'd be in this thing without you guys. That's why I'm afraid to do anything that might mess with something I need very much—and so does he."

"All valid concerns. What did he say about them?"

"He agrees that we need to proceed with caution. He said he can't imagine us ever not being friends at the very least. I'd like to think that, too, but you know how these things can turn ugly."

"I do. I also know that you two have traveled a path that few others get to experience."

"Lucky for them."

"Indeed. But you have a better appreciation than most people do of how precious life and love and friendship are. I have to believe you'd protect the friendship, no matter what happened between you."

"We would. At least we'd try to."

"That's all you can do, Wynter. If you have feelings for him, and vice versa, then you can either act on them and hope for the best or decide it's too risky. That's up to you."

"I don't like either of those choices."

Iris laughs. "There is no perfect choice in a situation like this."

"I'm really scared of how much I like him."

"Aw, sweetie. That's a wonderful thing. If nothing else, you're discovering there's a new life after loss, whether it's with Adrian or someone else."

"I never wanted a new life. I loved the one I had."

"I know."

"Thanks for listening. I'm not sure how you take care of three kids and all of us, too."

"I love you and the others like family. You know that."

"It means everything to me, Iris. I'm not sure if I've said that enough..."

"That means everything to *me*. When Taylor and I first started this group, we had no idea what we were doing. I look around now at what it's become, and I'm so proud."

"You should be. Xavier and I are off to lunch with Jaden's mom."

"Oh wow. Are you okay with that?"

"Yep. It'll be fine. I'll text you later. Give Gage a big hug from me."

"I will."

"Thanks again for always being available to chat."

"Any time, honey."

God, I love her. If I can someday help just one person the way she's helped me, that would make me so happy.

As I transfer the laundry to the dryer, I hear Xavier chattering in his crib. I get him dressed in one of my favorite outfits —a navy striped pullover with cute little jeans. I want Eileen to think he's as adorable as I do.

Fifteen

Wynter

The drive to Jaden's parents' home takes about thirty-five minutes thanks to traffic. We get there right on time, which was important to me. Eileen is the most punctual person I've ever met. I didn't want to keep her waiting.

I carry Xavier, his bag of toys and the lunch I packed for him before we left the house. I never get over how much stuff is required to take him anywhere. I've learned to be ready for any disaster with changes of clothes and all his favorite things, so he won't get cranky from wanting them.

Eileen meets me at the front door with a big smile and a warm hug. "It's so nice to see you!"

"You, too."

Before Jaden died, we saw each other every day. That was when we were practically living at the hospital.

"This is Xavier Smith Parker."

"Oh my goodness. Isn't he a cutie?" She shakes his hand and makes a big fuss over him.

He's not quite sure what to think of her yet, but he'll warm up to her. He loves meeting new people.

"I love his name."

"Smith was his mother's last name."

"It's so sad that she died."

"Yes, it is. From what Adrian has told me, she would've been a wonderful mother."

As I follow her into the kitchen, I'm struck by the familiar sights and scents of what was once my home away from home. The memories hit me like a punch that takes my breath away. Jaden juggling grapefruit while his mother yelled at him to cut it out. Jaden sitting on the counter bothering his mother while she made dinner. Jaden kissing me behind the open pantry door, stealing a second to ourselves while surrounded by his family.

I'm so overwhelmed, I can barely breathe as I sit on a barstool with Xavier on my lap.

"Do you still like Diet Coke?"

"Sure, that's fine."

I haven't had one in a year. Diet Coke also reminds me of Jaden because he liked it, too. What doesn't remind me of him? I take a sip from the icy glass of soda she puts in front of me, and even the taste of the drink is almost too much to bear. I should be used to it by now, the pain that resurfaces often without warning to remind me of what's been lost. Of course, I knew it would be tough to come here. I guess I just hoped it wouldn't be as tough as it was the last time I was here.

"How've you been, honey?" Eileen asks as she puts a tray of fruit on the counter.

I take a grape. "I'm doing okay. It's still hard. I don't have to tell you."

"No, you don't."

She's stopped bothering to color her hair, so there's more gray than blonde now, and she's gained about twenty pounds since Jaden died. She sits next to me at the bar and eats a slice of orange. "I keep thinking it'll get better, but it only seems to get harder."

"I hear year two is harder than year one."

"I read that, too. You wonder how that's possible."

Xavier keeps trying to grab at the fruit, so I push the tray out of his reach.

"You're good with him."

"Oh, thanks. He's a sweet boy. He makes it easy."

"I used to tell Bob that you and Jaden would have the most beautiful babies."

"You used to tell *us* that," I say, smiling. Jaden would be mortified when she'd say that, back when we were too young to be thinking about kids, before we knew he would die young.

"I guess I did," she says with a small smile. "I've been excited to be a grandmother for as long as I've had kids."

"How're the girls?"

"They're good. Kelsey is working hard at school and wait-ressing on the weekends, so she doesn't get home very often. Kristina has a great first-grade class this year, so it's been a lot better than last year. They've had a rough time of it losing their baby brother, but they're carrying on. We're proud of them."

"No boyfriends?"

"Not that I know about, but I'd probably be the last to know."

"They're so secretive about that."

"Always have been. What about you? Any new friends?"

Is she asking me if I have a boyfriend? "I, uh…"

"It's none of my business. I don't mean to put you on the spot."

"No, it's fine. I'm not seeing anyone."

"It's probably too soon to be thinking about that, but I

hope you know that we'd support you in whatever you decide to do. You've got your whole life ahead of you."

"Thank you for saying that. It means a lot to me."

"We love you, Wynter. You know that."

Her sweetness brings tears to my eyes.

She squeezes my arm before she gets up and goes to the fridge, returning with sandwiches. "I made that chicken pesto you like so much."

Another thing that reminds me of Jaden. It was his favorite and became mine. "That's so nice of you."

She shrugs. "It feels good to have you here. Like old times."

I need to come more often.

After we've eaten in silence for a few minutes, she says, "I want to talk to you about something, and I want you to tell me how you really feel about it."

"Okay..."

"I've been wanting to talk to you about this for a while now, but it never seemed like the right time."

"Talk to me about what?"

She pauses before she dives into it. "Before Jaden started treatment, the doctors told him he could end up sterile. While we were going through his things, we found this." She pushes a piece of paper across the counter to me that looks like a receipt of some sort.

"What is it?"

"Apparently, he froze his sperm."

"*What?*" I'm shocked. I knew nothing about this.

"We were as surprised as you are. He didn't tell any of us about it."

Immediately, I know why. "It was because I was so scared about medical stuff. He knew that and probably figured I'd get anxious about it if I knew."

"Probably so, but I guess he wanted to have the option available for whatever you guys decided later."

"Wow. So it's just sitting in a freezer somewhere?"

"Yes, it is." After a pause, she says, "Do you think you might want to do something with it?"

I stare at her, as if I don't understand what she's saying. "I, uh…"

"Never mind," she says with a laugh. "What am I thinking?"

"You're thinking that we might have a chance to have part of Jaden."

Her eyes fill as she nods. "The thought did cross my mind, but that would be entirely up to you."

I want to say no. Absolutely not. I'm in no position to become a single parent. It's not something I'd ever want, but I can't bring myself to say that to her. Besides, I have serious fears about medical stuff and childbirth that haven't gotten better since I've learned more about what happened to Sadie. But the thought of Jaden living on in our child is tantalizing, to say the least.

"I've shocked you. I'm sorry. Bob told me I shouldn't drop this on you out of the blue, but I thought you'd want to know that the possibility exists. If you're interested, that is." After another long pause, she says, "You're not upset, are you?"

"I don't know what I am. I've been upset for so long, I wouldn't know how not to be."

She puts her hand on top of mine. "I know, honey, and we say all the time how lucky Jaden was to have you. We're so glad he got the chance to be in love and to be married, even if it was only for a few days. That meant so much to him—and to us."

"You guys have always been so good to me."

"We love you like one of our own."

"I love you, too. I don't know what to say, Eileen. I'm still in such a weird place after losing him. I'm sure you are, too."

"I am. I've accepted that I probably always will be."

"Same."

"There's one other thing... Everything happened so quickly at the end that Jaden didn't have time to add you to his accounts or anything. He had a life insurance policy from when he worked for the town that only recently paid out. Bob and I agree that he'd want that to go to you."

"Oh. I, ah..."

"It's two hundred and fifty thousand dollars."

I'm sure my eyes must pop out of my head. "*What?*"

"We think Jaden would want you to use the money to do something that would make you happy. Whether it's travel or college or your own home."

"Or raise his child?"

"That's completely up to you." She hands me an envelope. "We want you to have the money either way. You were his wife. It should go to you."

Xavier picks that moment to get fussy.

I stand to put him down on a blanket with some of his toys.

"Is he walking yet?"

"Not quite. Any minute now."

"He's so sweet."

"I love him so much." And I'm relieved to be focused on him as I spin from the news she's shared with me.

"I can see that. He's lucky to have you."

"I'm the lucky one. He gives me a reason to get up and get going every day."

"I'm glad to see you bouncing back, as much as one can bounce back after such a loss."

"It's a day-to-day thing."

"Yes, it is."

We chat for a while longer before Xavier starts rubbing his eyes.

"I'd better get him home for his nap."

"Take this." She pushes the envelope toward me. "Do something amazing in Jaden's honor. He'd want you to follow your dreams."

"Thank you." I put the envelope in my bag. "I'll think about the other thing."

"Okay. No pressure from us. We wanted you to know the option exists."

"And now I know. Thank you for lunch and everything else you've done for me over the years. You and your family showed me how it's supposed to be, and I'll always appreciate the way you made me part of things here."

"You'll always be family to us, Wynter. That'll never change."

We hug at the door, and she gives Xavier a kiss on his forehead.

I drive home to Adrian's in a state of shock and disbelief. Two hundred and fifty thousand. And the possibility of having Jaden's child. I'm not sure which is the most unbelievable.

Back at the house, I move through the motions of changing Xavier and getting him down for his nap. When I go downstairs, I retrieve the envelope from my purse and open it to find a check for two hundred and fifty thousand dollars made out to me, one last unexpected gift from Jaden that brings tears to my eyes as I long for him. I'd so much rather have him than all the money in the world.

Revisiting the pain of losing him is lacerating. He was my everything—my past, my present and my future. For months after he died, I wasn't sure I'd survive losing him. I wasn't sure I *wanted* to survive it. On many a day, I still can't believe he really died. We'd begun making plans for after he got out of the hospital. We wanted to travel. London was first on our list and then Paris and Rome. He wanted to go to Tokyo after seeing a movie set there. I was willing to go anywhere as long as I got to go with him.

Tears roll down my cheeks when I think of the plans we made, the things we'll never get to do now. We talked about having kids a lot. We wanted one of each. A girl named Willow and a boy named Joshua. He brought up the subject of kids often enough that I could tell he really wanted them, even if I was scared of the medical stuff. I wanted to make him happy, so I'm sure we would've had them eventually if he'd lived. We would've been great parents, even if we worried about the world burning up.

A fresh wave of grief leaves me staggered and shocked by how much it hurts after all this time.

I'm still sitting on Adrian's sofa, wallowing in the past, when he comes in from work to find me in a dark room.

He turns on a light.

I wince.

"What's wrong?" he asks.

"Just having a day."

"Did you see your mother-in-law?"

"Yeah."

He sits next to me. "Did she upset you?"

"No. We had a nice visit."

"What's this?" He picks up the check I put on the coffee table and has the same reaction I did when I first saw it. "Whoa! Holy shit, Wynter."

"Jaden's life insurance. They wanted me to have it."

"That's amazing. Is that what upset you?"

"The whole thing is upsetting. He should be here, with me, not getting life insurance payouts because he's dead."

Adrian slides closer to me and puts his arm around me.

As I lean my head against his chest, I immediately feel better.

"It's so wrong," he says softly. "Every single thing about it is wrong."

"I don't want the money. I want him."

"I know, sweetheart. I get it. I got fifty thousand from a policy Sadie had through her work, and it made me sick to get that check. I didn't want the money. I wanted her."

"It's unfair."

"So unfair."

"What the hell am I supposed to do with that kind of money?"

"You could invest it and forget about it until you need it or put it toward something that makes you happy."

"Eileen said Jaden would want me to use it to follow my dreams, but I don't know what they are anymore. He was my dream. Our life together was my dream. Maybe that makes me silly or ridiculous, but he was everything I ever wanted. I didn't dream about things that didn't involve him."

"Why would you when you thought you had a lifetime to spend together?"

"People would tell us we were too young to know what we wanted forever, but I wanted him, and he wanted me. It was that simple for us, and it had been that way for years when he died."

"Sometimes you just know."

"Was it like that for you with Sadie?"

"For me, it was. Not so much for her. I was the assistant manager of a grocery store when we met. It was a good job that I liked, but I wasn't exactly on fire with ambition to figure out what was next. She encouraged me to go to school, to get my degree, to work hard for the life we wanted. I never would've gone to college without her pushing me. I went nights and weekends and graduated two years ago from George Mason."

"That's amazing, Adrian. I didn't know that."

"It was a slog, and on many a day, I felt like quitting, but I wanted her to be proud of me. She was my biggest cheerleader, telling me I could do anything I put my mind to. She'd graduated with honors from Old Dominion at twenty-two and made twice what I did. We waited until I finished school to have Xavier."

"Is that when you went to work for your brother-in-law?"

"Nah, that happened after Sadie died and the job I'd only just started said they couldn't put things on hold until I was ready to come back. They had to move on."

"What was that job?"

"It was with a government contractor, working in IT. I was going to love it."

"They should've waited for you to come back."

"I understood why they couldn't. They were really nice to me and gave me three months' salary and paid my health insurance for a year."

"I'm sorry your loss was compounded by another one."

"I was so messed up after losing Sadie that I didn't even care about the job. My brother-in-law asked me to come work with him, and I took it because I needed to do something. But it's just a job."

"It's what you need right now. Something that doesn't require too much of you."

"That's it exactly. I'm thankful to him for giving me the opportunity."

A little squeak from upstairs has us pulling apart.

How long have we been wrapped up in each other?

I stand and head for the stairs. "I'll get him."

Adrian follows me. He's always eager to see Xavier after a long day apart.

The little guy is so excited to see us. His arms and legs are moving around like crazy.

I bend over the crib rail to pick him up and give him a kiss on his plump cheek. "That was a long nap, mister."

"I hope he's not up all night," Adrian says.

"I read that they go through growth spurts where they eat and sleep more than usual. That might be what's going on."

I take him to the table to change his diaper and then hand him to his daddy.

"Wyn," Xavier says, making us laugh.

"I'm right here. Give Daddy some love. He missed you today."

"Do you want to stay for dinner? I was going to make pasta."

"Sure, that sounds good."

After the day I've had, I don't want to be alone.

Sixteen

Adrian

My heart goes out to her. The hits keep on coming long after the loss of the ones we loved the most. Every new development is a reminder that the lives we thought we were going to lead are gone now.

She oversees Xavier's dinner while I cook some chicken to go with the pasta and make a salad.

I keep thinking about Jaden and the insurance payout. His parents did the right thing giving it to Wynter. She was his wife, and even if he never got the chance to change the beneficiary, it should be her. However, I certainly understand the guilt that comes with benefiting financially from losing someone irreplaceable.

"That smells delicious," Wynter says when I put the plate in front of her. "Thank you."

"You're welcome."

I give Xavier some animal crackers to gnaw on while we eat.

Her phone buzzes with a text that has her frowning.

"Everything okay?"

"My mother is asking if I still live with her."

She fires off a reply and then puts the phone down.

"What did you say?"

"I told her I'm working, and I'll be home later."

"The insurance money could set you up in your own apartment," I remind her.

"Yeah, I thought of that."

"What else would you like to do that you couldn't do before you had the money?"

"I don't know. I haven't given much thought to anything beyond get up, shower, go to work, go home, try to sleep, rinse and repeat."

"The first year is tough that way. We're so focused on trying to function that we don't think beyond the basics. But you should think about what you most want now that you can afford to do anything you want."

"Sometimes I think about maybe going to college."

"Is that something you want?"

"Jaden and I were both accepted at George Mason before his cancer came back. He said I should go without him, but that wasn't an option. I never could've concentrated on anything else when he was so sick."

"You could do it now."

"I guess. I don't know. The thought of studying again is kind of revolting. I never liked school that much."

"College is different from high school. Most of the time, you're studying things that interest you."

"I suppose that's true. It's not something I give much thought to, honestly. I only applied to Mason because Jaden wanted me to. I was actually shocked when I got in."

"I bet if you reached out to them and told them why you didn't take the acceptance the first time, they'd welcome you whenever you're ready to start."

"You make it sound so easy."

"It is, Wynter. And now you can afford to pay for it."

"I'm still wrapping my head around that." She glances at me with a vulnerable look that tugs at my heart. "You're encouraging me to go to school even though it might complicate things for you with Xavier."

"If it's what you want, we'll figure something out. Don't worry about us. Think about yourself."

"It's hard to think about myself without thinking of him, too."

The look of pure love she directs at my son is beautiful. I love the bond they have, and she's right that it would be a bummer if she couldn't care for him anymore. But I'd never want to be responsible for holding her back from chasing her dreams.

I notice that she's poking at her dinner rather than eating it.

"Do you want something else?" I ask.

She looks up at me, seeming surprised. "No, this is great."

"Then why aren't you eating?"

She puts down her fork and wipes her mouth with a napkin. "There was something else Eileen told me today that I can't stop thinking about."

"What's that?"

"Jaden froze sperm before his treatment so we could have kids when we were ready. He didn't tell me because he knew how I feel about medical stuff. I'm sure he also didn't want me to feel pressured."

"Wow. That's a big thing to keep from you."

"I get why he didn't tell me. We had so many other things to think about then. And with the doctors telling him he could be sterile after treatment, it was the smart thing to do."

"Why did she tell you about it now?"

"They're wondering if I might want to have his child."

I'm stunned. "*What?* She asked you that?"

"She said she wanted me to know about it in case that was something I might want."

"Was the insurance money contingent on you agreeing to that?"

"No! Nothing like that. She said they all agreed that should come to me. But of course, the money would make single parenthood possible."

"Jeez. That's a lot to put on you."

"It's all a lot. What's one more thing?"

"That's a pretty big thing." I'm already full of anxiety at the thought of her being pregnant and having a child. I want to scream from the rooftops for her not to do it. I force myself to stay calm and be a good friend to her when she needs one. "What do you think of the idea?"

"I don't know what to think. Before today, I didn't even know it was a possibility."

"What's your gut reaction to the idea?"

"Not as clear-cut as it would've been before Xavier came into my life."

"How do you mean?"

"Babies used to be something we talked about in the abstract. Like, wouldn't that be fun someday, even if it scared me, too. They're so unpredictable and needy. I thought I would hate that. But I don't. From the time I first met you and Xavier, he's shown me that babies can be quite awesome. Once you understand what they need, it's actually pretty easy."

"I hear the baby stage is the easiest. It gets harder from here."

She shrugs. "I can't wait to see him at every stage."

I realize she's seriously considering the possibility of having Jaden's child, and I want to wail. I want to beg her not to. Instead, I keep it light, so I won't lose my composure. "Even the talking-back, willful, disobedient stage?"

"My sweet Xavier will never have that stage," she says with a smile for the baby.

He returns her grin with one of his own. He's made a mess with the animal crackers, but he's so cute, who cares about such things?

"Sure, that's what we'd like to think, but they all have that stage. I remember Iris saying how Laney nearly drove her crazy saying no to everything. She still loves that word."

"I know," Wynter says, laughing. "It's so funny."

"Not for Iris, it isn't. From what she tells me, the first year is the easiest in many ways because all they do is eat, sleep and poop. Things get more complicated when they get into school and sports and make friends. She talks about how she lives in her minivan. They spend so much time in the car, she keeps snacks and drinks in there."

"So what you're saying is that my sample size of Xavier isn't adequate to make any big decisions about having kids."

"Something like that."

"It's weird because I'm not as freaked out by the thought of it as I used to be, and the only thing that's changed is that Xavier has come into my life."

"That's not the only thing that's changed. You've also seen some really difficult things that may have you reevaluating how you feel about everything."

"True. I can't believe I'm even thinking about this. I'm still terrified of childbirth and all that, especially after hearing more about how Sadie died, but I'm not scared of being a mother. I know I could do it now, thanks to my little pal over there."

"You shouldn't dwell too much on what happened to Sadie," I say, even though I'm terrified for Wynter, and she hasn't even decided anything for certain. "Her complication was very rare. It only occurs in like two to eight out of every hundred thousand pregnancies."

"Two to eight is a lot if you're one of the two or the eight."

"You still shouldn't dwell on that. It's not at all likely to happen." Why am I trying to talk her into this when it's the last thing in the world I want her to do?

"A million other things can happen."

"Most women come home with perfectly healthy babies after perfectly normal deliveries."

"I have hospital trauma after what I saw Jaden endure. That day we went to the hospital when Iris had the lumpectomy brought it all back. The smells, the sounds... I never want to step foot in a hospital again."

"I get that. They're not my favorite place either, but it's not realistic to expect to go through life without ever again being in a hospital."

"I suppose you're right. Thanks for talking this out with me. I've been kinda spinning since she brought it up."

"I'm sure you have. That must've come out of nowhere."

"It did. I had no clue it was even possible, and now that I know it is, it's all I can think about."

No, no, no. Please, Wynter. Just no. "Keep in mind you don't have to do anything about it any time soon. You've got time to decide if that's what you want."

"That's true. I'm all over the place since that visit with Eileen."

"She gave you a lot to think about."

Xavier starts fussing to get out of his chair.

I get up to get some wet paper towels to clean him up before I set him loose. When I stand him up on the floor, I expect him to drop into a crawl the way he usually does, but instead he teeters.

"Wynter..." I use my chin to direct her attention to him.

She immediately sees what I do and jumps up to position herself on the floor to catch him. "Get your phone."

I scoot around him to get my phone off the charger. When I turn back to them, I'm just in time to record his first tentative step toward her.

"That's it!" She holds her arms out to him. "Come see me, sweet boy."

With a big, spitty smile, he takes another step and then a third before collapsing into her arms. "You did it! What a big boy you are!" She hugs him tightly. "Did Daddy get that?"

"I sure did."

She hands him up to me.

I hold him with one arm while I reach out to help her up with the other. "I'm so glad we were both here for that."

"Me, too. I was afraid it would happen when you were at work."

I gather her into a group hug with me and Xavier. "I wish..."

"What?" she asks, sounding as breathless as I feel.

"I wish we were a real family. You, me and Xavier. I wish you didn't have to go home at night."

"Adrian..."

"I know. That's a lot to drop on you after the day you've already had, but that's what I wish for."

Between us, Xavier squirms to get down, probably to further test out his newly acquired skill.

We pull apart, and I put him down to roam. Then I return my attention to Wynter. "That was too much. I'm sorry."

"No, it wasn't. It's nice to hear that you feel that way, especially since it gets harder every day for me to leave after you get home. All I want is to be here with you guys."

I put my hands on her hips and gaze down at her sweet face. "Then be here. As much and as often as you want."

"That simple?"

"And that complicated. This feels good to me, and after feeling like complete shit for so long, it's nice to feel good again."

"Yeah, it is. It feels good to me, too. I just still have the same worries I did the last time we talked about this."

"I know, and I do, too. But God, Wynter, I want to start living again rather than just existing, and I want to start living with you."

She stares at me for the longest time before she goes up on tiptoes to kiss me.

Wynter

THIS IS STILL A BAD IDEA. Even as I make the first move by wrapping my arms around his neck and kissing him, I know it's a bad idea.

The thing is, I don't care.

I feel good when I'm with him, and after months of feeling terrible, being with him is like watching the sun come out from behind dark clouds. I can't resist my feelings for him any longer. I don't *want* to resist.

His arms encircle me as he pulls me close enough to feel what my nearness has done to him.

I rub against him shamelessly, which makes him groan.

"Xavier," I whisper against his lips.

As we pull apart, I can tell he's as stunned as I am that we both nearly forgot there's a toddler on the loose.

"To be continued," he says as he releases me to go find his son.

I shiver with anticipation.

It's been ages since anything like this has happened to me. The last time was more than eighteen months ago, on what turned out to be a rare series of good days for Jaden. His family was out of town for the weekend attending an event at Kelsey's college, so we spent most of the weekend in his basement bedroom. We had no idea then that it would be the last time we'd ever be together that way.

Thinking about that now, as I stand on the cusp of something new with Adrian, puts a huge lump in my throat. I hope that wherever he is, Jaden knows I'd never go near another man if he was still here.

As I follow Adrian upstairs to give Xavier a bath and put him to bed, I'm in all my feels as the past and present collide in this complicated thing called life. One of the things about having had something special in the past is that I recognize it when I encounter it in the present.

Adrian is special. I feel the things for him that I once did for Jaden, which is sad and exciting at the same time. I never wanted to feel things for anyone but Jaden. Since he's not here anymore, I have no choice but to follow my heart toward something new and exciting, while never forgetting the man I'll always love.

The push-pull of past, present and future is one I've heard the other widows talk about as they've taken steps toward new relationships and new lives after tremendous loss. Without my widows, I'd be questioning my sanity. But thanks to them, I know it's a normal part of the grieving process.

Roni and Derek have talked about honoring the past while they create a future for themselves and the children they had with their late spouses. Gage has wrestled with falling in love with Iris and becoming a father again to her three young children after losing his wife and daughters so tragically.

Like all things in this messed-up journey called grief, you don't really understand the emotions that come with moving on with someone new until you feel them the way I do now.

Their stories have given me the courage to look beyond the fog of my grief to see what else might be possible. When I picture what I want my future to be, I see Adrian and Xavier as clear as day. Maybe there'll be other things, too, such as college and more kids and other adventures. Whatever happens, I hope they'll experience it with me.

"Want to read with us?" Adrian asks.

"Sure."

I follow them into Adrian's bedroom, stretch out on the bed next to them and listen to Adrian read his little boy a story about a talking train. Though he's tired, Xavier hangs on his father's every word and watches the pages turn with interest.

"Choo choo," Adrian says.

Xavier giggles.

"Your turn, Wynter."

"Choo choo."

More giggles.

Adrian smiles. "He loves that sound."

"Choo," Xavier says.

"Choo," Adrian and I say together, leading to more help-less giggles from Xavier.

My God, I love him. I love them both. If I had this, with them, and only this for the rest of my life, I'd be so happy. That scares me so bad because I've learned that right when you think you've got life figured out, the universe has other plans.

To hell with that. I'm going to enjoy this moment for as long as it lasts and focus on the here and now. That's another thing I've learned from my widows—to live in the moment because that's all there is. Nothing else is guaranteed.

"Give Wyn a kiss night-night," Adrian says.

Xavier gifts me with a spit kiss and a big smile.

"Night, sweet boy. See you in the morning."

"Wyn."

He reaches for me, so I take him and give him a tight squeeze. "Love you."

"Love."

"That's a new one," Adrian says, smiling.

"He's so smart."

"I'll be right back."

I hand Xavier to his daddy and blow kisses at him as they leave Adrian's bedroom. A twinge of anxiety overtakes me when I realize I'm reclined on his bed, waiting for him to return to do what, exactly? In the ten minutes it takes him to tuck in Xavier, I've worked myself into a full-blown panic. I sit up and pull my knees to my chest, focused intently on breathing. Deep breath in. Hold it. Release. Repeat. Just keep breathing.

"Wynter."

I look up to find Adrian watching me with a concerned expression. "What's wrong?"

"Nothing."

He comes to sit next to me. "Don't say it's nothing when it's clearly something."

"I just started to feel a little nervous about, you know, what might happen when you came back."

"Sweetheart, nothing happens unless we're both ready and willing. I'm happy to have your company. I get to look at your gorgeous face and your sexy smile and watch you with my son, which is one of the sweetest things I've ever seen. I'm perfectly satisfied with that for now."

As he speaks, he runs a finger lightly over my face that sends shivers down my spine, waking up every part of me that's been asleep since long before I lost Jaden. It takes all my courage to say, "I don't know that I am."

"What do you mean?"

"I don't know that I'm perfectly satisfied with what we already have when I know it could be so much more."

"Wynter..." He exhales. "I just caught you in a panic."

"It's passed."

"Just like that?"

189

"It's a big deal to be thinking the kind of thoughts I am about you when you've been through what we have."

"Yes, it is, and we don't need to rush anything if you're not ready."

"I want to be ready." I lean closer to him, hoping he'll take the hint and kiss me again before I lose my nerve.

He takes the hint.

Damn, the man can kiss like nobody's business, and this kiss... *Whoa*. This one includes tongues and hands and a level of desperation I wouldn't have thought myself capable of anymore. I would've been wrong about that.

"Tell me to stop if it's too much too soon," he whispers against my neck. "Just say stop."

"I'm not saying that."

"At any point, Wynter. Say the word."

Seventeen

Wynter

I appreciate that he's giving me an out, but I don't want out. I want in. I want him. I want this. We slide down on the bed and reach for each other in a moment of perfect harmony that makes my head spin from the rush of desire. It reminds me of a limb coming back to life after "falling asleep," with pins and needles attacking all my most important places.

His hand slides under my top to rest against my back, making me gasp from the sensation that comes with being touched by a man for the first time in a long time.

"Is this okay?"

"I hate acting like a scared virgin."

His low chuckle makes me smile.

"Why is that funny?"

"Because you're the most fearless person I've ever met."

"Oh my God! That's so not true."

"Yes, it really is. You're the youngest of us, but we all wish we could be more like you."

"No way."

"Yes way. You're bold and courageous and funny. You're the one who says what everyone else is thinking."

"That makes me obnoxious. Not those other things."

"No, Wynter. Those things make you who you are, and we all love who you are."

"Half the time, I feel like you guys want to muzzle me."

"Never."

I raise a brow in disbelief. "Come on. Sometimes you do."

"Not me. I find myself waiting to hear your take on the topic of the moment because I know it's going to be the most interesting and entertaining one of all."

"Just in case you're saying all this to butter me up, I'm already in your bed and acting rather willing."

He laughs hard. "Stop it."

"You stop it. You're blowing smoke up my skirt."

"No, I'm not." His hand moves from my back down to cup my butt as he pulls me in closer to him.

My mouth waters at the feel of his hardness pressed against my belly. It occurs to me that I could touch him there if I wanted to.

I want to.

I slide my hand from his chest, over well-defined abdominals, bumping up against the head of his hard cock and drawing a sharp gasp from him. "Is this okay?"

"Uh... yeah." He pushes himself against my hand to make the point.

Cruising over his T-shirt and sweats, I explore the full length, which is impressive. It's hard not to compare when you've been with only one other guy, but Adrian is bigger. Quite a bit bigger if I'm being honest.

"Wynter," he whispers. "You're driving me crazy."

"Do you want me to stop?"

"God no. Don't stop."

The urgency I hear in his voice has me doubling down. As

I stroke him through his clothes, his hand moves from my butt to my leg and then back to where he started, squeezing and shaping and generally turning me into one big nerve ending that's completely focused on him.

Then he moves so he's on top of me, gazing down at me with fire in his gorgeous eyes. "Hey."

"Hey, yourself."

"I want to tell you something."

"Okay..."

"When you saw me with those women..."

"What about it?"

"I was picturing you when I was with them. I didn't want them. I wanted you."

"Adrian..."

"I swear it's true. They were nice, and we had a good time, but when I'd close my eyes, it was you I saw, not them. That makes me feel awful because I don't behave that way with women. I never have. But I couldn't help it."

That might be the sweetest thing I've ever heard, and I've heard lots of sweet things from the man who loved me. But hearing Adrian confess to wanting me while he was with other women is overwhelming in so many ways.

I wrap my legs around his hips and my arms around his neck.

He keeps his gaze fixed on mine as he comes in for a kiss that quickly becomes intense.

For the first time in longer than I can remember, I'm entirely focused on something other than grief. And wow, does it feel good. I tug at his T-shirt and pull it over his head, breaking the kiss for only the second it takes to get his shirt off.

Then I feel his hand under me, inching my shirt up as he continues to kiss my face off.

Again, we part only long enough for him to get the top over my head, leaving me only in a sheer bra, which soon comes unhooked and gets pushed aside, putting my breasts in contact with his chest.

The feeling takes my breath away and brings tears to my eyes that I deeply resent. This is no time for tears. I close my eyes tightly, hoping they'll go away. One slides down my cheek, and naturally, he notices.

"What, babe?"

"Just all the feels."

"Should we stop?"

"No, don't stop. Please don't."

He moves from my lips to my neck and down to my breasts. I'd forgotten how good it feels to be held and kissed and caressed. When he tugs my nipple into the heat of his mouth, I moan so loudly I fear I'll wake up Xavier. I bite my lip to contain the noise while he gives the other side equal attention.

"Still okay?"

"Mmm, you can't tell?"

"Just want to be sure."

He plants a kiss smack in the middle of my belly before he pulls back to remove my leggings and underwear.

My whole body goes hot as he takes a long, perusing look at my naked body spread out before him.

"You're even sexier than I imagined, and my imagination has been vivid where you're concerned."

I run my hands over the bulging muscles in his arms. "Same to you."

Then he drops his head to kiss my inner thigh, using his shoulders to push my legs apart.

"Tell me to stop."

"Don't you dare."

He laughs as he gives me his tongue in deep thrusts that have me so close to coming, I can barely hang on. I can't help but remember the first time Jaden and I did this, and how mortifying it was until we got to the end, and I came so hard, I saw stars. That's about to happen again with Adrian, so I force the memories from my mind and focus on the now, rather than the then.

Now is feeling pretty damned good.

He pushes his fingers inside me and sucks on my clit, triggering an epic orgasm, the first I've had since disaster struck.

I'm still gasping when I feel him press against me.

"Condom."

"All set."

Wow. How long was I out of it?

"Tell me to stop."

"Shut up."

I love his laughter and how it completely transforms him from a grieving widower into a man with so much left to give. How lucky am I that he wants to give it to me?

As he pushes into me, I realize this is going to pinch a bit. Thankfully, he goes nice and slow, making sure I'm with him every step of the way.

"Look at me."

I tip my gaze up to meet his, which is intense and focused.

"Are you okay?"

"I'm good. You?"

"I'm very good, but this isn't my first time."

"I'm okay, Adrian. I swear." I raise my hands up to frame his handsome face. "I'm so glad it's you. I wouldn't be okay if it wasn't."

"I'm glad it's me, too. I'm so, *so* glad."

As he says that last part, he pushes the rest of the way in, triggering a series of orgasms that has me clinging to him, digging my fingers into the dense muscles of his back.

"Oh damn, Wynter..."

We stay like that for the longest time, our bodies joined as we breathe the same air and stare into each other's eyes. It's a searingly intimate moment that fills me with hope for a future that might include joy and love and *this*. God, more of this.

Then he starts to move, his hands grasping my ass as he takes me on a wild ride that has us both reaching for the big finish that hits me like a tsunami of emotion and pleasure and so much love for this incredible man.

He comes down on top of me, his head on my shoulder as he breathes hard. "Talk to me."

"Hello, Adrian."

He snorts out a laugh. "Hello, Wynter. How're you doing?"

"Remarkably well, actually."

"I'm glad to hear that."

"You?"

"Spectacular, in fact."

With his arms around me, he rolls onto his back, taking me with him so I'm sprawled on top of him as he continues to throb inside me.

I shiver from the overload of sensation.

Mistaking my shiver for being cold, he pulls a blanket over us.

"So," he says, "that happened."

"So it did."

"I slept with my nanny. Serious single-dad cliché."

I laugh along with him. "I'd prefer to think you slept with your friend."

"That, too." His hands move over me, sparking another twinge of desire when I would've thought that was done for now. Apparently not. "This feels so good to me, Wynter. Tell me it does for you, too."

"It does. I was thinking earlier that when you've had what we did with Jaden and Sadie, you recognize it when it comes along again. I hope I'm not giving myself too much credit by saying that about Sadie."

"You're not, and you're right. There's a feeling that comes with being with the right person, and if you know it, you know it."

"Yeah, that. Exactly that. Although I'm not sure this is forever and ever or anything like that, it feels good to be with someone who gets it."

"Same."

"I had widow sex."

"Yes, you did, and may I say you're very good at it."

That has me cracking up. "Whatever."

It feels so good to laugh, to love, to be with him this way.

"After I first lost Jaden, I thought I'd never do anything like this again. I thought that was over for me."

"I think we all believe that at first until it becomes clear that way of thinking isn't sustainable."

"I believed everything was over. I was in a very bad place when I first joined the group."

"We knew that. We worried about you. I thought about you a lot after we first met. I couldn't believe someone as young as you were had been through what you have."

"I don't feel young anymore."

"I get that, but you are, and you have your whole life ahead of you to do whatever you want. And now, thanks to Jaden, you can afford to do anything."

"Funny, the only thing I really want to do is take care of Xavier and be with you guys."

"We can make that happen."

I'M TOTALLY sleep-deprived after spending the night with Adrian. We were up most of the night, talking, having sex and laughing. We did a lot of laughing, which was a relief. I was afraid it would be awkward after we had sex, but it wasn't. It was more like now that we've crossed that line, we could fully indulge and not sweat the ever-present consequences. Every muscle in my body hurts today, especially the ones between my legs that haven't been used for anything like what we did in a very long time.

I'd forgotten what it was like to be sore there.

Jaden and I were having sex by the time we were fifteen, so it's been a while since I had a sex hangover.

But it's all good. Being with Adrian was amazing, and I can't wait for more time with him.

Hovering in the back of my mind and messing with my bliss after being with Adrian is the info about Jaden freezing his sperm. I have no idea what to do about that, so I decide to run it by the Wild Widows at our weekly meeting. They always know what to do.

On Wednesday, Adrian's sister takes Xavier for an overnight since she doesn't have to work until noon the next day. As much as I love early mornings with my little buddy, I'm excited to be able to sleep past seven o'clock for the first time in a while.

I'm also excited to spend the night completely alone with Adrian. Not that Xavier is any trouble, but I'm aware of him in the next room while I'm getting busy with his daddy.

After a few nights together, I feel better than I have in a very long time. Life seems hopeful again, and the pervasive gloom I've lived with since Jaden died seems to be lifting. That's not just because of Adrian, though. I have to give myself some credit for having survived this last year, for having found an amazing source of support with the Wild Widows (okay, my mom gets the credit for making me go, but I'll take the credit for the friendships I now have with them) and for finding a new purpose as Xavier's nanny.

I dropped Xavier at Nia's, so I'm the last to arrive at Iris's house.

Adrian seems relieved to see me when I come in carrying the seven-layer dip and corn chips I picked up at the grocery store on the way.

"Sorry I'm late."

"You haven't missed anything," Iris says as she hugs me and takes my coat.

As always, I feel like I've come home when I arrive at her house, which is entirely thanks to the way she makes us feel so welcome there.

"All good with the little guy?" Adrian asks as he greets me with a warm smile.

"Yep. Nia and the kids were thrilled to have him."

"Did he cry when you left?"

"No, he was too busy playing. I don't think he noticed."

"That's good." He places his hand on my back where no one else can see and gives a subtle squeeze that has me counting the hours until we can be alone.

We exchange smiles before moving on to talk to others, as neither of us is willing to go public with the change in our relationship. Not yet, anyway. Although, I'm sure we're not fooling anyone. I've never met a more intuitive group of people than these Wild Widows. They see things that haven't even happened yet, or at least that's how it seems to me.

"Update on Aurora," Iris says as we fill our plates from the wide variety of food that everyone brought. "Her husband was convicted. He's looking at twenty years in prison on each of the three counts."

"Did you hear that from her?" Naomi asks.

"I saw it on the news," Iris says. "I reached out to her to tell her we're still here if she needs us. She responded for the first time in ages and said she might come by one of these weeks. She also said to thank you all for thinking of her."

"I hope she comes," Brielle says. "She's rebuilding her life the same way we are and deserves the support."

The others agreed.

"Wait till she finds out Derek is engaged to Roni," Gage says with an evil grin.

"Stop," Derek says with a groan as the rest of us laugh.

Aurora had her sights set on Derek until it became obvious he was interested in Roni. Shortly after that, Aurora stopped attending the meetings.

"Where's Hallie?" I ask when I realize she isn't there.

"She had another date with her new friend tonight," Iris says. "I talked to her earlier, and she seemed excited about it."

"Are we worried about her in this situation?" Christy holds a piece of celery that she dips into ranch dressing. "I'm worried about this woman experimenting with a lifestyle and breaking Hallie's heart if she decides it's not for her."

"I know," Iris says with a sigh. "I worry about that, too, but Hallie said she's trying to be realistic and not get too far ahead of herself. She said she's sorry to miss the meeting, but tonight was the only night her friend could get together."

I'm not sure why I feel worried about Hallie, who's perfectly capable of taking care of herself. I don't want any of these precious people to ever hurt again the way they have in the past. While I know that's not a realistic goal, I still hope for it. They deserve the best of everything.

Eighteen

Wynter

We take our seats in the usual circle in Iris's living room, most of us juggling drinks and dessert.

"Who wants to start?" Iris asks.

I raise my hand. "Me."

They all look at me with surprised expressions.

"Don't stare at me."

"It's just that you never share voluntarily," Brielle says.

"First time for everything." I'm amused by how well they know me. "I saw Jaden's mother this week, and she told me something I didn't know, but if you guys don't want to hear about that..."

"Spill it, sister," Naomi says. "Leave nothing out."

"Apparently, my husband froze his sperm before his treatment in case he was left sterile afterward. He didn't tell me because I've always been super queasy about medical stuff, and he didn't want me to feel pressured in any way."

"*Whoa*," Gage says.

"Right? I have no idea what to do with this information."

"You know you don't have to do anything with it if you don't want to, right?" Roni asks.

Nodding, I say, "Yes, for sure. It's just that Eileen asked me if I'd consider having his child, and she seemed so hopeful. That's what I can't stop thinking about."

"You're under no obligation to her, Wynter," Lexi says. "It's a huge thing for her to ask of you."

"She said as much, and I know I'm under no obligation. It's just that ever since I found out it's a possibility, I can't stop thinking about it."

"Do you want to have a baby?" Iris asks.

"I mean... I hadn't been sitting around thinking about that, but I also didn't know I could still have Jaden's baby."

"Are you upset that he didn't tell you?" Derek asks.

"No, I get why he didn't. We were in no way ready for anything like that. But spending time with Xavier has changed how I feel about babies. Now it doesn't seem quite so impossible or overwhelming, even though the medical side of it still terrifies me."

"As delightful as Xavier is," Iris says, "it's a whole other ball game to be a single parent to your own child. For one thing, it's very expensive to raise kids."

"Another thing Eileen did was give me Jaden's life insurance. It's two-hundred-fifty large, which would make it possible for me to be a single mom."

"Wow, Wynter," Roni says. "That's amazing."

"I know! We hadn't been married long enough for him to get around to changing the beneficiary."

"It's really great of them to do that for you," Gage says.

"I've been in a state of disbelief ever since she handed me the check with all those zeros. Knowing I could afford to have a baby has me thinking about it in a way I wouldn't have without the money."

"They didn't make it contingent, did they?" Derek asks.

"No, not at all. She said the money is mine either way."

"Oh, that's good."

"They were awesome to me the whole time he and I were together. They showed me what it's like to be a family, and I have no doubt they'd be there for our child, too. If I have one, that is."

"You should take your time and really think this through," Iris says. "It's a huge commitment, as you certainly know. But until you're in it, you can't possibly know how big the commitment really is."

"I'm sure." I appreciate her honesty. If anyone understands the challenge of single parenthood, it's her. "Enough about me. Thank you for listening."

"We're here for you as you work through this, Wynter," Christy says. "And as a single mom myself, let me add that Iris is right when she says you can't possibly know how challenging it is until you're doing it."

"What's up with you and the guy?" I ask her, ready to move on from my own stuff.

"I still haven't responded to him," Christy says. "He texts me every day to say he's thinking of me and the kids and hoping we're doing okay and wishes he could see me."

"So what's stopping you from replying?" Joy asks.

"I can't get past him needing a break to decide if he can stand to be around my kids every day."

"I get that," Gage says, "but if I may speak from personal experience..." He smiles at Iris. "It's a very big deal to take on someone else's children, especially when they've been through what yours have. Like what we said to Wynter, I'd be concerned if he dove in without careful consideration."

"See, I know that," Christy says. "And I even understand it. But it still bugs me that he said it in the first place."

"Your kids are your life," Derek says. "You're offended on their behalf."

"Yes!" Christy pumps her fist. "That is it exactly. I am offended that anyone would hesitate to love them. As I say that out loud, I can hear how preposterous it is." She laughs as she says that.

"Doesn't mean you don't feel the offense," Derek says.

"I know how difficult they can be," Christy says. "They drive me crazy every day, and I love them more than anything."

"He knew you had kids from the beginning," Gage says, "that you were a package deal. It's not really fair to want to press pause to think about whether he can actually handle it now that there're feelings involved."

"That's the part that bothers me the most," Christy says. "He was fine with me having kids until he spent time around them and got a better idea of what that meant. Then he needed time to think? It's such bullshit to me."

"It is," Adrian says tentatively, "and I get why it's hurtful to you. But I can see his side of it, too." He holds up his hands to stop her from going off on him. "I'm always on your side, and you know that. It's just that there's a difference between 'kids' in the generic form and 'kids' in the real form. He's never had them, so he has no clue how all-consuming parenthood really is. Maybe after seeing that up close, he wasn't sure he could handle it. This could have nothing to do with your kids, specifically, and everything to do with him evaluating whether he has it in him to be a father figure to them."

"I hate that you're right," Christy says. "But you're right. I immediately took it personally when it might not be about them at all."

"There's only one way to find out," Iris says.

"Yeah, I guess so," Christy says.

"You should talk it out with him," Roni says. "Whatever the outcome, it would be better than this limbo you're in now."

"Thanks, guys," Christy says. "As always, this helps."

It helps the rest of us to focus on someone else's crap for a while and take time away from our own worries. The meeting is about to break up when Hallie comes in the front door. I do a double take when I see that her face is red and swollen from crying.

We jump to our feet as a group.

"What's wrong?" Iris asks as Hallie falls into her arms, sobbing.

I notice that she's changed the streak at the front of her blonde bob from pink to purple. I'd rather focus on that than her swollen face and obvious despair.

Several tense minutes pass before she pulls herself together enough to speak. "I was with Robin tonight."

Iris helps her out of her coat and into a chair that Gage brings from the kitchen.

Roni gets her a glass of ice water.

"What happened?" Lexi asks.

My stomach hurts from seeing Hallie so upset. I can't bear to see any of them unhappy. Before disaster struck my own life, I'd never experienced that kind of empathy before, except for Jaden. It hadn't extended beyond him. Now I feel everything.

Adrian puts his arm around me, and I lean into him, thankful for his presence.

"She told me more about herself." Hallie wipes her face with a tissue that Joy hands her. "She has stage-four metastatic breast cancer."

Iris gasps.

Gage puts his arms around her.

After her own bout with early-stage breast cancer, it must be terrifying to hear of a diagnosis like that.

"Shit," Brielle says.

My thoughts exactly.

"Apparently, she's doing fine and has no reason to believe

she won't live for a good long while yet. She left her husband after the cancer came back because she wanted to live the rest of her life authentically. I just... I don't know if I have that in me, you know?"

"Of course we do, sweetie," Kinsley says as she crouches in front of Hallie. "We understand that better than anyone ever could."

"I wasn't sure I had real feelings for her until she told me that, and then suddenly, all this emotion just surged to the surface, and I had to get out of there."

"Did you tell her the rest of the story with Gwen?" Roni asks gently.

"Not yet." A sob shakes her entire body. "Tell me I did the right thing by leaving. I feel awful about it."

"You took care of yourself," Derek says. "No one could fault you for that."

"She was so disappointed, though. I could see it. I hated doing that to her."

"You don't owe her anything at this point," Lexi says. "That may sound harsh, but it's true. Tell me you know that."

"I do, it's just that she was so sweet and sincere telling me how much she's enjoyed getting to know me and how spending time with me has validated her decision to change her life. Then she said there was something she hadn't told me that she felt I needed to know before things went any further. After that, it's all a bit of a blur."

The phone she's gripping in her hand chimes with a text.

She hands the phone to Lexi. "See if it's from her."

Lexi looks at the phone. "It is. Do you want me to read it?"

Hallie nods.

"'I know you're upset,'" Lexi reads, "'and with good reason. It's a lot to throw at anyone, especially a widow. I'll understand if I don't hear from you again, but I'll be sad, too.

As soon as I met you, I had a feeling you were the one I was supposed to find in this new life I'm making for myself.'"

"Damn it," Hallie says as tears spill down her cheeks. "Why does she have to be so sweet?"

"What do you want to do?" Iris asks her.

"I have no freaking clue."

"Stay with us tonight," Iris says. "You shouldn't be alone when you're upset."

"I don't want to put you out."

"You're not. We want you. Please stay."

"If you're sure."

"We are," Gage says as he hands her a glass of her favorite rosé.

"You all are the best. Seriously, the best."

"So are you," Roni says, "and we're going to get you through this."

"I'm counting on that."

I TEXT my mom to tell her I'll be home tomorrow night and follow Adrian to his house. Along the way, my mind is full of thoughts about Hallie and Christy and the many dilemmas and challenges that come with widowhood. It seems like we barely get through one crisis before another erupts.

Being part of a group like ours means you're on the front lines in many other people's turbulent lives while you have enough of your own stuff to contend with. Even with all the drama, though, I wouldn't want to be doing this without them, and I know they feel the same way. But it's a lot on top of a lot, and the hits just keep on coming.

My mom replied to my text while I was driving. *I'm glad you're coming home. We need to talk.*

Oh jeez. What's that about? Any time she wants to "talk,"

it usually means she wants to critique my choices and take apart my life.

She must see that I've read her text. *What time will you be home?*

After work.

I'll see you then.

Awesome. Something to look forward to. Not.

"What's the matter?" Adrian asks as he waits for me in the garage.

"My mom wants to 'talk,' which is never a good thing."

"Do you need to go home?"

"No, I'm meeting her there after work tomorrow."

"You want a drink?"

"Very much so." I'm still so upset about Hallie that she's almost all I can think about. I follow him into the kitchen, where he pours vodka on the rocks for both of us.

"Cheers," he says, smiling as he holds up his glass.

"Cheers."

We drink in silence for several minutes before I share the thought that's most pressing. "Life is so incredibly screwed up sometimes."

"Sure is." He puts his glass on the counter and takes mine to put it next to his. "But other times, it's incredibly sweet."

As he wraps me in his warm embrace, I feel myself start to relax a bit.

"I couldn't wait to be alone with you," he whispers.

"Same."

I'd forgotten how nice it was to have someone to lean on when things go sideways—even if the sideways things belong to someone else. When you care for others, their things are yours. I have no idea how long we stand there in the kitchen, simply holding each other and soaking up the comfort.

At some point, Adrian takes my hand and leads me upstairs to his room.

We undress each other and fall into bed in a tangle of arms, legs and desperate desire. It's amazing to me that it feels like it's been years since we were together when it was only this morning, a quickie before Xavier woke up. Now, even though we have all night, we're still in this urgent rush that has him joining our bodies in one deep thrust that makes me scream.

He stops short. "Did that hurt?"

"God no." I pull him into me, raising my hips to meet him. "Don't stop."

It's wild and earthy and so, so exciting. My heart beats a crazy staccato, and I can barely catch my breath.

"Wynter... *Fuck*..."

The desperation I hear in his voice only feeds mine as we chase the thrill.

I'm not sure what happens, but one minute I'm right there with him, and the next, I'm hurled into the past. I'm in Jaden's hospital room at the end. All hope had been lost. The pain sucks the air from my lungs. I'm a sobbing mess before I realize anything has occurred.

"Wynter, babe, what is it?"

Poor Adrian has no idea what to do with me. I don't know what to do with myself.

He withdraws and stretches out next to me, holding me close as I cry it out.

What am I doing in this bed with this man? I was supposed to spend my life with someone else. We had a plan. Where did he go?

"I'm... I'm sorry."

"Don't apologize."

"I should go."

He puts his arm around me. "No, no. Don't go. Please don't go."

"You don't need this."

"I'm here for all of it, Wynter. Talk to me. Tell me what I can do."

"There's nothing anyone can do. I had a flashback, and it set me off. I'm so sorry that happened when I was with you." I'm mortified that it happened while I was having sex with him. What the actual fuck? "I... I don't know why. Why now. I d-don't know."

"Shhh, it's okay, Wynter. It was bound to happen at some point."

"It was?"

"Sure. It's a big deal for both of us to be taking this first big step forward in the aftermath of disaster with someone we care about so much."

"How do you do that?"

"What?"

"Sum up everything I'm feeling in one perfect sentence?"

He laughs. "Nothing about any of this is perfect except for the way I feel when I'm with you."

"How do you feel?"

"Calm in a way I haven't been since before Sadie died. Everything has been such a huge freaking mess since then, but this, with you... It's not a mess."

"Well, it wasn't until I made it into one."

"You have no control over when the PTSD shows up to remind you who's boss."

"I hate that."

"We all hate that. It's the worst."

"Has it happened to you?"

"A few times. Once when I was at the park with Xavier, there was a mom there with two older kids and a newborn. Seeing the mom with the newborn really triggered me. It was like it hit me all over again that I'll never have a picture of Xavier with his mother, the person most responsible for him being here. I totally lost it."

"Oh, Adrian, I'm so sorry. That must've been awful."

"It was embarrassing more than anything. People were looking at me. One lady came over to see if I was okay. I blubbered out the whole story to her. I was mortified after the fact. She was so nice, but we haven't been back there again."

I put my arms around him and hold him as tightly as I can. "As much as I'd do anything to have had none of this happen to either of us, I'm thankful for you and this and whatever it turns out to be—or not be. For right now, it's... Well, it's what I need."

"Same goes. I wish you'd never lost Jaden and I'd never lost Sadie, but if that had to happen, at least we've made some amazing new friends."

"I think about that every day and how my mom made me go to that first meeting with the Wild Widows, probably because she had no idea what to do with me and my staggering grief. It made her uncomfortable."

"Aw, poor her."

"Right?" I ask with a laugh. "But I don't blame her. She's twenty-three years older than me and has never lost anyone close to her, so she had no clue how to deal with me. I appreciate that she found people who knew what to do with me as much as I didn't want help from anyone then."

"I get it. My sister heard about the group and urged me to go. I finally went to shut her up more than anything."

"Everyone wants to fix the unfixable. Jaden's family drove me crazy at first, wanting to see me every day and make me part of their grieving process when it was all I could do to handle my own. I blew up at them one day and said enough already. I felt bad about that for weeks afterward."

"It was what you needed at the time."

"Yeah, but they didn't deserve to have me lash out at them when they'd been so good to both of us."

"They knew you were hurting."

"I guess. I felt bad about it after and texted to apologize. They were very nice, as always. I think the hardest part for me then was realizing he'd actually died, which wasn't supposed to happen. During his last hospitalization, the doctors kept saying he was doing so much better until that last week, when it was clear he wasn't. It was like we had no time to prepare for it, even though he'd been fighting it for like two years at that point."

"God, that had to be so awful."

"Not as awful as losing your perfectly healthy wife out of nowhere."

"It's all awful, Wynter."

"Yeah," I say on a long exhale as I rest my head on his chest with my hand on his tight abs. "By the way, all that time you spend in the gym?"

"What about it?"

"Keep it up. It's seriously working for me."

His snort of laughter makes me smile, too. "I'll keep that in mind when I don't feel like working out."

"Don't you dare skip a workout."

"Yes, ma'am."

"How would you feel about showing me what to do in a gym? I'm like a big pile of pudding over here next to you."

He cups my ass and gives it a squeeze. "Sexiest pile of pudding I've ever met."

"Whatever."

"I'm not kidding. If this is pudding, sign me up for more."

"You're crazy."

"Maybe so, but you're perfect just the way you are. If you want to work out with me, though, I'd love to have you."

"I'd like to learn."

"I'd be happy to teach you."

"I'm sorry I freaked out before we got to finish what we were doing before."

"Don't worry about it."

"I am worried about it." I push myself up so I'm hovering over him and plant a kiss between his pecs.

His hands slide over my arms, leaving goose bumps that make my nipples tight.

I move down, kissing and licking soft, salty skin and outlining the shape of the washboard abs that fascinate me.

"Wynter…"

"Yes, Adrian?"

"What're you up to?"

"Nothing much."

He grunts out a laugh. "Feels like something to me."

"It might turn out to be something."

As I nudge the head of his cock with my chin, I realize he must've removed the condom at some point.

"As you might've noticed, it's already turning out to be something."

I smile up at him, our gazes colliding as I touch my tongue to the head of his cock before running it down the full length of him.

His hips come off the bed, and his fingers tangle in my hair as he gasps when I take him into the heat of my mouth, lashing him with my tongue as I take as much of him as I can. Even then, it's only half. I wrap my hand around the base and stroke him as I lick and suck him to a quick orgasm.

"*Whoa*," he says on a long exhale.

"Feel better?"

"I feel great. How about you?"

"Feeling better all the time."

Nineteen

Wynter

We're up late and wake to Adrian's alarm at eight. I slept better than I have in a long time. I'm facedown next to Adrian, who has an arm around me.

He kisses my shoulder. "Morning, sleepyhead."

"Morning."

"How do you feel about breakfast in bed?"

"Do you have time for that?"

"I took a few personal hours this morning."

"Did you now?"

"I did. So, breakfast in bed. Your thoughts?"

"Like in concept or in reality?"

"I'm thinking reality."

"I could be down with that."

"Stay put. I'll be back."

"I'll be here."

When he gets out of bed, I turn on my side to watch him move around the room in all his naked, sexy glory. He is a beautiful man, and I feel so lucky to be spending this time with him. Do I worry where it's all going? Not so much. I've learned that we can make all the plans in the world, but life has a way of saying to hell with all that. We're just along for the ride, and this ride with Adrian is making me happy. It seems to be making him happy, too, which matters greatly to me.

And then I remember the date with my mother tonight, and my good mood plummets. What does she want to talk about, and how will it upset me? I don't want to be upset when I'm feeling so good. As if she knows what I'm thinking, she texts me. *Still on for tonight?*

I'll be there.

Even though I don't want to hear whatever it is she has to say. I love her. I really, really do, but her life is so chaotic and always has been, which means mine was, too, when I was growing up. I hated that. Chaos makes me shut down mentally, emotionally, physically. I'm all about order, which is another reason Jaden's illness was so hard on me. No two days were ever the same. I couldn't plan anything or prepare myself for whatever new development might send us spiraling into... you guessed it, chaos.

My mother, on the other hand, thrives on it. The crazier things get, the happier she seems to be. That's why I tend to keep my distance from her. Jaden helped me see a long time ago that I can love her from a distance and not be caught up in all her craziness. He helped me install boundaries in my relationship with her that have helped me tremendously.

She was never the kind of mother who told me what to do or when to do it. Her parenting style was very hands off, which allowed me a tremendous amount of freedom. That wasn't always a good thing. For instance, maybe I shouldn't have been having sex with my boyfriend when I was fifteen.

Not that I am judging my fifteen-year-old self, but we took a lot of risks that thankfully didn't lead to more than we could handle at that age. No one took me to a doctor or taught me about birth control. I eventually figured that out for myself. My mom was oblivious to how quickly things with Jaden got serious.

My trip down memory lane is interrupted by a text from Lexi. *Had another huge fight with my parents. Can we do the move on Saturday rather than Sunday? I'll take whatever help I can get.*

I respond to her right away. *Will be there. Just tell me when and where.*

The others chime in one after the other saying they'll be there, too.

Adrian comes in wearing an apron and carrying a tray. "Breakfast for the lady." He puts the tray on the bed.

"Let me see the back of you."

He does a fancy spin that shows he's wearing *only* the apron.

I lose it laughing. "Please let me take a video of that performance."

"Only if it's just for you."

"Who else would I show it to?" I get the phone ready. "Okay, action."

I'm laughing so hard, I can barely hold the phone still to get the video, which I end with his smiling face. "Service with a smile."

"You know it, baby. Dig in."

He's made eggs and pancakes with sausage and fruit. "Wow, this looks so good."

"Don't be too impressed. The pancakes were frozen."

"They're not now, and I am impressed." He hands me a cup of coffee. "Thank you."

"Welcome."

I pop a strawberry into my mouth. "Did you see Lexi's text?"

"Not yet. What's up?"

I fill him in on her move happening Saturday rather than Sunday.

"I'll respond to let her know I can help. Between the two of us, we can juggle Xavier, I suppose."

"I'll help with him. She'll need you for the heavy stuff. Did you hear from Nia yet?"

"Just a quick text that said he slept well and was having fun with the kids, who have a day off for parent-teacher conferences. She said her noon meeting got moved to two, so I can take my time coming to get him."

"I'm glad the sleepover went well."

"Me, too. As much as I love him, it's nice to get a morning off."

"Yes, it is."

We enjoy breakfast and then shower together before he leaves to pick up Xavier from his sister.

While I wait for them to return, I decide to take a nap since I'm seriously sleep-deprived. It was totally worth it, though, I think as I fall asleep smiling.

Adrian

ALL I CAN THINK about is Wynter as I drive to my sister's house to pick up Xavier. She's so hot, sexy, funny, smart, gorgeous and so, so fragile, even if she'd hate to be described that way. I can't stop thinking about what happened last night and how upset she was afterward. I certainly understand how the trauma can resurface out of nowhere, even when you're thoroughly enjoying a new relationship. Maybe especially then.

We might be moving too fast, a thought that fills me with concern for her. If I've learned anything about Wynter in the time I've known her, it's how good she is about portraying a strong outer shell even when she's hurting on the inside.

I'm still thinking about her when I walk into my sister's house.

Xavier is thrilled to see me, squealing as he comes toward me on legs that aren't quite steady under him. That greeting makes a day that's already been great that much better. I hug him to me and breathe in his sweet baby scent. "Daddy missed you, buddy."

"Daddy!"

"That's me! I'm your daddy!"

He giggles and then squirms to get down to play with his cousins.

The family room is a disaster of toys and kids.

My sister is taking it all in from the sofa, where she's nursing what's probably her third cup of coffee.

"Is there more of that?" I ask her after fist bumping Chantelle and Malik.

"Help yourself."

After I get a coffee, I return to the family room and sit next to her. "Thanks for this. I really enjoyed the break."

"Glad to do it any time. The kids love having him, too, but I forgot how early little ones wake up."

Wincing, I say, "Sorry about that."

"It was fine. I got a couple of hours all to myself with him. That never happens with the kiddos around. The minute they show up, Auntie Nia is left in the dust."

"Aww, he loves you."

"I know he does, but he loves them more."

We laugh at the truth of that. "He loves them more than me."

"He doesn't love anyone more than you."

"Maybe Wynter. He's all about her when she's around."

"Are you all about her, too?"

Yikes, that came out of nowhere. "Um, well, I like her."

"I know. I can tell."

"How can you tell?"

"You look at her the way you looked at Sadie when you were first together."

"I do?" That's truly shocking to me.

"Yeah, you do," she says softly. "That's a good thing, Adrian."

"It feels odd to have someone notice that."

"I'm not just anyone. I know you better than most, and I can tell when you're into someone." She takes a sip of her coffee. "She's young, though, huh?"

"No one who's been through what we have is young anymore in the way you mean."

"I suppose that's true."

"She's very mature for her age, and she understands where I am better than just about anyone ever could, except for our other widows."

"I'll never pretend to understand the magnitude of your loss—or hers. I just want you to be careful." She glances at Xavier, who's playing with a truck as my niece and nephew play next to him. I appreciate how great they are with him. "There's so much at stake."

"I know what's at stake. There's Xavier and the many mutual friends we both rely upon to get through the days. We've promised that no matter what transpires between us, we won't let it get in the way of any of that."

"I'm glad to hear you've talked about the possible pitfalls."

"Widows talk about everything in a way that other people don't. We've learned the hard way that there's no time to waste."

"Have you talked about the pitfalls of a younger white woman dating a Black man?"

"Not specifically."

"You know how some people will react when you take this relationship public."

"I hate that people react that way."

"So do I, but it's reality, and you should prepare her for it."

"I hear you, but knowing Wynter, she'll just tell them to fuck off and mind their own business."

"I can see that," she says with a laugh. "Have I told you lately how proud of you I am?"

"Shut up."

"No, seriously. I'm incredibly proud of the way you've stepped up for Xavier and become a wonderful father under the most difficult of circumstances."

"What choice did I have, Ni?"

"You had no choice, but you've risen to the occasion so brilliantly, and I'm proud of my baby brother. You have to let me be."

"If you say so." I'm unreasonably touched by her kind words.

"I say so."

"I suppose I should confess to you that I brought women home when Wynter and Xavier were sleeping upstairs, and she heard us."

"Adrian! What? *Why would you do that?*"

"Desperate times and all that," I reply, feeling mortified to be sharing this with her. But I share just about everything with her, and I always have.

"I ought to kick your ass for disrespecting her that way, but I won't, because life has kicked your ass enough. What did Wynter say when she caught you?"

"She didn't tell me that right away, but when she did, she said it was hot."

Nia laughs. "Have I mentioned that I like Wynter a lot? I don't want you to think I was saying otherwise when I said she's young or that an interracial relationship is going to be challenging at times."

"I like her a lot, too. This thing with us is new. We're enjoying it and trying not to get too far ahead of ourselves."

"I'm happy for you."

"I'm happy for me, too."

Xavier toddles over to bring me the truck he's playing with. "Truck."

"That's right! So many words lately."

"Words."

He returns to his cousins on unsteady legs that make him look like a drunken sailor as he makes his way across the room, tripping twice and nearly falling.

"I wish Sadie could see him," I tell Nia.

"She's right here with us. I know she is."

I hope she wasn't watching me with Wynter last night. "Do you think she'd be okay with me being with someone else?"

"Oh hell no. She'd claw her eyes out."

I wince. "You think so?"

"I know so. You know she hated the way other women looked at you. It drove her crazy."

That's true. "But do you think she'd be okay with me being with someone else when I can't be with her?"

"Yeah, I suppose she would. She'd want you to be happy, but she'd still be pissed."

We share a laugh, even if I feel sad once again that she isn't here. Good old grief. It's always there to remind you that nothing is like you thought it would be.

I get a text from Mick. *Things are slow today. Take the full day. I'll see you tomorrow.*

Wow, thanks, man.

You got it.

I text Wynter to tell her we've got an unexpected full day off. *I'll still pay you for today, of course.*

No, you won't. I don't need it. I'll head home now to see what's up with my mom and see you back here after a while?

Sounds good. Hope it goes okay with your mom.

Me too!

I'm thinking about Sadie and how pissed she'd be to see me with someone else as I leave Nia's and take Xavier to the park to make him feel better about leaving his cousins. We stop for chicken nuggets and fries on the way home for a nap. I cut the chicken and fries into tiny bites that he devours. I try not to feed him junk food—mostly because I'm afraid Sadie will come back to haunt me if I do—but an occasional treat never hurt anyone.

Besides, what's a childhood without chicken nuggets and fries?

I do laundry and catch up on paying bills and other stuff around the house while Xavier naps. By five o'clock, I'm ready to see Wynter again.

It's odd that I haven't heard a word from her all afternoon.

I hope everything is okay.

Wynter

MY MOTHER IS WAITING for me when I get home, which is concerning. She's usually at work this time of day. I texted her to say I was coming sooner than planned, and she said she was home. Another thing to know about my mother is that she's gorgeous. Like movie-star gorgeous, which has been more of a problem for her than a blessing, if you ask me. She has reddish-brown hair, brown eyes and a face that stops traffic. Men fall all over themselves when she's around, which has only added to the chaos.

"Drink?"

"Sure, I'll have an ice water."

She hands me the glass and takes a seat next to me on the sofa.

"Thank you."

"No problem."

"What's wrong?" I ask her because I can't stand the tension of wondering.

"Nothing is wrong. I have some news to share with you."

"What kind of news?"

"Well, it seems I might be getting married."

If she had told me she'd decided to go live on the moon, I wouldn't have been more surprised. My mother disdains marriage. She makes fun of it. She told me not to marry Jaden even when we knew he was dying. "You sacrifice your independence when you tie yourself to a man," she said then.

I remember being infuriated at her for lecturing me when it was clear the man I was going to marry had days to live.

"You're getting married." I honestly have to try not to laugh at the sheer absurdity of it.

"Don't give me that look."

"What look should I give you when I've heard you shit on marriage my entire life? Including when I was about to marry Jaden when we knew he was dying."

"I'm sorry about that. I never should've said that. I've felt bad about it ever since."

This is truly shocking. My mother never apologizes for anything.

"What? I'm sorry. I really am."

"Well, thank you. I guess."

"I want you to know that watching you and Jaden go through what you did broke my heart. I had no idea how to help you through it, and that made me feel awful. Losing him and seeing you so sad was the worst thing I've ever experienced."

"You helped a lot by finding the Wild Widows for me."

"I'm so glad, even if I'm jealous of your tight bonds with them."

"You are?"

"Of course I am. I wish I had the wisdom you need right now and that you'd turned to me when you were sad. I get why you didn't, but I still wish you had."

"Mama... You know I love you so much. I always will."

"I do, even if I also know I don't deserve that."

"Yes, you do. Stop being hard on yourself. It's pissing me off."

We share a smile that reminds me again of how damned pretty she is. She's forty-four but looks thirty.

"Who's this guy you say you're going to marry?"

"His name is Lou, and for some reason, he truly loves me."

"Show me a picture."

She gets her phone and calls up some shots of the two of them together. The first thing I notice is that he's a bit older than her and that she's smiling in every picture.

"He's nice-looking."

"He is, but he's nice on the inside as well, which I've learned is what truly matters."

"You know I want you to be happy, no matter what, but having heard your thoughts on marriage many times, I guess I'm surprised."

"You and me both, baby."

"How long have you known him?"

"Almost a year."

That year coincided with my widowhood, which is why I probably didn't notice she had something new going on.

"That's a record for you."

"I know! I keep telling him I'm a bad bet, but he doesn't

want to hear that. He makes me feel like a queen. He's the nicest man, and he can't wait to meet you."

"So wow, you're really getting married."

"He asked me a week ago. It was so romantic. Remember when I told you I was going to Middleburg for the night?"

"Vaguely."

"He planned a whole day of winery tours. We had the best time. At dinner that night, he proposed, and I couldn't think of a single reason to say no." She extends her left hand to show me a stunning diamond ring.

"That's beautiful."

"Isn't it? I couldn't believe it. No one has ever treated me the way he does."

"Have you googled him?"

"What? No, why would I do that?"

"Mom, come on. You watch enough *Dateline* to know why you should google him."

"I just feel like at some point you have to trust people. He's given me no reason not to trust him."

"Then it shouldn't be an issue to make sure his story checks out before this goes any further."

"You really think I should?"

"I really do."

"Fine. You do it."

She gives me his full name, which I punch into my phone along with his date of birth that she provides.

The first result that pops up is his title as the chairman and CEO of an aerospace company. "Is that him?"

"Yes."

"So he's loaded, huh?"

"I guess. I don't really know."

"Look at what he does, Mom." We scroll through the information about the company he founded in the late '90s that holds contracts with all the US services as well as other militaries around the world, providing high-tech deliverables to forces on the front lines. "Sounds impressive."

I scroll further, looking for more on his personal life, which shows he was married for two years in the early 2000s and has no children.

"Seems legit and loaded."

"That's not why I'm with him. I knew he was successful, but I fell for his kindness and the way he treats me. I've never experienced anything like it."

"I'm happy for you, even if I'm still shocked."

"I am, too. Believe me. I never expected anything like this when I met him online. We talked for weeks before we saw each other in person, and it just kind of took off from there." With her head resting against the sofa, she turns toward me. "I'd love for you to meet him."

"Sure. I can do that."

"The other thing I wanted to tell you is that he's asked me to move in with him in Arlington while we plan the wedding. I'm thinking about that, but I wanted to talk to you first."

"How come?"

Her small smile has a tinge of sadness to it. "You and I have been a team for a long time. Even when you were with Jaden, we were still a team. I don't want to leave you if you're not ready to be left."

"I'm fine, Mom. You should go live your life and not worry about me."

"I'll always worry about you."

"You don't need to. I'm doing much better."

"I'm glad to hear it. Does your Adrian have anything to do with that?"

"Maybe. A little. But it's more than that. I'm starting to emerge from the fog to find that life is still worth living, even if it's harder now that I don't have Jaden."

"I've been so proud of you over this last year. Jaden would be, too."

"I hope so." I take her hand. "Go move in with your fiancé and have a happy life. You deserve it."

"You really think so?"

"I do. I'll take over the rent on this place for now, until I figure out what I'm doing."

"Can you swing that?"

"As a matter of fact, I can." I tell her about the life insurance. "I can pretty much do whatever I want."

"That's amazing, honey. It was so good of the Hartleys to give it to you. It was the right thing."

"That's what they said. Eileen told me something else when I saw her."

"What's that?"

"Jaden froze sperm before his treatment in case we wanted kids later on."

"Oh wow. And you didn't know that?"

"Nope. He didn't want to put pressure on me when we were still so young."

"Why did Eileen tell you?"

"In case I might want to have Jaden's child."

Her eyes go wide. "Do you?"

I shrug. "Maybe."

"Wynter... Wow. And here I thought I was sitting on some big news."

"Your news is very big."

"This is bigger."

"Don't get too excited about it. I'm still deathly afraid of all things medical, and the childbirth thing really freaks me out, especially since that's how Adrian lost his wife."

"You shouldn't let fear stand in the way. Childbirth is no fun, but it's one day of your life, and then you have a beautiful kid who'll always remind you of your Jaden."

"I keep trying to imagine what he or she would look like. Jaden was so blond, and I'm not, so which one of us would the baby look like?"

"It's amazing how babies can resemble both their parents."

"Do you think I should do it?"

"Only if you really, really want to. It's a huge responsibility, as you know after taking care of Xavier."

"Yeah, I do know, but I think I might be interested in hearing more about what it would entail."

"Then that's what you ought to do."

Twenty

Adrian

Wynter comes in around six thirty, bringing a blast of early spring chill with her. Her cheeks are rosy, and her eyes are bright.

"Wyn!"

"Hey, buddy!" She leans in to kiss Xavier and then looks up at me. "You won't believe it."

"What won't I believe?"

She plops down on the sofa next to us. "My mother, who thinks marriage is for fools, is getting *married* to a guy who owns his own aerospace company. Can you believe it?"

"Wow."

"I know! I couldn't believe it. She told me I was crazy to marry Jaden when we knew he was dying. Something about tying yourself to someone who can control you or some such thing. That made me so mad. Clearly, this wasn't going to be your traditional marriage, you know? Anyway, she apologized for saying that, which I appreciated. We had the best chat, and then we did takeout for dinner. She's moving out of the apartment, and I'm going to take over the lease until I figure out what's next."

"That's a lot all at once."

"It was, but it was like the best conversation we've ever had. I'm really happy for her. Lou seems like a nice guy."

"Lou Harris?"

"Yeah, do you know him?"

"I worked for his company before Sadie died."

"That's crazy! No way. I bet we could get your job back if you wanted it."

"Look at you, already settling in to having a step sugar daddy."

"Ew, don't make it gross, but I'm sure my mom would ask him if you wanted her to."

"That's okay. I'm set for now. I can handle this job with a one-year-old."

"Well, the offer is on the table if you change your mind."

"Good to know."

"So, wow, my mom is getting married."

"Life keeps marching forward."

"It really does."

I reach for her hand. "You know, you could move in with us if you don't want to live alone." After a beat, I start to laugh. "Are you speechless? I never thought I'd see that."

"You surprised me."

"You're here most of the time anyway. This would just make it official."

"I don't know what to say."

"You don't have to say anything now. Think about it." I lean Xavier toward her. "Say night-night to Wyn."

"Wyn."

She kisses his cheek. "Night-night, Xavier."

"Wyn!"

"I'll see you in the morning."

"Be back in a few," I say as I carry Xavier upstairs.

I can't believe I came right out and asked her that, but I don't regret it. Being with her feels good, which means I want to be with her as much as I can. If we lived together, that would make everything easier. To an outsider looking in at us, it might seem as if we're moving way too fast. To me, however, it's been a slow roll. We've known each other for almost a year and have grown a friendship we both enjoyed long before she became my nanny or anything happened between us.

That friendship, forged in grief during the most difficult time in our lives, has put a strong foundation under the romantic relationship that's recently developed.

Since I've already bathed Xavier and read three books to him, I kiss him good night and put him down in his crib. "Love you, buddy."

"Dadadadada."

Smiling, I blow him a kiss as I walk out of the room.

He's so cute and sweet. I love watching him grow and learn, even as the heartache of missing his mother never really goes away. For every new thing he does and says, I can only imagine what she would think of it. I hope wherever she is now that she can see him and knows how wonderful he is.

It's amazing and sad to me that I can be so excited about this new relationship with Wynter while I continue to mourn Sadie. The two of them exist side by side in my heart, which is such an odd thing. I still feel married to Sadie, even though I know I'm not anymore. It makes what's happening with Wynter feel wrong when I think of it that way.

There's nothing wrong about being with Wynter.

I don't care what anyone says—even my own conscience. Being with Wynter makes me happy, and I'm so ready to be happy again.

Wynter

I can't believe he came right out and asked me to move in with them—or how much I want to. I feel like I've lost what's left of my mind by wanting to fully jump into this thing with Adrian as if there's nothing at stake.

"Slow your roll, girl. Just take a breath and calm your ass down."

"Are you talking to yourself again?" Adrian asks as he comes downstairs wearing only basketball shorts.

I'm so busy staring at his amazing pecs and abs that I forget to reply.

"Wynter?"

"Huh?"

"I asked if you were talking to yourself again."

"Oh, yeah. I guess I was." With him standing right in front of me, I can no longer remember why I thought it was important to slow my roll one minute ago.

He sits next to me and takes my hand. "Are you okay?"

"Yes, I'm good."

"Did I freak you out asking you to move in with us?"

"No. Of course not."

He gives me a skeptical look. "Not even a little?"

"Okay, maybe a little, but I'm fine. It's nice of you to ask."

"I want you to know that I asked you now because you said your mom is moving out, but I would've asked you soon anyway. You're here all the time, and we love having you with us. The three of us have become a little family in the last few months, and that feels good to me."

My heart can't take the overload of emotion that his words cause. "It feels good to me, too." I take a second to think carefully about what I want to say. "I appreciate you asking me to move in, but I think I need a little more time on my own to make a few decisions before I take such a big step."

"How much time?"

"I don't know, but I need to live alone for a time and figure out my own life before we take this to the next step. It's been a lot this week, finding out about the insurance money, Jaden's banked sperm and my mom's engagement. I need a minute to process it all and figure out what's next."

"I want to be what's next for you."

"I want that, too, but I need to make sure I'm ready for it. Does that make sense?"

"Of course. I get it, and I don't mean to pressure you or ask for more than you're ready to give. I just like feeling good again with you."

I lean my head on his shoulder. "I feel good with you, too, and I definitely want more of that."

"Will you keep me posted on what you're thinking and planning?"

"I will." I raise my head off his shoulder and lean in to kiss him. "I don't want you to worry. We're on the same page. I just need a little time to think about a few things."

"Are you thinking about having a baby?"

"Possibly, which is something you need to think about, too. If we make a go of this, we'd be raising each other's kids."

"Yes, I suppose we would." After a pause, he says, "It sounds like you've decided to pursue that."

"I've got an appointment with my doctor to discuss it. I want to hear more about what's involved before I go any further."

"Makes sense."

Is it my imagination, or is he not happy to hear that I'm looking into it? "What's wrong, Adrian?"

"Nothing."

"Don't start lying to me now. I know you too well. I can see that you're unhappy."

"I'm not unhappy. I'm worried."

"About me?"

Nodding, he says, "It's the childbirth thing..." He shudders. "Scares me."

"I know, and I'm so sorry. I don't want you to be worried about me."

"Too late. I already am."

"I should skip the whole thing. I'm a total baby when it comes to medical stuff anyway. I'm already freaked out, and I haven't even looked into what I'd have to do."

"Don't skip it on my account. You need to follow your own path wherever it might lead you. I shouldn't factor into your decision."

"You do factor in. I mean... You could end up being the man who helps me raise this child. Your opinion matters tremendously."

"I'm scared of losing you."

"You won't. What happened to Sadie is so rare."

"Other things can happen."

I've never seen him so tense. "I'm young and healthy, and nothing has been decided yet. I'm merely considering it."

"I know."

His fear is palpable, and it has me rethinking whether I should even pursue this if it's going to upset him this way. I wasn't even thinking about having kids until I started taking care of Xavier and then learned Jaden froze his sperm.

"Can I ask you something?"

"Sure," he says. "Whatever you want."

"Before you and I were you and I, when you thought about someday remarrying, did you want more kids?"

He shakes his head. "No more kids. I couldn't bear to go through that again."

I'm shocked to hear him say that so forcefully, but I shouldn't be surprised. He went through hell losing Sadie after she gave birth to Xavier. It's only natural he'd avoid what caused that going forward.

But what does that mean for me and for us?

"I hear what you're saying, and I respect why you're saying it. When Eileen first told me that having Jaden's child was an option, I expected to think 'no way.' But that's not what I thought. It was more like 'what if?' I want you and Xavier, Adrian. I want this. I want it so much that it scares me, because I honestly thought I'd never want something like this again after I lost Jaden."

"I want it, too. Just as much."

"That said... I can't stop thinking about what it would be like to have Jaden's baby. To see him live on in our child the way you can see Sadie in Xavier. Can you understand that?"

"I do."

"But you don't want to be part of it?"

"I don't know if I can. I just don't know, Wynter. The very idea of it terrifies me."

His words land like a punch. I completely understand why he's saying what he is, but where does that leave me?

My heart is in my throat. "I think, maybe... We should press pause on this for now."

"Don't say that."

"It's the smart thing to do, Adrian. We might be heading in very different directions."

"We're not."

I turn to face him, to share the painful truth with him, even as my heart is breaking. "I love you and Xavier so, so much. You know I do. I'd love nothing more than to take what you're offering me and build a whole new life with you two."

"Then let's do it."

"But..." I force myself to say it. "I think I also want to try to have Jaden's child. Everything has changed now that I know it's possible—and I have the money to afford single parenthood. The genie is out of the bottle, and it can't be put back in, even though I understand and respect your feelings on it."

"I don't want to lose you, Wynter. These last few weeks have been the best I've had since my life imploded."

"Me, too, and I don't want to lose you either. But I have to do what's best for me—and what's best for me might be the worst possible thing for you."

"Even if we aren't together as a couple, I'll still suffer over you being pregnant, because I love you, too. You know I do."

"I don't want you to suffer."

"Can't help it. So if I'm going to suffer either way, maybe I could suffer with you by my side rather than living a separate life from me."

"Our lives will never be separate. I'm Xavier's nanny and your friend, no matter what."

"I want to be with you."

"We need to take some time to think this through before we make any big decisions." I have no idea where the courage to walk away is coming from. I only know that I need to do it, or I might take a pass on something I want so I can be with him. I honestly believe I'd regret not at least trying to have Jaden's baby.

I lean into his hug. "I'm going home. I'll be back in the morning."

"I don't want you to go."

"That means a lot to me. And it means a lot that you were honest about how you feel. You could've said what I wanted to hear rather than sharing the truth."

"I wouldn't have been able to hide the fear from you."

"If you and I are meant to be, we'll make it work somehow. But if we aren't, I just want you to know that I've enjoyed every second we've spent together as friends and as lovers."

"Same," he says gruffly.

I kiss his cheek and get myself out of there before I can decide that his needs are more important than mine. If there's anything I've learned from being a widow, it's that I have to put myself first as I figure out the rest of my life. That's not always easy to do, especially when you love someone like I love Adrian—and Xavier. But I know it's the right thing.

For now, anyway.

Adrian

I'M GUTTED after she leaves. The feeling reminds me all too much of the dismal days after Sadie and Alyssa died. I'm so freaking sick and tired of feeling horrible. I grab the baby monitor and head for the basement to work out my frustrations in the gym. An hour later, with my muscles trembling with fatigue, I stand under a hot shower, realizing that no amount of weightlifting or anything else will fix this latest ache.

We want different things.

I want to go back to before she knew having Jaden's baby was a possibility, before she knew his life insurance would make single parenthood—or anything else she might want to do—possible. Everything was great before that. We had each other. We had Xavier. It was enough, or so I thought.

She probably would've wanted kids with me. We hadn't gotten around to discussing that, which might be proof that we rushed into this thing without thinking it all the way through.

The hell with that. We didn't rush into anything. I know her. She knows me. Being with Wynter made me grateful to have survived losing Sadie and Alyssa, when there was a time, not that long ago, when I couldn't imagine being grateful to have survived such massive losses. I'm thankful every day for Xavier, but even he couldn't fill the gaping hole inside me the way Wynter did.

It's all so incredibly screwed up.

My sister calls, and I debate whether I feel like talking to her. If I don't answer, though, she'll worry.

"Hey," I say.

"Am I interrupting anything?" she asks with a laugh.

"Not at all."

"What's wrong?"

I'm not surprised she can tell with three little words that everything is wrong. She's always seen right through me. "Wynter and I are taking a pause."

"Why? Didn't you just tell me you guys are having a great time together?"

"We were."

"So what happened?"

"She found out her late husband froze sperm before he started cancer treatment, and now she's looking into having his baby."

"*Oh…*"

"Just the thought of her being pregnant, of giving birth… It triggers the fuck out of me." I feel cold all over and filled with dread.

"I'm sure it does and with good reason. You probably did the right thing if you're not up for that."

"Then why do I feel like absolute shit?"

"Because you love her."

"I really do. If you'd asked me a year ago if loving someone who isn't Sadie was even possible, I would've laughed. And now…"

"Now you love Wynter and so does Xavier, but you're terrified of losing her, too."

"Yeah."

"There're a million ways you could lose her that have nothing to do with childbirth. You know that, don't you?"

"That doesn't make me feel better, Ni."

"It's true, though. Anything can happen. Every time she drives off in a car or crosses a street or has a weird health issue or fill in the blank."

"How does anyone survive loving someone else?"

"It's not easy, but the good times are so worth the worry, right?"

"I guess."

"They are, Adrian. You know they are."

The good times with Wynter were worth everything to me. It's inconceivable that we could be over just like that.

"It's going to come down to which is worse—seeing Wynter through a pregnancy and childbirth or living the rest of your life without her."

Her words *living the rest of your life without her* scare me more than the childbirth stuff, and that's saying something. But still... "I just don't know if I can do it."

"Then you should take this time apart to really think about it, but you should know that you'll worry about her whether you're together or not."

"I said as much to her. Anyway, I'm sure you didn't call to hear all my drama. What's going on?"

"I was going to invite you, Wynter and Xavier to dinner tomorrow night."

"Is it okay if it's just me and Xavier?"

"Sure."

"Thanks. That'll be fun. What can I bring?"

"Nothing but your little guy."

"Thanks, Ni."

"Any time, little brother. Hang in there. It was nice to see you happy again."

"It was nice to be happy, for a little while, anyway."

"Don't give up on her. I have a good feeling about you two."

"I'm glad you do. See you tomorrow."

"See you then."

I end the call feeling slightly better thanks to Nia's unwavering support. Hearing she has a good feeling about me and Wynter helps, even if I'm not as optimistic.

Twenty-One

Lexi

I'm so thankful to my Wild Widows for helping me move out of my parents' home. They made what could've been an upsetting day into something fun. Adrian, Gage and Derek were amazing—and funny—as they lugged a sofa, love seat, entertainment center and bed up the stairs from my parents' basement into the truck Gage borrowed from his dad.

My friend Tom has made a bedroom and sitting area available to me for rent I can easily afford, which I still can't believe. I really hope it's not one of those cases of something being too good to be true. I also hope he's not hoping I'll be so thankful that I'll have sex with him in exchange for a nice place to live.

According to mutual friends, he's not like that. I sure as hell hope not.

I'm so not interested in that.

That's not to say that Tom isn't attractive, because he is. He's tall, muscular and still broad-shouldered like he was when he was the captain of the high school football team. I wonder how it's possible that a guy like him isn't married with a bunch of kids by now. But according to sources, he hasn't been in another serious relationship since ending an engagement years ago.

So, it's not him. It's me. I'm not ready. I was with Jim for ten years total, and he was battling ALS for the last four. I gave up my job to care for him and have been digging out of the financial hole his illness put us in since he died two years ago. Thankfully, my parents let us live in their basement during the worst of his illness, and I'll be eternally grateful to them not just for that, but for being dedicated caregivers, too.

I wouldn't have managed it all without them—before or after his death—so it breaks my heart to see their tearful faces as we carry the last of my things out of the basement. As I go over to hug them both, the fights of the last few months are forgotten. They've been my ballast through the worst time in my life.

"Thank you for everything," I whisper to my mom. "Please don't be sad. This is a good thing. I'm taking a step forward."

"We'll miss you around here," my dad says.

Jim's illness took a toll on us all. They wear their grief for the son-in-law they adored on faces that aged under the strain of watching his torturous decline.

"I'll be back so often, we won't have time to miss each other."

This is one of those times when being an only child is difficult. If only I had siblings to pick up the slack with them while I try to figure out my life. But nope, it's just me, which makes this move that much harder. I've been living back at home for six years, since shortly after Jim was diagnosed and we realized we were going to need more help than I could provide on my own. They got used to having me around, even as they picked at me recently to figure out my next steps.

The minute I decided to move out, they objected to it. *Who is this man?* they asked. *What do you know about him? How can you be sure he's trustworthy?*

I get in my car and wave to them as I lead the way to my new home.

Gage pulls out behind me in the truck, with Iris riding shotgun.

Five other cars follow them.

I wouldn't wish widowhood on anyone, but there have been blessings. Chief among them is the group of friends who are helping me move on a Saturday, when they all have better things to do.

My new place is six miles from my parents' house and is off a dirt road that leads to a big, beautiful contemporary. The first time I saw it, I couldn't believe I was being offered the chance to live there. Tom built it himself. He told me it took him four years of nights and weekends while building houses for other people to finish his own.

I was blown away by the house. Every detail is spectacular, from flooring to backsplash to lighting. I described it to a friend at work as an HGTV wet dream.

She thought that was funny.

I can't wait to live here.

As our caravan pulls into the driveway, I'm filled with excitement, which I haven't felt in so long, I've nearly forgotten what it's like.

I get out of my car and meet the others next to the truck.

"Holy. Shit." Wynter's eyes are wide as she looks at the house. "This place is gorgeous."

"I know, right?"

Tom comes out through the garage to greet us. "Hey," he says, giving me a quick hug. "Welcome home."

The hug throws me off my game for a second because it was so natural and unforced. And it reminded me of years of having the most ferocious crush on him in high school. "Thank you. Let me introduce you to my friends."

Tom pitches in with the other guys, and they have my stuff set up in no time.

My space is over the garage and includes a full bathroom. I want to pinch myself to believe that I really get to live here, that I'll have the time and the space to figure out my life without the added financial strain of paying a huge rent. Tom will never know what he's done for me by making this place available.

"This is awesome," Iris says as she helps me fold towels and put them in the linen closet. "I like how your part is separate from the rest."

"I do, too."

"He seems really nice and happy to have you here."

I give her a wary look. "Not too happy, right?"

Iris laughs as Christy comes in to check out the bathroom.

"I love this for you," Christy says. "It's perfect, and hello, you didn't tell us your new roommate is hot AF."

"Is he? I hadn't noticed."

"Right..." Christy laughs.

"You guys... That's not why I moved here. I hope you know... I'm just... I'm not ready for that yet."

"We know that, sweetie," Christy says. "I'm just teasing you. Sorry if I was out of line."

"You weren't, and of course I've noticed how handsome he is." I'm appalled when my eyes fill with tears that have no place in a great day like this one. "I see you guys getting on with it, and I want to be like you. I'm just not there yet. Sometimes I wonder if I ever will be."

"You will," Christy says.

"When the time is right, you'll know," Iris says. "I was years out from losing Mike when things happened with Gage.

And he was years out from losing Nat and the girls. It didn't happen overnight for us."

"That's true. Some days, I feel so stuck. I hate that Jim died. I hate my job. I'll never dig my way out of debt. I couldn't stand living with my parents."

"Well, you've solved one of those problems today," Iris says.

"I predict you're going to be very happy here," Christy adds.

"I sure hope so."

Wynter

ON A SATURDAY MORNING in early April, I take the check that's been sitting on my bedside table to the nearby branch of the bank I've used since I was a teenage bus girl at a local restaurant. I have mixed feelings about depositing the check. On the one hand, the money will come in handy as I take steps toward possibly having a baby. On the other hand, depositing that money is just further confirmation that Jaden is really gone.

As if I needed further confirmation. It's just another step on this surreal journey of widowhood—cashing in on my husband's premature death.

However, I'm afraid I'm going to lose the check if I don't do something with it, so off I go.

I haven't been inside the branch office since I set up the account as a teenager. With everything online these days, I haven't had any reason to come in.

I'm not sure what to expect, showing up with a massive check that I want to deposit, but I guess I'll find out.

Four people are in line ahead of me, all of them older.

They probably haven't figured out online banking. The thought amuses me while I wait my turn.

A young female teller with dark hair and a welcoming smile waves me over to her window. "What can I do for you today?"

"I'd like to deposit this." I put the check on the counter and push it toward her.

She takes the check and gives it a close look, her eyes widening at the number. Then her gaze darts toward me, probably judging my half-shaved head and the piercings that line the ear on that side as well as the one in my nose. I recently removed the lip ring when I realized that kissing Adrian was easier without it.

"May I ask the source of the money?"

"Do I have to tell you that to deposit it?"

"I'm afraid so. We're required to ask on amounts over ten thousand dollars."

"It's a life insurance payout for my dead husband."

My reply shocks her. "I'm so sorry."

"Thank you."

"The check isn't from an insurance company."

I bite back the nasty retort that's dying to get out that would tell her it's none of her business. But apparently it is. "The payout went to his parents. They decided to give it to me."

"Oh, I see. That's very nice of them."

"Yes, it is."

"Were you married long?"

"Four days. But we were together for six years."

"I'm so sorry that's what brought you in today."

"Thank you. Can you deposit the check for me?"

"Yes, I can. There'll be a ten-day hold on the funds."

"What does that mean?"

"You won't be able to access the money for ten days."

"Why?"

"Because that's how long it takes for the check to clear."

I'm not sure what that means, but whatever. "Okay."

"I also need my supervisor's approval before I do the deposit. I'll be right back."

She returns with an older woman, who gives me a long once-over that raises my hackles. "I understand this is a life insurance payment?"

"Yes," I say through gritted teeth.

"I'm sorry for your loss."

"Thank you."

"Could we see some ID?"

I hand over my license, which they examine closely.

The older woman signs something and hands it back to the younger woman.

"Have a nice day," the older woman says as she walks away.

The teller types something into the computer and puts the check into a machine that spits out a receipt that she pushes across the counter to me.

"Good luck to you."

"Thank you."

I take the receipt and head for the door with my heart aching over how I just became financially secure because of Jaden's death.

I feel sick.

THE NEXT FEW weeks are brutal as Adrian and I pretend we don't want each other fiercely while we navigate Xavier's care like two cautious strangers.

It's funny because after Jaden died, I barely gave sex a thought for close to a year. But after being with Adrian, I think about it all the time.

I miss him, even though I see him regularly.

I sit across from him at Wild Widows meetings and think about how it felt to take him inside me, to hold him close, to kiss him and love him and touch him. The memories of him and us make me feel feverish with desire.

Iris asked me what's going on between us, but it was too painful to get into, even with her.

I have my first appointment today with the specialist to discuss my options for having a baby. I read that because of my age, I have a much higher chance of a positive result than older women would, and I discovered that frozen sperm is just as effective as live, which was interesting to me.

My doctor said I'd probably be a candidate for Intrauterine Insemination (IUI) because I haven't had fertility problems. As far as I know, there's no reason I couldn't conceive and carry a baby to term. I really hope I can do IUI, in which they inject the sperm directly into my uterus. That's much simpler than having eggs harvested and fertilized in a lab like they do with IVF. Both ways are supposedly painless, but I'm still anxious about it.

Dr. Nancy Bauer is right on time, which I appreciate. She's younger than I expected her to be and very pretty. Her friendly demeanor puts me right at ease.

"I understand you're interested in IUI," she says, scanning my chart.

"That's right."

"Have you tried to conceive naturally?"

"No."

Her brows furrow with confusion.

"I should explain that my husband passed away more than a year ago, but he froze his sperm before he began cancer treatment."

"Oh, I see. I'm so sorry for your loss."

"Thank you."

"I'd like to do a full exam to make sure you're a good candidate before we go any further."

That's the last thing I want to do. "I should tell you that all things medical freak me out, especially after seeing my husband go through cancer treatment."

"I'll make it as easy on you as I possibly can."

I suppose I couldn't ask for much more than that.

Thirty minutes later, I've been thoroughly poked and prodded. I've endured a vaginal ultrasound as well as blood work.

The nurse who takes my blood tells me to get dressed and meet Dr. Bauer in her office across the hall.

She's on her computer when I step through the door.

"Come in, Wynter, and have a seat."

I try to prepare myself for bad news, because anything is possible.

She clicks around on the screen. "I see you've listed the lab where your husband's sperm was stored. We can reach out to them to retrieve it with your permission."

"So does that mean I'm a good candidate?"

"You're in perfect health. Everything checked out. I think you'd be an excellent candidate for IUI. If that doesn't work, we can try IVF. You should know there can be some costs above and beyond what insurance may cover."

"My husband left me some money."

"That's wonderful. Shall we make an appointment for the procedure?"

Here it is. Put-up-or-shut-up time. The medical stuff still scares me, but when I imagine one day holding a baby who looks a little like Jaden, I can't see anything but pure joy.

"Yes, please."

After careful examination of my cycle and ovulation dates, the procedure is scheduled for ten days from now, when I should have the best chance of conceiving.

"I don't want you to get too excited yet," she says. "We don't always get lucky the first time out. This can be a marathon, not a sprint. Okay?"

"Okay." I give her the response she wants, but I'm already excited. How could I not be?

And I'm scared, but in a good way.

I can't think about Adrian and what he'd have to say about this, or I might not go through with it. I'm positive I'd have regrets later if I didn't at least try to make this happen. So that's what I'm doing, even if my heart is broken over what might've been with him.

I totally understand his reluctance. Before I met him and heard about what happened to Sadie, I had no idea such things were even possible. I liked it better when I didn't know. As terrifying as it is to consider complications, I'm pressing forward anyway.

After I saw her, Eileen emailed me all the info I needed to use the gift that Jaden left me. She said, *Whatever you decide, we support you.*

I thanked her for the details and decided to keep my plans private until something comes of it. *If* something comes of it.

I haven't told anyone about today's appointment, and I won't say anything about the procedure in ten days. There's no sense involving others until I have something to tell them. Would I like to have someone with me for support? Sure, but I'm not going to ask anyone. I need to get used to doing things on my own if I'm going to be a single parent. There's no time like the present to start that.

The next ten days go by so slowly, it's like time is moving in reverse.

Every time I see Adrian, it's like a knife in my heart. He's the same old friendly, sweet guy he's always been, but the distance between us is painful. We keep our focus on Xavier, which helps us get through the brief time we're together every day.

I'm still up watching TV when he comes in from the bar early Sunday morning.

"Hey, you're up late," he says.

"Couldn't sleep." I have three more days until "the day." I told Adrian I needed to take a half day on Tuesday, and he said he can work from home for the afternoon. He didn't ask me why, and I didn't tell him. We speak only about Xavier while we pretend like we haven't known each other as intimately as two people can.

If I didn't love Xavier so much, I'd give Adrian my notice, because being around him is torturous in this bizarre limbo state we're in these days.

Thankfully, our friends haven't tuned in to the weird tension between us, or if they have, they're waiting for us to say something about it. I'm not going to, and I doubt he will either.

My mom is moving out tomorrow, and after that, I'll have the apartment to myself.

"I think I might head home as long as I'm awake."

"Are you sure? It's so late."

"I'll be fine." I run upstairs to gather my things. When I turn to leave the room, he's in the doorway, taking up most of the space.

"I miss you."

His words break my heart. "I miss you, too."

"Maybe we could talk and figure this out."

"It's better if we don't."

"How is it better?"

"I'd like to go now."

He steps aside to let me pass, but the devastation on his face stays with me long after I leave his home.

Twenty-Two

Wynter

The late-night encounter with Adrian haunts me as I meet Lou and help my mom move the next day, and then as I drive to work Monday morning, both excited to see him and dreading it, too. After such long, difficult ordeals, we found something we both needed in each other. Living without it sucks, but he was honest about his understandable feelings on the baby topic, and I'm determined to make that happen.

We're moving in two different directions, even though we intersect twice a day.

I'm even more aware of him after his late-night confession. I see the way he looks at me and feel the pain of loss all over again. How can it hurt this much when we were barely together before we decided to cool it?

Shortly after Adrian leaves for work, Iris calls me.

"Hey, what's up?" I ask her.

"That's what I'd like to know."

"What do you mean?"

"What's going on with you and Adrian? And don't say it's nothing. We can all see that something has changed between you guys, and we're worried about you."

"We realized we want different things, so the personal relationship isn't happening."

"Oh crap, Wynter. Are you all right?"

"I'm better than I was, but it was a setback. For both of us. We were enjoying it."

"I could see that. Everyone could."

So much for thinking we were fooling anyone. "I really miss being with him that way."

"Surely whatever it is isn't insurmountable."

"I think it might be. I've decided to try to have Jaden's baby."

"Oh, Wynter! Oh my goodness. That's amazing."

"I'm very excited and nervous about it."

"That's totally normal, especially when you know you're going to be a single mom."

"I'm not worried about that. I was raised by one. I turned out okay."

"You turned out better than okay. So when is this happening?"

"Tomorrow, but I haven't told anyone. I'm feeling superstitious about it."

"I won't tell a soul, but I'd be happy to come with you if you don't want to go alone."

"You would? Really?"

"Absolutely."

"I would love that. Thank you."

"Anything for you."

"Iris..."

"What, honey?"

"I might be having a baby. Jaden's baby. It's all so..."

"Overwhelming?"

"Yeah, that for sure, but amazing, too."

"Oh God, this is why you and Adrian called it off. Because he can't deal with you being pregnant."

"Yes."

"The poor guy. And poor you!"

"I know. It's very sad. I thought about not pursuing the baby because I could see how upset he was about it."

"You can't not do it because of someone else, even if you love that someone else."

"That's it exactly. I do love him. I hate to see him suffering or worried about me. It's just that I want this, Iris. I really want it."

"Then go get it, sweetheart. Adrian will either decide he wants to be part of it, or not. But either way, you should have what you want."

"I didn't even know I wanted it until I found out it was possible. And then it was all I could think about."

"Which means you're doing the right thing."

"I hope so."

"You are, and I think Adrian will come around. His loss is still raw in so many ways. You get that."

"I do."

"If Adrian had the same cancer Jaden had, you might not be able to handle being in a relationship with him."

"I hadn't thought of it that way. You're right. That would be torturous."

"Pregnancy and childbirth are going to be fraught for him for the rest of his life, whether it's you or someone else he cares about."

"I suppose so. That makes me sad for him. He's a wonderful father. He should have a bunch of kids."

"I know. It's all so freaking sad. Maybe after you have your baby—"

"Don't jinx me."

"After you successfully have your baby—knock on wood —he might feel differently."

"Possibly."

"I just can't believe you two are over for good. Roni and I were talking about how you two had gotten your sparkle back."

"And we thought you were the only one who knew."

"Haha, wishful thinking. We all knew, and I didn't tell anyone. We were happy for you both."

"I was happy for us, too. I knew how lucky we were to have found what we did with each other."

"It's a rare and beautiful thing."

My throat closes around a huge lump. "I miss him so much, even though I see him just about every day."

"I can't imagine how difficult that must be."

"It's sad more than anything. What we both want is right there, but out of reach." I expel a huff of laughter. "I sound so dramatic saying that."

"I understand what you mean. I want you to know how proud of you I am for going after what you want."

"I'm probably crazy to think I can do this on my own."

"You'll never be completely on your own. Tell me you know that."

"I do," I say softly. "Thank you for the reminder."

"Any time you need it. What time and where is the appointment tomorrow?"

I give her the details.

"I'll see you there."

"Thanks again, Iris."

"You got it. Love you to pieces."

"Love you, too."

As always, I feel a thousand times better after having spoken to her, and I'm relieved to know I won't go through the procedure alone tomorrow.

. . .

Adrian

I'M miserable as I trudge through life without being able to look forward to being with Wynter at the end of every long day. We had such a brief relationship, but as I look back on the long months since Sadie died, the time with Wynter stands out as the single really bright spot, other than every minute I've spent with Xavier, of course.

I love my son so much. He brings joy to every day. But being with Wynter gave me hope for a future that might not totally suck for the first time since Sadie died. And now that's gone, too.

The grief isn't as intense as it was when Sadie and Alyssa died, but it's bad enough to drag me down to lows I haven't seen in a while.

"What's going on?" Mick asks at the end of a workday when he catches me staring off into space. We're the last two in the office. "You're not at all yourself lately."

"Sorry. Everything is done."

"I'm not worried about work. I'm worried about *you*."

"I'm dealing with a small setback, but it won't interfere with the work. Don't worry."

"Again, I'm worried about you. I told Nia you seemed better for a while there, and now we're back to this, but she wouldn't tell me what's going on. What gives, man?"

"I was seeing someone for a while, and it didn't work out."

"Wynter?"

"Yes."

"I knew it! I said there was something brewing there, but, dude, she's your nanny."

"Believe me, I know. She's also my very good friend."

"So what's the problem?"

"We want different things."

"What does that even mean?"

"She found out she might be able to have her late husband's baby, and I'm not... I mean... I just can't, Mick. You know?" I look up at him, hoping he'll understand without me having to spell it out for him. "I can't."

"Shit." He sits in the cube across from mine and rolls the chair so he's right in front of me. "I get it, and I don't blame you one bit."

"But?"

"No buts. I'll only say it was nice to see you smiling again. I hadn't realized how much I'd missed that."

"Felt good to have something to smile about again—not that Xavier isn't enough."

"Naw, man, I get it. You mean something all your own."

"Yeah."

"What happened to Sadie..." He shakes his head as his eyes fill. "It's the worst thing that's ever happened to *me*. I can't begin to know what it was like for you. You've been a trouper, though. She'd be proud of you."

"You think so?"

"I know so, but here's the thing... I don't know anyone else who's lost a wife in childbirth. I don't know anyone else who's died in childbirth, and I know a lot of kids. What happened to Sadie—and to you and Xavier—was horrible. It was also a very rare complication."

"So many other things can happen."

"Granted, but the way I see it, you have one of two choices. You can live in fear of what *might* happen, or you can live in the moment and enjoy every damned minute of happiness you can find wherever you can find it."

"I don't want to live in fear."

"Then don't, Adrian. You could be with her right now. Loving someone, really loving them, takes tremendous courage because there's always a chance you could lose them. I worry about Nia and the kids every time they leave the house, especially since Sadie died and reminded us that everything is so incredibly fragile. But it would never occur to me to not love them anymore simply because it's possible I could lose them. You know?"

I nod because I'm so choked up, it's all I can do.

"I love how much support you've gotten from your widow friends, but I've worried about how it might impact you to hear so many sad stories. That's a lot of grief to carry around with you, when you have enough of your own."

"It's not like that. There's so much love and support."

"But there's a ton of grief, too, and perhaps you're letting that color your perceptions about the way forward, huh?"

I didn't think of that. I look at my brother-in-law with new respect. "Thank you."

"For what?"

"You said some things I needed to hear. I appreciate it."

"I'm here any time, and I hate to see you suffer any more than you already have." He stands and returns the chair to the other cubicle. "Let's get out of here."

As I drive home, I think about what Mick said. He's right. I know he is. I'm preconditioned now to expect the worst. I suppose anyone would be after losing two people close to them suddenly, one right after the other. The one thing he said that really resonates with me is that he doesn't know a single other person who's died in childbirth.

Neither do I.

I also appreciate his perspective on how the grief of others might be weighing on me. Even if that's true, the benefit of being with my widow friends far exceeds any downside. That said, it's quite possible my grief load has been heavier than it needs to be, and that could be affecting my judgment when it comes to Wynter and her desire to have Jaden's baby.

Life is so complicated sometimes.

Other times, it's simple. I love Wynter. I want to be with Wynter. Am I extremely freaked out at the thought of her being pregnant and delivering a baby? Absolutely. Which is worse, though? Staying away from her out of fear of something that may or may not happen, or committing fully to her, come what may?

The former.

Definitely the former.

I press the accelerator, eager to get home to Xavier —and her.

Wynter

SOMETHING IS different when he gets home. He seems lighter than he has in days. And he actually smiles a few times as I gather my things to leave.

"Can you stay for a bit? I'd like to talk."

"I can't tonight. I have plans."

"Oh. Okay. Another time, then."

"You remember about me having to take a half day tomorrow, right?"

"Yes, I'll be home by noon."

I kiss Xavier goodbye. "Thank you."

I'm almost to the door when Adrian says my name.

I turn back to him. "Yes?"

He stares at me for a long time before he shakes his head. "Nothing. It'll keep."

"See you in the morning."

"See you then."

I leave before I can lose my nerve. I don't have plans tonight, but I'm so worked up about tomorrow that I don't have the emotional capacity for whatever he wants to talk

MARIE FORCE

about. I'm eager to know what's on his mind, but it has to wait for now.

I'm awake all night in the quiet apartment where I now live alone, staring up at the ceiling, thinking about the enormity of what I'm about to do and missing Jaden so much, I ache. For the first time, I start to have serious doubts about whether I should be doing this. What business do I have thinking I can raise a child when I still feel like a child myself?

Except I'm not a child.

I'm a fully grown adult who's seen the best and the worst that life has to offer. I know how to take care of a baby and a child. I know what's important to teach them. I'm willing and able to do whatever it takes to make sure our child has every advantage. Thanks to Jaden, I not only have the chance to be a mother, but I can also afford to care for our child.

I can't help but see these final gifts from him as blessings, and I won't let anything, even Adrian's fears, take away from the joy I feel when I imagine myself holding our baby.

I take a long shower in the morning and down two cups of coffee before I get to Adrian's.

Xavier must've been up early because I can hear him chattering in Adrian's room.

I'm about to head back downstairs to wait for them when Adrian comes through the door wearing only his underwear.

As I stare at him, I've forgotten that I'm not supposed to do that anymore.

"Oh, hey. Thought I heard you. We'll be right down."

I lick my lips and try to recover my ability to breathe. "Um, sure. Okay."

I scoot down the stairs and wish for a stiff drink to calm my nerves and libido. I'd give anything for thirty minutes in a bed—or even against a wall—with Adrian right now. But since that's not going to happen, I take a seat at the kitchen table, cross my legs and focus on my phone until they come down.

Xavier squeals when he sees me.

Adrian puts him down to toddle over to me.

I reach for him and bring him in for a hug and a kiss.

He quickly squirms to break free.

"He's not very snuggly now that he's got wheels," Adrian says as he fixes his coffee.

He still snuggles me, I want to say, but I never would.

"Also, he's discovered the stairs, so keep an eye on that. He gets up but can't get back down."

"I spent most of yesterday chasing him off the stairs. We might need a gate."

"I'll pick one up. I also took everything off the tables in the living room."

"Good call. He's all hands."

"Yep." He picks Xavier up to give him a kiss. "Be good for Wynter."

"Wyn."

To me, he says, "I'll be back by noon."

"Thank you."

He gives me another of those searching looks before he goes out through the garage, while I wonder if it's possible to want someone so much, you can spontaneously combust.

After he eats breakfast and watches a few episodes of *Paw Patrol*, Xavier is ready for a nap.

While he sleeps, I curl up on the sofa and try to nap, too.

I'm certain I won't sleep, but I wake to the sound of Adrian coming in through the garage and sit up.

"Is he still asleep?"

"He is."

"Long one this morning?"

I check the time on my phone. "About ninety minutes."

"Hopefully, he'll take another one this afternoon so I can finish up at work."

"He will. He still loves his naps." I put my coat on. "Thanks for coming home early."

"No problem."

"I, ah, I guess I'll see you tomorrow."

"See you then." After a heartbeat, he says, "Damn it, Wynter. This is horrible. I miss you. I want you."

The words explode out of him, leaving me speechless.

He comes over to me and puts his hands on my shoulders. "I love you."

As I look up at him and hear him saying words that should mean everything, I remember he doesn't know where I'm going today, and if he did, he'd take it all back. "I can't right now. I'm sorry. I just can't."

Twenty-Three

Wynter

I feel terrible leaving after he said what he did, but if I don't go now, I'll be late for the appointment. My emotions are all over the place as I drive the thirty minutes to the clinic.

Iris is waiting for me in the parking lot.

"What's wrong?" she asks after taking one look at me.

"Adrian... As I was leaving, he said he loves me, misses me, wants me. That this is horrible."

"What did you say?"

"That I couldn't talk about it right now. I had to leave so I wouldn't be late, but I couldn't help but think if he knew where I was going, he wouldn't have said any of that."

"Maybe he would have." She puts her arm around me as we walk inside. "Maybe he's realized that seeing you through pregnancy and childbirth isn't as bad as being without you."

"I'm so nervous and wound up that I can barely process this right now."

"Then don't try to process it now. Focus on the appointment, and then afterward, you can decide how you feel about what he said."

"Thank you for being here. I didn't know I would need you this much."

"I'm happy to be here and very excited for you."

"I'm trying not to get excited until I know if it works."

"It's okay to be a tiny bit excited."

"I keep thinking how funny it is that we tried so hard for years *not* to get pregnant, and now, all I want is to be pregnant with his child."

"It is funny how that happens."

Inside, we go to the second floor and check in with reception.

They call me back twenty long minutes later. I'm given a gown and told to take everything off from the waist down. When I'm ready, the nurse brings Iris in.

She stands by the exam table and holds my hand. "I read up on this last night. It's supposed to be painless."

"Yeah, that's what they told me, but I'm shaking anyway."

Dr. Bauer comes in a few minutes later, and I introduce her to Iris.

"I'm so glad you brought a friend," the doctor says. "How're you feeling today, Wynter?"

"Nervous and excited."

"Both are understandable, but this will be quick and painless, so try not to be nervous."

"Trying."

She already told me that the procedure is similar to having a Pap smear, so I'm ready when she scoots me to the end of the table, puts my feet into stirrups and inserts the speculum.

I cling to Iris's hand through the ten-minute ordeal and breathe a sigh of relief when the speculum is removed.

"That's all there is to it," Dr. Bauer says as she removes her gloves and washes her hands. "You may have some cramping and spotting, but that's normal. Any sign of fever, give us a call. After two weeks, I'll have you back for a blood test to check for pregnancy. You can take a home test before then, but I advise you to wait until day fourteen to ensure the most accurate result."

"Thank you so much for this."

"My pleasure. I've got my fingers crossed for you."

After she leaves the room, I notice tears in Iris's eyes. "What's wrong?"

"Nothing at all. I'm just so happy for you and so proud of you."

"You always know just what to say."

"Not always, but in this case, 'happiness' and 'pride' are the words of the day. Shall we go to lunch to celebrate?"

"That sounds good."

Adrian

I'VE BEEN miserable since yesterday when I blurted out those things to Wynter when she had somewhere to be and no time to talk. I had to talk myself out of texting her a thousand times to apologize for my timing. But I'm not sorry for what I said. I'm glad she knows I love her, miss her, want her and hate this awful never-never land we've been in for weeks now.

This whole thing is my fault. I own that. I just wish I could figure out how to fix it.

I'm puzzling that over after a shower when Gage calls me.

"Hey, is everything all right?" I ask him.

"Yeah, sorry to call so early, but I need a favor."

"Anything for you."

"Will you come up with a reason for why you suddenly need to host the meeting this week?"

"Sure. What's going on?"

"I want to propose to Iris, and I want to have all of you and our families there, but I can't sneak them into her house."

"Ah, gotcha. I'm down for that. And PS, congratulations."

"Thanks, man. I'm excited. Is it okay if I bring Wynter in as a coconspirator to help me get everyone in place ahead of time?"

"She'd love to help."

"Thanks again."

"Glad to be part of such an amazing moment."

"I hope it will be."

"It will. I have faith in you."

We say our goodbyes, and I stand there holding my phone, thinking about my friends. I'm so happy for Gage and Iris, two people who deserve this happily ever after more than just about anyone I know. However, their good news only makes my current situation with Wynter more excruciating. Gage and Iris have it all figured out, and we're stuck in this horrible limbo.

I hear her come in downstairs, and just that quickly, I feel better knowing she's close by.

I ache from wanting her. I want to know what's going on with her. She hasn't said anything to me, except about Xavier, for weeks now. Is she having a baby? I'm going crazy wanting to know.

I get Xavier from his crib and change his diaper before carrying him downstairs to greet his favorite person.

She's so beautiful, she takes my breath away, especially when she smiles at my son.

While she has him, I backtrack to the stairs to put up the gate I bought last night.

"That'll make my life a thousand times easier," she says. "Thanks."

"You got it. So Gage called this morning." I fill her in on

the plan. "He wondered if you might help by letting everyone in before the meeting."

"That's so exciting! I'll text him, and I'll make sure this place is meeting ready."

"Thank you."

I want to scream for how cordial and businesslike we are when the sight of her sets my blood on fire with desire.

"I wanted you to know…"

She has my full attention.

"I heard what you said yesterday, and I feel the same."

I take a step toward her.

She holds up a hand to stop me. "There are things we should talk about at some point."

"Any time you want. Just say when."

"We'll talk when you get home."

"Okay."

After I kiss my son goodbye and tell him to be good for Wynter, I drive to work wondering how I'll make it until tonight. One thing she said keeps echoing through my mind.

I feel the same.

Have four words ever meant more?

Wynter

XAVIER IS NAPPING around three when I hear the door from the garage to the kitchen open. I've just finished folding a load of his laundry when Adrian comes into the living room, looking a little wild in the eyes.

"What?"

"You. That's what."

"What did I do?" I ask, genuinely confused.

"All you have to do is breathe to make me crazy. I can't sleep or eat or work or do anything other than want you."

I fan my face. "It's getting warm in here."

"Wynter... Please. *Please.*"

Even though we've resolved none of the things that drove us apart in the first place, I get up and go to him because I can't resist him.

He hauls me into his arms and kisses me with such ferocity that I wonder how I made it this long without his kisses. "How long has he been down?"

"About fifteen minutes."

"Thank you, Jesus."

Before I know what hits me, he's lifted me and is headed for the stairs, where he's stopped by the gate.

I giggle as I watch him try to open it.

"Don't laugh at me. This isn't funny."

"It's very funny. Flip that latch."

He flips the latch and pulls the gate open so hard, he nearly takes the whole structure down.

I'm laughing helplessly as he surges up the stairs and into his bedroom, kicking the door shut behind him.

God, it feels good to laugh again, to be held by a man who cares about me, to be wanted so fiercely.

He holds me tight against him as he stares down at me with a heated gaze. "I missed you, Wynter. I missed you so fucking bad."

"Same."

"Not just in here." He uses his chin to point to the bed. "I missed you everywhere. Seeing you every day, but having that distance between us, was..."

"I know, Adrian. I know." I pull him down to me, and our lips meet in an incendiary reunion that's so hot, I wonder how we don't set the place on fire. I pull back from him only because I feel like I need to tell him I might be pregnant. "Adrian, there are things... Things you should know—"

"Later."

Okay, then.

We pull and tug at clothes until we're both standing naked next to the bed.

He wraps his arms around me and drops his head to my shoulder. "I worried I'd never get to hold you like this again, and I was sad like I haven't been since I lost Sadie."

"Adrian..."

"I was so, so sad without you, Wynter."

"I don't want either of us to be sad anymore."

"Neither do I."

He kisses me, and we land on the bed in a blaze of desire that makes my head spin.

It's hard to believe I've found something like this twice in one short lifetime, but thanks to Jaden and how I lost him, I know to be thankful for every minute I get with Adrian.

He stops only to grab a condom, and then we're on the bed, with him looking down at me as he fills me. "I love you, Wynter. I love you."

"I love you, too."

His eyes close as he seems to release weeks' worth of tension.

Whereas we've been all about the fast and frantic in the past, this time is all slow reverence.

"Wynter..." His lips are soft against my neck and send shivers down my spine. "You can't leave me again. You just can't. I won't stand in the way of anything you want."

As I realize what he's saying, my heart swells to overflowing with love for this amazing man who's willing to put aside his greatest fear if it means he gets to be with me. How lucky am I?

I no sooner have that thought than the grief shows up to remind me not to get too comfortable in my newfound happiness.

To hell with that shit.

I'm as happy as I've been since my world imploded, and I'm going to enjoy it to the fullest, starting with an orgasm for the ages that rocks my whole body and has me clinging to him as he comes with me.

Afterward, he holds me so tightly, I can barely breathe.

"You can't ever leave me again."

"I won't."

"Do you promise?"

"Yeah." That's an easy promise to make because I don't want to be without him either.

"We're going to do this, you and me. We're going to make a life together and raise Xavier and be happy. I can't stand to spend another minute of my life feeling like absolute shit."

"I'm here, and I'm not going anywhere if this is what you want."

"I want everything with you."

I take a second to breathe before I say the one thing that could pop this happy bubble we're in. "Including my child with Jaden?"

"If that's what you want, then that's what I want, and I'll love him or her the way you love Xavier."

"Really?"

He nods and raises his head off my chest to look at me. "I'm scared for you—and for me. I'm not going to lie to you about that."

"I wouldn't want you to."

"Having to take a step back from you these last few weeks, when that was the very last thing I wanted to do, made me see that I can't live my life in fear of what might happen. I have to live for the minute we're in, right now. And where we are is something I never thought I'd have again after I lost Sadie."

I reach up to caress his gorgeous face. "Same. I thought this was over for me, even if I can see now that it would've happened eventually. I'm glad it happened with you and Xavier."

"Me, too. You'll be the only mother he'll know."

"We'll make sure he knows the woman who gave him life as well as he knows me."

"Thank you for that."

"You don't have to thank me."

"I really do. You've been so amazing with him. He loves you more than anything."

"Not more than you."

"On many a day, you're in first place. But that's okay. I get why my son can't help but love you."

"You should know…"

"What, babe?"

"The half day I took yesterday?"

"What about it?"

"It was to have an insemination procedure."

"Oh, so are you…" He swallows hard. "Are you pregnant?"

"I won't know for sure for two weeks."

"Wow, so how are you feeling and stuff?"

He's so, so cute. "I'm fine."

"Did it hurt? I know how much you hate medical stuff."

"It was nothing. Took ten minutes."

"I'm sorry I wasn't with you for that. I should've been."

"Iris was there."

"I'm glad you weren't alone."

"Me, too."

"I want you to know…" He drops his forehead to rest against mine and closes his eyes. "It scares the living hell out of me to think that anything could hurt you or…"

"I'm fine, and I'm going to be fine. I promise."

"We both know you can't promise that, but despite how I reacted to this news initially, I'm excited to welcome your baby into our family and maybe…"

"What?"

"Maybe we could have one of our own at some point."

"I'd love that."

"I'll always be afraid of losing someone I love so much."

"I know, and I'll be right here to hold you when the fear gets to be too much. And when we're wrangling teenagers, I'll be there, too."

"I'm going to hold you to that."

"I'm counting on it."

Twenty-Four

Christy

I've put this off long enough. I finally respond to one of Trey's texts.

Hi.

He writes right back. *Hello, beautiful. I've missed you.*

See what he does there? He never misses a chance to tell me I'm beautiful, and the thing is, I believe he really thinks that. He's not one to spout platitudes.

I've missed you, too.

I'm really glad to hear that. Thought maybe I'd pushed you away.

You almost did.

Can I see you? Can we talk?

As I stare at his words on the screen, I take a deep breath and then type my reply. *When?*

Now?

Like, right now?

Sweetheart, I've been hoping for weeks that I would hear from you, so yes, right freaking now. Where are you?

As much as I want to stay calm, that response sparks a slight bit of swoon. *Home.*

May I please come see you? (Please note use of proper grammar.)

Did I mention he's funny, too? As I'm laughing, I type my reply. *Yes, you may, but only because you used proper grammar.* I ranted to him about a guy I was seeing having the worst grammar of any adult I know and how it totally turned me off wanting to date him.

I'm already on the way.

I run for the shower, shave everything and get dressed in the leggings he once told me make my ass look hot. I pull a top off a hanger, causing the hanger to come flying at my face. I manage to deflect it with my hand as I tell myself to calm the hell down.

The top is black, off the shoulder and sexy, if I do say so myself.

I put my hair up in a clip and apply mascara and lip gloss.

I don't want to look like I tried too hard, but some things are essential.

Downstairs, I pour a glass of unsweetened tea and sit at the bar in my kitchen to wait.

He works twenty minutes from me, but I'm not sure if that's where he's coming from.

Ten minutes later, the doorbell rings.

As I get up to answer it, I'm aware that the next few minutes could truly change the new life I've made for myself and my kids since my husband died suddenly four years ago. Opening the door to Trey could mean opening myself to much more.

I open the door.

I forgot how cute he is.

He has a tanned face from working outdoors, wavy dark

hair, brown eyes and a really nice smile that's on full display as I move aside to let him in.

When he reaches for me, I step into his arms for the best hug I've had since the last time I saw him.

"There you are. I'm so happy to see you."

I also forgot how good he smells and how great his hugs are. "Me, too."

"Really? Because I wouldn't blame you if you weren't."

"You wouldn't be here if I hadn't really missed you."

"That's the best thing I've heard since the last time I saw you."

When we finally pull apart, I realize that quite a bit of time has gone by in which we held each other and breathed the same air.

"Come in." As I lead the way to the kitchen, I hope he's appreciating the leggings he's complimented in the past.

I turn and catch him checking me out.

"Sorry. You're just a sight for very lonely eyes."

"Tea?"

"Sure."

I'm glad to have something to do to calm myself down before I welcome him back with open arms—and legs—without resolving any of the issues that came between us.

We sit at the kitchen table with glasses of iced tea.

"It's so good to see you," he says.

"You, too."

"You made me suffer."

"Good."

His huff of laughter pleases me. "I guess I deserved that."

"You did."

"I know, and I'm sorry for how I handled this. It was all wrong."

"Not if it was what you needed to do. I don't blame you

for that. We're a lot, and I know it. Believe me. It's a lot for me, and I love them."

"They're great kids. You should be so proud of them."

"I am. They've seen things that no one should ever see, and it's been a long, hard road to where we are now. We're still a work very much in progress."

"You know what I thought a lot about while we were apart?"

"What's that?"

"The way you sparkle when you talk about them, even when you're telling me how they did something that drove you crazy." He puts his hand over mine. "I feel your love for them. It's in every fiber of your being."

"Yes, it is, and when someone tells me he needs time to think about whether he wants them in his life, and then takes three weeks of complete silence to decide..."

"It's a very big deal to me to possibly be part of their lives. I have next to no experience with kids. My nieces and nephews live in Montana and Oregon. While I see them at least once a year and talk to them on FaceTime and send them birthday presents, I've had nothing to do with raising them. Some of my friends have kids, but they're little or grown. Nothing in the middle where yours are. I realized that if we were going to make a go of this, I needed to get some experience with young teens. So I've been volunteering at the Boys and Girls Clubs of Greater Washington."

I'm so flabbergasted, I can barely process what he said.

"I wanted to know what they're interested in, what excites them and what challenges them. I wanted their advice on how I could connect with my girlfriend's kids. Three days a week, I do homework with kids in eighth, ninth and tenth grades, and let me tell you how stupid I am next to them. I'm basically faking it as I pretend to know what to do to help them.

Mostly, I make sure they do their work before moving on to something more fun.

"In addition to learning about kids the same ages as yours, I've learned about the struggles of young people who don't have the strong support system at home that yours have. One of them has been in six different foster homes since he was four. Another has both parents in rehab for the fourth time while he lives with his grandmother."

My reaction to this information is one hundred percent emotional. While I thought he was taking all that time to think about whether he could stand to be around my kids, he was off doing research so he could better connect with them.

I reach for a napkin from the basket on the table and mop up my tears.

"I was thinking I could invite Shawn to a Feds game, since he loves baseball so much, and I thought Josie might like going to the workshops they have at Home Depot on Saturdays where you can learn how to build things. I remember she told me she wants to figure out how to build flower boxes so she can plant a garden where the deer can't get to the plants. They have this other thing about gardening later in the spring—"

I'm up and out of my chair before I take even a heartbeat to consider what I'm doing.

Since he's sitting sideways on the chair, I straddle his lap and put my arms around his neck.

"What is happening?" he asks with a sexy smile.

"This." I kiss him with everything I have, everything I'll ever be and all the love I tried to deny I felt for him when I was busy making assumptions that were completely false.

He cups my ass and pulls me in tight against his immediate erection.

The kiss is one of the best of my life because it's so full of hope.

"I'm sorry," I say to him when we come up for air quite a bit later.

"For what, honey?"

"For ignoring your texts for so long. I shouldn't have done that."

"You did what you needed to do, and so did I."

"What you did... I can't believe it."

"What can't you believe? That I love you enough to do whatever it takes to make it work between us and between me and your kids?"

"Yes. That."

"Well, I do."

"I see that now. I'm sorry if I ever doubted it."

"I understand why you did. I didn't handle it as well as I could have. I should've better articulated my specific concerns rather than making you think I had a problem with being around your kids. I'll admit, it was a lot for me at first, but only because I'm not used to it. I want to get used to it. I want to be there for you and them—as much or as little as they'll allow—and I want us. I want this. If you do, that is."

"I do."

"Oh, those are two *very* loaded words."

Laughing, I say, "I'm not saying yes to *that*."

"We'll get to it."

"Thank you for what you did by volunteering."

"I'm still doing it. Those kids are in my life to stay. I could never give them up now."

"I love you, too."

"I'm so glad to hear that."

"I'll never get over Wes. Not ever."

"I wouldn't want you to. Whatever we are together, he'll be part of it. Please don't ever feel like you can't talk about him to me or mention things about him. I want to know him."

"This feels like a dream to me. I've been so upset about this situation for so long, and to think, all this time..."

"All you had to do was text me back."

I laugh even as I cry, and then he kisses me again. For the first time in a long time, everything is right in my world.

I'm wise enough to know by now that this may not last forever, so I plan to enjoy every minute of it while I can.

He breaks the kiss. "How long until you have to pick up the kids?"

I check my watch. "Two hours."

With his arms tight around me, he stands and then sets me on the counter as he raises my top over my head. "That should be just enough time to properly seal the deal."

Gage

I SWORE I'd never get married again. I laugh at how funny that seems to me now that I'm completely absorbed in my new life with Iris and her three adorable, sweet kids. At the time I made that promise to myself, I was shattered by grief after losing my wife and daughters to a drunk driver.

I couldn't imagine a scenario that would have me down on one knee, loving someone enough to ask her to spend the rest of her life with me. The very idea of it would've been preposterous to me a few years ago.

But then came Iris to show me how silly I was to think I could go it alone when she was right there, offering me everything I could ever want or need.

She is *everything* and then some.

And tonight, in front of our families and the friends we share, I'm going to ask her to marry me.

She has no clue this is coming.

We haven't discussed marriage at all, probably because she

knows it was a very big deal for me to enter into a real relationship with her and the kids, to move in with them, to make a new family together. She's probably afraid to hope for anything more than what we already have because I was so reluctant to be in a real relationship again—at first.

I'm not reluctant anymore.

Grief takes an enormous amount of energy. On the bad days, it sucks the will to live right out of a person. On the good days, it's an ache that no amount of medication could ever make go away. I still have bad days with grief, such as on my twin daughters' birthday or on my anniversary with Nat or on other days that meant something to us. But the bad days are fewer and further between these days, which makes me feel guilty.

How can I move on with my life when my gorgeous, sweet girls will never be anything other than eight years old? How can I be happy with someone else when my Natasha is gone forever?

Despite all the reasons why I shouldn't be, I'm happy, or as happy as I can possibly be in the after without them. I'm happy with Iris. I adore her kids. I want us to be a family in every possible way.

I receive a text from my mother-in-law, Mimi. *On the ground at Reagan. See you soon, love. We're so excited.*

Natasha's parents, Mimi and Stan, have flown in to be with us tonight. It means so much to me to have their support as I take this next step with Iris and the kids. We had the best time at their house in Florida over Christmas. Iris and Mimi have become daily text pals, which is so lovely.

My parents love Iris, my sister loves Iris, her parents and family love me. Her mother and stepfather cried when I asked their permission to propose to Iris. It's all good.

And yet...

I ache for Nat and my girls. How can I be doing something so important without them? Years after the accident that took them from me, I've come to realize I'll always feel their absence. I'll feel it at the best and worst of times. Joy coexists with sorrow in the aftermath of disaster.

Today is about the joy, and all I can do is hope my girls are cheering me on as I step forward into a new life with Iris and the kids.

I arrive at Adrian's an hour before the Wild Widows are due. I told Iris I had an appointment and I'd meet her there.

Her mother's job was to deliver the kids to Adrian's. He told her that Xavier was having an awful time with teething when he asked if we could meet at his place this week. Naturally, Iris gave him every teething remedy she's ever heard of as she said of course we could hold the meeting at his house.

The kids are waiting for me when I come in the front door.

Laney rushes me the way Ivy and Hazel used to when I got home from work. I had no idea how much I missed that until Laney started greeting me the same way. I sweep Laney up and into my arms and give her a noisy kiss that makes her giggle.

"Tyler got in trouble at school."

"I thought you weren't gonna be a tattletale anymore."

"I'm trying, but this was big."

It's all I can do not to howl with laughter.

I put her down and let her tug me toward the kitchen with her little hand wrapped around mine.

I give Iris's smiling mom and stepfather quick hugs and then sit at the kitchen table with Wynter, Xavier, Tyler and Sophia, who are coloring as they enjoy a snack.

"Thanks for all the help, Wynter."

"My pleasure. I'm so excited for you and Iris."

"Thanks." Well, here is the moment of truth I've been anticipating for weeks now. "Kiddos, can I talk to you about something?"

"Daddy Gage wants to know what you did at school," Laney says to Tyler.

He gives her a filthy look.

"We'll talk about that later." I give him a wink and a smile, so he won't worry about later. "What I want to talk about now is your mom." I waited until the big day so there was no chance they'd accidentally give away the surprise.

"Is she okay?" Tyler asks with furrowed brows.

"She's wonderful and beautiful and loving."

"She's the best mommy," Sophia says.

"She sure is, and I was thinking I might ask her to marry me so we can all get married and be a family forever. What would you guys think of that?"

"We're getting *married*?" Sophia asks, her eyes wide.

"If Mommy says yes," I reply, moved by her reaction.

"Duh," Tyler says, "she will. She's all silly over you."

"She laughs all the time now," Sophia says. "I like that."

"I do, too, sweetheart. She makes me laugh, too, and so do you guys. I'd forgotten what it was like to laugh so much. I want to do a lot of laughing and loving with you and your mom. So will you guys marry me?"

"Yes!" Laney says with her fist in the air.

"I will," Sophia says, her expression serious, as usual. Making her laugh is always a big accomplishment and one I try to achieve daily.

"Tyler? What do you think, buddy?"

"It's cool."

"Are you sure?"

He looks at me and nods. "I'm sure."

"It means the world to me to have you guys in my life. I love you very much, and I always will."

"We love you, too," Sophia says.

I look over at Wynter and catch her swiping at tears. "Good job, Daddy Gage," she says.

I never imagined that I'd consider someone young enough to be my daughter such a close friend, but she's one of my favorites, and her opinion means a lot to me. "Thanks, pal."

"I can't wait for Iris to get here," her mom says as she wipes away tears, too.

I can't wait either.

Twenty-Five

Iris

I hate being late. It gives me so much stress. I had a rare afternoon free after my mom asked to have the kids, so I decided to get a mani/pedi. The salon was busier than it should've been on a Wednesday, and the traffic is hideous at this time of day. That's easy to forget when you're rarely out at rush hour.

A car cuts me off, forcing me to slam on my brakes. Fortunately, there's no one right behind me, or that might've been bad.

I resist the urge to give the offending driver the finger, fearing I might end up dead. As a single parent, you have to keep those things in mind when you want to tell a stranger what you think of them.

Although... These days, I'm not really a single parent anymore. Since Gage moved in with us, he's stepped up in so many ways to take some of the load off my shoulders. He loves driving the kids to school in the morning and picking them up in the afternoon. He's the best thing that ever happened to homework, and he's brought laughter back into our home.

I'm so thankful to have him as part of our lives and to see him fully committed to our relationship and the kids when it would've been so much easier for him to stay uninvolved and uncommitted. It was a huge risk for him to take us on, and I hope we're making it worth it for him every day.

All the visitor spots near Adrian's are taken, so I have to park about a quarter mile away. I grab the cupcakes I picked up at the Giant on the way and half walk, half jog toward Adrian's, where the light is on over the front door.

It's nearly six thirty by the time I walk in to find the widows already gathered in the living room. "I'm so sorry I'm late." I dump my coat in the pile by the door and go into the kitchen to put my cupcakes on the counter with the other desserts. I pour myself a small glass of wine, since I have to drive, and take it with me to the living room, where I give Gage a quick kiss before I take the seat next to him that he saved for me. "You guys are down to business early tonight. What'd I miss?"

"Christy was just telling us that she finally returned Trey's texts," Brielle says.

I already know all about that. I smile at Christy, who's beaming. There's no other word for it.

"I can't believe he volunteered to get experience with kids the same ages as yours," Joy says. "That man is a keeper."

"Yes, he is," Christy says with a satisfied smile.

"And how's Lexi doing in her new home?" Roni asks.

"It's really great. Tom is an amazing cook and makes me dinner every night. I'm enjoying it."

"Ah, that's the best news," I tell her. "And how is our Hallie?"

"Still talking to Robin, but just not sure where it's going. I'm okay, though."

"You know where to come if you're ever not okay," Christy tells her.

"I do, and it means everything."

"What's going on with you two?" I ask Wynter and Adrian, who are back to sitting next to each other after several weeks of barely exchanging glances at the meeting.

"We're working it out," Adrian says with a smile for Wynter.

"He realized he can't live without me," she says, making us all laugh as only she can do.

I think I'm seeing things when my children come down the stairs, holding flowers that they bring to me. "What? What's going on?"

I look to Gage, but he has nothing to say as my mother, stepfather, his parents, sister and... Mimi and Stan? What the hell is happening? I start to look at him again when I realize he's now in front of me and on his knees. *Oh my God.*

When the kids position themselves on either side of me, I start to cry.

Everyone is in tears.

Gage looks up at me with so much love and devotion and grief and every other emotion all directed at me and my kids. "Iris, my love, my friend, my savior... Tyler, Sophia, Laney, my sweet little friends. I love you all so much. That wasn't supposed to happen."

I laugh, recalling how hard he fought the "relationship" tag and then how easily he later surrendered to the inevitable.

"But you guys made it impossible for me to resist you, and now that I get to spend my days and nights with you, I'm as happy as I could possibly be."

There's so much he doesn't say there that I instinctively understand. We're both as happy as we could be without the people we loved before.

"Laney, sweet Laney, I'd like to marry your mom and be your Daddy Gage forever. Will you have me?"

"Yes!"

Laney's enthusiastic reply has everyone laughing and sniffing and wiping away tears.

He puts a gold heart-shaped necklace on her.

"Sophia, my reading buddy and Harry Potter pal, I'd like to marry your mom and be your Daddy Gage forever. Will you have me?"

"Absolutely," Sophia says with a loving smile for him.

She receives the same necklace as her sister while I mop up a flood of tears at realizing how much thought he's put into this.

"Tyler, my football-watching, model-building, wrestling buddy, I'd like to marry your mom and be your Daddy Gage forever. Will you have me?"

"Yeah," Tyler says gruffly. "I'll have you, but only if it's okay with my mom."

He's so protective and grown up for his age, which makes me proud and sad at the same time.

Gage straps an impressive-looking watch onto Tyler's wrist. I'm sure it's got all the bells and whistles that my son will love. "Let's see what she has to say, shall we?" he asks the kids, who giggle. "Iris, you know how much I love you because we tell each other all the time. We've learned to never let a minute pass without saying it, living it, showing it. I want to spend every second that I possibly can with you and the kids. Will you please marry me and share what's left of this life with me?"

As I look at his arresting face and listen to his beautiful words, a stream of memories runs through my mind from the life I thought I was going to have with Mike to the one I have now with Gage. He's become my rock, my north star, my everything, and though I'm completely shocked that he's actually proposing when he planned to never love anyone again, there's only one answer I can give him.

"Yes," I whisper softly. "Yes to everything."

And then I'm in his arms as everyone around us laughs and claps and whistles.

The kids are jumping up and down with excitement.

Gage pulls back to look at me before he kisses me and slides a ring on my finger. I'm so focused on him that I don't even bother to look at the ring. Those things don't matter to me the way they once would have. He stands and helps me up for another hug.

We pull apart only because the kids are demanding our attention.

With Laney in his arms and Tyler and Sophia standing in front of us, we pose for photos to document this exciting moment.

Everyone hugs us and congratulates us.

"That was so amazing," Roni says, wiping away tears. "I'm so glad we were part of it."

"Of course you were," Gage says. "We never would've gotten here without the support we've received from this group."

Adrian and Wynter come in carrying trays with champagne glasses on them.

"A toast," Joy says, "to Mom and Dad."

Everyone laughs.

"No, really, if this group has a mom and dad, it's you two," Joy says. "You're the ones we all turn to in times of need, in times of sorrow and joy. If anyone deserves this, you do, and we're all so happy to have been part of it from the beginning as a great friendship borne out of tremendous loss turned into an epic romance full of hope. We love you. Congratulations to Gage and Iris!"

I'm so moved by her words, I can barely speak. This group

has meant everything to me as I navigated young widowhood. I still can't believe what's come of a small idea that my friend Taylor and I had years ago. Look at us now.

Mimi and Stan come over to hug us.

"That was so lovely, Gage," Mimi says. "Thank you for including us in such a joyful event."

"We couldn't have done it without you," I tell her. She's become my close friend since we met at Christmas, which is still so incredible to me. His late wife's mother is my dear friend. Only a widow could possibly appreciate such a unique relationship.

I was so scattered when I arrived with my cupcakes that I failed to notice the foil-covered trays in the kitchen.

Gage went all out with a fully catered meal to celebrate our engagement.

"This is amazing," I tell him as the house buzzes with excitement and energy. The kids are so wound up, they'll never sleep tonight. "Thank you so much. It was perfect."

"I'm glad you think so."

"I hope you know this means you're in a real *relationship*."

"Ah," he says, laughing, "there it is. You had to go and ruin it."

I flash my sauciest grin at him. "I'm just making sure you *fully* understand the implications of your actions."

He leans in for a kiss. "I'm very much aware, and I couldn't be happier."

"Same, love."

Wynter

THE NEXT TWO weeks are the best and the longest I've had in a while. I'm still floating after witnessing Gage and Iris's engagement. They're two of my all-time favorite people.

Seeing them get their happily ever after gives the rest of us so much hope.

Things with Adrian are amazing since we decided to try again. I've spent every night since at his place, even though I plan to hold on to the apartment for now. He's asked me again to officially move in. I'm not sure why I feel hesitant. Things have moved quickly between us, even if we've known each other for more than a year. I want to be careful to make the best possible decision for myself—and possibly my baby.

Even though he's said and done all the right things, I'm not under any illusions that we're fully out of the woods on the matter of me carrying and delivering a child and his very real fears.

I'm planning to take a pregnancy test tonight after work. I bought four of them just so I could be certain one way or the other.

It's been torturous to wait.

I keep recalling what Dr. Bauer said about how it often takes several attempts before it works, and I might have to be patient. I've been waiting for some physical feeling or sign to come over me to indicate I could be pregnant. So far, there's been nothing. I'm tired all the time lately, but I can't chalk that up to pregnancy. I've been staying up way too late with Adrian, which has us both dragging.

Tonight, we're going to do nothing but sleep. Or else.

While Xavier naps, I do, too, waking up quite a bit later when I hear Adrian come in. I feel guilty napping on the job, but it's his fault I'm so tired—a thought I share with him when he comes looking for me.

"I'm running on fumes myself," he says as he stretches out next to me, wrapping his arm and leg around me.

"Man cannot live on sex alone," I tell him.

"Ah, but what a way to go."

We're still there fifteen minutes later when Xavier starts chirping upstairs.

Adrian is out cold, so I gently extricate myself, hoping he might rest for a while longer.

Xavier is jumping up and down in his crib by the time I get upstairs. He's always so happy to see me. I lift him out, change his diaper and tell him we have to be quiet because Daddy is sleeping.

He puts his finger over his lips and says, "Shhh."

Could he be any cuter? Nope. Not possible. "That's right."

I take him downstairs to the kitchen and put him in his high chair with some crackers while I get his dinner ready. He's having chicken and pasta cut into tiny bites along with the green bean baby food he loves.

He's munching on little bites of sliced apple for dessert when Adrian comes to find us.

"There's my family."

I smile up at him as he stands behind me.

"Dada."

"Hey, buddy. What's for dinner?"

"Yum."

"Can you take over for a few?" I ask him.

"Sure."

I get up to give him my seat. "I'll be right back."

Upstairs, I retrieve the tests and take them to the hall bathroom. I've already read the instructions at least ten times, so I'm ready to get this done. I'm doing two of the tests now and will save the other two for the morning in case these are negative. I read that early pregnancy shows up more readily first thing in the morning. After two very long weeks, I can't bear to wait another minute.

I pee on both sticks and set them on the vanity.

Before I can get my jeans back on, they both have plus signs showing.

Holy. Shit.

Oh my God.

I'm pregnant.

It worked.

I can't believe it.

It actually worked.

And then I'm crying like I did after I first lost Jaden. Unlike those tears, however, these are tears of joy mixed with a healthy dose of sorrow. I've come to realize the sorrow will always be there, no matter how happy I am. That's the tremendous price you pay for loving someone the way I loved Jaden and then losing him.

"We did it, babe," I whisper to him. "We made a baby."

The pain is right there next to the joy, coexisting in this weird state of reality that makes up my life as a widow.

But now there's a baby. His baby. Our baby. My baby.

A soft knock on the door pulls me out of the past and into the present.

I open the door to Adrian with Xavier in his arms.

"Wynter, honey. What's wrong?"

"Nothing's wrong." I hold up the stick so he can see it. "I'm pregnant."

The change comes over him almost immediately. His face loses all expression as his body goes tense. "Congratulations."

"You really mean that?"

"I want you to be happy."

"I want *you* to be happy."

"I'm going to do my best to support you in every way that I can." He makes a visible effort to say the right thing. "But this is hard for me. I won't lie to you about that."

"I'd never want you to lie, and I'm sorry it's hard. I wish it wasn't."

"It's okay. Please don't let me and my fears take anything away from your happiness. You deserve it so much."

"You do, too."

"We all do."

"So where do we go from here?"

"I was going to give Xavier a bath. You want to help?"

"I'd love to."

Twenty-Six

Adrian

I'm sick to my stomach. I love her so much. I meant what I said about wanting her to be happy, and having Jaden's baby will make her happy. I'm sure of that. She'll be an amazing mother. I just wish I could push the clock forward about thirty-eight weeks to seeing her and the baby safely through the delivery.

Thirty-eight weeks is a long-ass time to live in utter dread.

She's asleep in my arms as I stare up at the dark ceiling, riddled with anxiety.

I'm as tired as I've been since Xavier was a newborn, but I can't close my eyes without seeing disaster. Images of lifeless Wynter torment me. My fears are irrational, and I know it. If only I could control them somehow.

Tomorrow, I'll reach out to the therapist my sister set me up with right after Sadie died. I need to do something about this wildfire of fear before I ruin this special thing I have with Wynter.

At some point, I must've fallen asleep, because I'm startled awake when the alarm goes off.

Wynter groans and rolls toward the other side of the bed.

I kiss her shoulder. "Sleep for a little while longer."

"Mmm."

I take my phone with me into the bathroom to get ready for work. Before I do a single other thing, I send a text to the therapist, Candace, asking if she can fit me in over the next few days.

Just had a cancellation for three o'clock today. You want it?

I should check with Mick first, but I'm sure he won't care. *Yes, please.*

See you then.

I'm so relieved to know that help is on the way as I shower, shave and get dressed. When I'm ready, I go check on Xavier, who's still asleep.

Back in my room, I kiss Wynter awake and smile at the grouchy look she gives me. "I have to go. He's still asleep. I moved the monitor to your side."

"K."

"Have a good day."

"K."

She's so cute when she's grumpy. Hell, she's cute all the time.

I kiss her cheek again and head downstairs for coffee. I hate feeling like I did in the early days after I lost Sadie and then her mother a short time after. Through the Wild Widows, I've heard about the concept of "anticipatory grief," such as what occurs when you know someone is going to die and you start grieving them before they're gone. That's what this feels like, and it's totally screwed up. Wynter is fine. She's young and strong and healthy as can be. But so was Sadie.

On the way to work, I call Mick and tell him I have a

doctor's appointment at three and ask if it's okay with him if I take a couple of personal hours.

"No problem, man. Do what you've gotta do."

"Thanks, Mick. I appreciate it."

"I appreciate you. Even with everything you've got going on, you're my best agent."

"I am? Really?"

"Hell yes. You're the only one who gets everything done on time, and the customers love you."

"I had no idea."

"Well, now you know, so you can quit thinking I'm keeping you around out of pity."

That makes me laugh. "Never crossed my mind."

"Sure, it didn't. Did you eat breakfast?"

"Not yet."

"I'll grab you something."

"Thank you. You're the best."

"Right back atcha."

Wow. I'm his top agent. I honestly had no clue. There was a time when that sort of thing would've mattered greatly to me, especially with how hard I worked to get through college. It just goes to show how much things have changed since Sadie died and Xavier became the most important thing in my life. Now there's Wynter, too, and another baby that could be part of my life as well.

I have no idea how I'm supposed to feel about any of this.

Work is busy, which helps the day to go by quickly. I arrive at Candace's office ten minutes before three and wait for her in a room that brings back memories of the darkest time in my life. I've come so far from there and done the hard work on myself. The possibility of a backslide is too much to bear.

Candace, who's about ten years older than me, opens the door with a friendly, welcoming smile. "It's good to see you, Adrian."

"You as well."

"I saw Nia at Giant a few weeks ago. She said you're doing well, and that Xavier just turned one. Time flies, doesn't it?"

"Sure does. I can't believe he's one and that Sadie's been gone more than a year."

"Nia said you're slaying single fatherhood."

"I don't know about that."

"I believe her." She crosses her legs, balancing a pad on her knee. "What brings you in today?"

"Did Nia mention I've been seeing someone?"

"She didn't, but I'm happy for you. What's her name?"

"Wynter. We met through our widow group. She's a very young widow at twenty-one, but an old soul, if you know what I mean."

"I do. What happened to her husband?"

"He died of bone cancer a few days after they got married in the hospital. They'd been together for years."

"That's so sad. I'm sorry for her loss."

"She's an amazing person. Funny, smart, caring. She takes care of Xavier for me when I'm at work."

"Ah, so that's complicated."

"You'd think so, but it's been great. We were friends for months before it became anything more."

"Are you in love with her?"

"Very much so, and vice versa. She's so, so good with Xavier. She's crazy about him."

"That's wonderful, Adrian. I'm glad you both have her and that you found each other through your widow group."

"It's been really nice to feel good again, you know?"

"I can only imagine. Are you feeling guilty about being with Wynter?"

"I did at first, a little, but not so much anymore. I have to hope that Sadie would want me to be happy, even if she'd claw Wynter's eyes out if she was here."

Candace laughs. "She'd want you to be happy for sure. Why aren't you?"

I take a deep breath and release it. This is so hard. "A while ago, Wynter found out that her husband banked sperm before his treatment. He didn't tell anyone at the time he did it, but his mother told Wynter about it, and now she's all fired up to have his baby. In fact, she found out last night she's pregnant."

"I see. It's a lot to take on, the parenting of someone else's child."

"That's not it at all. I have no doubt I could and would love Wynter's child because I love her. It's the fear of losing her the way I lost Sadie."

"Oh, Adrian... Oh my goodness."

"And before you say it, I know that was a very rare complication, but it was one of so many things that can happen. People think childbirth is no big deal when it's a huge deal from a medical standpoint."

"It is. You're right. But the complications are rare."

"I know they are. Intellectually, I get that the odds are very much in her favor. But every time I closed my eyes last night, I saw Wynter looking like Sadie did after, lifeless..." I shake my head. "It's horrifying to think about what could happen to her."

She puts her pad and pen aside and leans forward, arms braced on her knees. "There're a million things that could happen to the people we love at any given time."

I think about the day Wynter and Xavier were missing and know she's right. "Nia said the same thing."

"What happened to Sadie was a terrible tragedy, but it was a rare complication of childbirth. There's no reason to believe that Wynter's pregnancy and delivery will be anything other than perfectly routine."

"That's what they said to Sadie. She was young and healthy and strong. And then she was dead."

"I want you to know that your fears are entirely valid."

"Even if they're ridiculous?"

"They're not ridiculous. You feel the way you feel and with good reason. The way I see it, you have several choices. One, you could consider anxiety medication to help manage your fears so you can support Wynter the way you want to during her pregnancy and delivery. Two, you can decide that it's too much for you after what you've already endured, and you can end things with her."

"I'll still love her, even if I'm not with her."

"Would you worry about her even if you're not together?"

"Yeah."

"Would it be easier to worry about her if you were together or apart?"

"It won't be easy either way, but the thought of being without her is heartbreaking. That's the problem."

"I think you'd be an excellent candidate for some low-dose anxiety meds."

"Would they help me to stop living in a place of utter doom?"

"That would be the goal."

"Then I guess I'll give them a try."

"I really think it'll help. I'll send a message to your primary care doctor with my recommendation."

"Thank you so much, Candace."

"I really hope it helps. You deserve every happiness, Adrian, and from what you've told me, your Wynter does, too."

"She does. That's all I want for her."

"Then let's try to make that happen. I want you to keep seeing me weekly as you get closer to her due date so you're as ready as you can be to support her through this."

"Sounds good."

I drive home feeling much better than I did before I saw

Candace. I appreciate that she didn't make me feel like I was being ridiculous for worrying about Wynter having a baby, even if I wouldn't have blamed her—or anyone—who did think that. It's crazy to project what happened to Sadie onto Wynter, and I know that. But that doesn't stop me from worrying about it. Wynter will be seven years younger than Sadie was having Xavier. Even that's an advantage, from what I've heard.

I'm stopped at a light when I get a message from my pharmacy that a prescription is ready for pickup.

Wow.

For all its many failings, modern medicine can also be quite miraculous, especially when the therapist and PCP work for the same company.

I take a left turn at the light to run through the drive-through at the pharmacy to pick up the prescription.

When I come into the kitchen from the garage, Xavier is in his high chair, and Wynter is standing at the sink doing dishes.

"Hi, honey, I'm home," I say, kissing the side of her neck where she's super ticklish.

She laughs as she shivers. "What've you got there?" she asks, using her chin to point to the bag I put on the counter.

"Anxiety meds."

"Really?"

"Yep."

"Do I need to ask what brought this on?"

"Probably not. I want to support you the way you deserve without projecting my fears onto you. I want to feel excited about your baby and not dread his or her arrival. I want to be there for both of you the way you've been there for me and Xavier. I saw my therapist, Candace, who was so great after Sadie and Alyssa died, and she suggested meds. Wait... Why are you crying?"

"Because you did that for me."

"I did it for both of us. I can't live in this purgatory of hellish fear for thirty-eight weeks and still go with you to birthing classes and hold your hand in the delivery room and be your coach. I had to do something."

She hugs me tightly. "I love you so much for this, for facing your fears head on so you can be part of this with me."

"I want to be part of everything with you."

Xavier starts howling from the high chair.

"He wants in on this." I kiss her forehead and go to get him. "How's my favorite boy?"

"Dada!"

I hug him and kiss him and bring him with me when I return to Wynter.

"Wyn! Dada!"

We're laughing and crying and hugging and loving. There's so much love, and there's much more to come.

"Thank you, Adrian. Thank you so much for understanding how important this is to me and for doing what needed to be done to support me. It means so much to me."

"You mean so much to me. You'd better not let anything happen to your perfect self. You hear me?"

She rests her head on my chest as Xavier tugs at her hair. "I hear you."

Epilogue

Nine months later

Wynter

L abor is a bitch. I mean, I knew it would hurt, but not like this. Not like someone is slicing my insides wide open with a machete.

Adrian has been a trouper. He hasn't left my side since my water broke at two o'clock this morning. Twelve hours later, I'm still not ready to push this invader out of me. I don't know what I'm having. I wanted to be surprised. Eileen is losing her mind waiting to hear what it'll be. She's in the waiting room with Jaden's dad, his sisters, my mom and step-father and the Wild Widows.

Everyone came when they heard I was in labor.

I heard the widows brought enough food to feed every person on the floor—patient and staff. That doesn't do me much good because they won't let me eat in case I need a C-section. I'm hangry and hurting and sweating, and this whole thing sucks.

This baby had better be freaking worth it.

If Xavier is any indication, the baby will be well worth it, but first, I've got to survive the birth. It's way worse than expected.

"I want the epidural," I tell Adrian.

He's been a mess all day, but he's held up well, just like he has throughout my entire pregnancy.

"I'll let them know."

"Tell Iris I need her, too."

"I'll get her."

Iris comes in a few minutes later and steps right up to my bedside, taking my hand in hers.

I feel immediately better having her there.

"I'm scared that it's taking so long."

"That's normal. Sophia took thirty-six hours!"

"Don't tell me that."

She laughs. "I'm sure it won't be that long."

"Every second this goes on takes five years off Adrian's life. I gotta do something to move things along."

My nurse, Maisie, comes into the room. "How's it going in here?"

"I need to talk to you."

"What's up?"

"My partner, Adrian... His wife died in childbirth. This is extra stressful for him. Is there anything we can do to move things along that would be safe for the baby?"

"I'm so sorry to hear that about Adrian's wife. That's so sad."

"Yes, it is."

"I was coming in to tell you that Dr. Bauer has prescribed Pitocin to get this party started. I also heard you're asking for the epidural."

"I was going to try to do it without, but I can't."

"We've alerted the anesthesia department, and they'll send

someone. After you have the epidural on board, we'll administer the Pitocin. Hopefully, it'll be quick after that."

"Great," I say with a deep exhale that's immediately interrupted by a sharp, stabbing labor pain. "Mother*fucker*."

Iris, that bitch, laughs. "Breathe."

"Fuck that shit! Doesn't do anything to help."

"I know, but it's something to do while you're being sawed in half."

"You could've told me it was like this," I say through gritted teeth.

"Why would I do that? You were freaked out enough about the medical stuff, which, I must say, you're totally acing."

"Whatever."

The anesthesiologist shows up to give me a shot in the back that would've sent me into a panic at any other time. That's the least of my concerns. The relief is immediate.

"Wow."

"Yep," Iris says. "It's lifesaving."

Next comes the nurse with the Pitocin, and true to her word, things start happening very quickly after that.

With Adrian on one side and Iris on the other, I push a baby girl into the world at just after five o'clock that afternoon. And she is, without a doubt, the most beautiful thing I have ever seen.

Hours later, the room is flooded with people—grandparents, aunts, friends. But all I see is her—and Jaden. She looks just like him, right down to the little dimple on the right side of her mouth. She has wispy blond hair and big eyes that remind me of his.

"My Lord," Eileen says through profuse tears, "she's him all over again."

"I know. It's amazing."

"This is the best gift that anyone has ever given us, Wynter. Thank you so much for her."

"Thank you so much for *him*."

She leans over the bed to hug me as we shed tears full of joy and grief and love. There's so much love.

"I can't wait to shop for baby girl clothes," Eileen says with a giddy squeal.

We share a laugh before she steps aside to let my mom have a turn.

She's elated and stunned to suddenly be a grandmother. "Nine months wasn't enough time to prepare for such a thing," she says.

I've been calling her Granny from the day I first told her the baby was on the way. "You had plenty of time to prepare."

"Nothing can prepare you for how much you'll love them," she says softly as the baby wraps her little hand around her finger. "I love her name."

"I do, too. Willow Jaden Hartley." I can't stop saying it. My daughter's name is Willow Jaden Hartley.

"She's beautiful like her mother. Welcome to the world, sweet Willow."

Iris takes pictures of everyone with me and the baby. The other Wild Widows come in to say a quick hello before they leave us to get acquainted with the baby. They threw the most epic shower in the history of baby showers for me, and thanks to them, Eileen and my mom, we have everything we could ever need and more.

A short time later, the night nurse comes in with the lactation specialist. They ask everyone to clear out to give the new mom and baby a chance to bond.

"We'll check in tomorrow," Eileen says as she leaves me and Willow with kisses.

Me and Willow.

I have a daughter named Willow.

"Is it okay if I stay?" Adrian asks me after the others have left.

"As long as Xavier is okay with Nia."

"He's doing great. She said to do whatever I need to. She's got him."

"Then I would love for you to stay."

The lactation expert goes over the basics of breastfeeding, and my girl and I get to work. It's the weirdest feeling at first, having her tug at my nipple, but she latches right on.

"She's a natural," the lady says.

The area between my legs is on fire with pain, but what do I care about that when I have a baby to feed and care for?

"Looks like you girls have got this." The lady puts a business card on the table. "Contact me at any time if you have any questions. Congratulations on your new daughter."

"Thank you."

Adrian lowers the light over the bed. "Is that better?"

"Yes, thank you. You know what would be even better?"

"What's that?"

"If you were up here with us."

"Is there room?"

"We'll make room."

I move carefully to the far side of the bed, grimacing from the pain of even the simplest movement. I hear that only lasts a few days. I hope that's true because I've got important stuff to do.

Adrian gets on the bed slowly. "Is this okay?"

"You can come closer."

He turns on his side to face me and puts an arm around me, under the baby. "Good?"

"Perfect."

"Yes, she certainly is."

I realize he has tears in his eyes.

"Are you okay?"

"I'm great. You were amazing. I'm so proud of you."

"I'm proud of *you*. Through it all, you never wavered." The anxiety meds had the almost-immediate effect of taking the sharp edges off his fear.

"You needed me. I stayed focused on that." He runs a gentle hand over Willow's little arm, which has broken free of the receiving blanket. "When Xavier was born, I never got to have what we did tonight with the family and friends here to welcome him. It was just a total catastrophe. I'm thankful to have new memories to associate with Willow's first day."

"I'm glad you have that, too."

When she has fed on both sides, I look to him. "Would you like to hold her?"

"I'd love to."

I transfer her into his arms and then curl painfully onto my side, so I won't miss a thing.

"Hi there, sweet Willow. I'm Adrian, and I already love you so much."

"She and I would very much like for you to be her daddy. If you're willing, that is."

He blinks back tears. "That would be the greatest honor of my life, next to being Xavier's daddy. But it would only be fair if you're his mommy."

"I feel like I already am."

"You are, and he loves you so much."

"I love him, too." As I watch the man I love hold the child I had with the other man I loved, my heart is full to overflowing. "Only in widow-ville would this make sense, right?"

"Yeah," he says with a laugh. "That's true."

"For two people who've experienced far too much of the worst life has to offer, we're actually pretty lucky, huh?" Not that everything between us has been smooth sailing. We've experienced the blatant racism his sister predicted might happen when we were first together, but we tell ourselves that other people's opinions aren't our business. Fortunately, it doesn't happen often. We also still experience frequent bouts of grief over Sadie and Jaden, but having the support of a partner who gets it makes even the worst days better than they would be otherwise.

"We sure are."

"Thank you for being here today, even though I know it was so hard for you."

"There is nowhere else I'd rather be than wherever you are."

"Even in a hospital birthing suite?"

"Well, that's probably in last place on my list of where I'd like to be with you, but our little Willow... She's worth all the worrying, isn't she?"

"Yes, she sure is."

There was a time, not that long ago, when I thought my life had ended when Jaden's did. I've since found out there's still so much more to do and experience, so much love to give and receive. I'm thankful for the people who propped me up in those early days of unbearable grief, who showed me a way through the pain to the light at the other end of a dark tunnel. They made it possible for me to have what I do now, and I'll be forever thankful to them, and I know Adrian feels the same way.

Sadie and Jaden will always be with us as we move forward together with the children they blessed us with and any we might have of our own.

I finally give in to utter exhaustion, knowing my little girl is safe with her daddy. I can't wait to watch our babies grow up together.

Meanwhile...

Lexi

I TELL myself to quit looking forward to dinner with Tom. He's just being nice to his widowed roommate by making me the most amazing meals every night and serving them with wine and candles and what can only be called romance.

Before I moved in, I wasn't completely sure if he was just doing me a favor or if he liked me that way.

Now I know, and I'm not sure what to make of it.

I like him, too. Of course I do. He's so nice and sweet and thoughtful and sexy. He's all the things. But he's also my roommate, which makes it sort of awkward. Moving out of my parents' house has been the best thing I've done for myself since my husband died.

I can't mess up this arrangement, no matter how much I'm enjoying being wined and dined by him for months.

I arrive at home after visiting Wynter and baby Willow, determined to tell him I can't do dinner because I have a meeting to attend that'll keep me from joining him for dinner. I use the device he gave me to open one of the four garage doors, where I park my car next to Tom's white Ford F-150.

I climb the stairs from the garage to the main floor and open the door, expecting to smell something mouthwatering like I do every other night.

But the house is eerily silent.

He cooks with classic rock on blast, usually Led Zeppelin, Aerosmith or AC/DC, among others.

I go up the next flight of stairs to the living area and flip on a light, gasping when I see Tom lying on the floor.

Oh my God. He looks dead.

"Tom!"

I drop everything and run to him and somehow find the wherewithal to check for a pulse in his neck. It's faint but present, thankfully. I find my phone and call 911, tripping and stumbling over the address as I tell them to please hurry.

"Tom." I give him a gentle shake that does nothing to rouse him. "It's Lexi. I'm here. Just hang on. Help is coming."

It's so quiet and cold and wrong in this house where I've found nothing but warmth and welcome.

"Please," I whisper as I lean over him. "Please don't do this to me."

Watch for Lexi's Wild Widows story, *Someone to Watch Over Me*, coming soon!

Acknowledgments

Thank you so much for reading Wynter and Adrian's story! I hope you enjoyed it as much as I loved writing it. These Wild Widows are some of my favorite characters ever, and I look forward to spending time with them again soon. Join the Someone to Love Reader Group at *www.facebook.com/groups/someonetolove3/* to discuss Wynter and Adrian's story. Also join the Wild Widows Series group at *www.facebook.com/groups/thewildwidowsseries* and the Wild Widows Grief Support Group at *www.facebook.com/groups/wwsupportgroup1*.

A special thank you to Renita McKinney, who provided a sensitivity read to help me with Adrian's story and the challenges of an interracial relationship. I very much appreciate her input.

My niece, Mary Gish, a banking professional, helped me with the details of Wynter trying to deposit a high-dollar check and how that transaction would unfold. I loved working on that scene with Mary!

Thank you to Dr. Sarah Hewitt, family nurse practitioner, for always checking the medical facts.

Thank you to my primary beta readers, Anne Woodall, Kara Conrad and Tracey Suppo as well as my continuity editor, Gwen Neff, who makes sure the storyline matches up from one book to the next. And to the Wild Widows Series beta readers, Jennifer, Juliane, Marianne, Karina, Mona, Amy and Gina, thank you so much for your input.

To my editors, Linda Ingmanson and Joyce Lamb, I appreciate you making time for me whenever I need you.

My home team of Julie Cupp, Lisa Cafferty, Jean Mello, Nikki Haley and Ashley Lopez keep the wheels on the bus going round and round while I write. I love them all and appreciate them more than I could ever say.

Finally, thank you to the readers who embrace every new book and make this the most fun "job" I could ever have. I appreciate you all more than you know.

Xoxo

Marie

Also by Marie Force

Contemporary Romances Available from Marie Force

The Wild Widows Series—a Fatal Series Spin-Off

Book 1: Someone Like You

Book 2: Someone to Hold

Book 3: Someone to Love

Book 4: Someone to Watch Over Me (coming 2024)

The Miami Nights Series

Book 1: How Much I Feel *(Carmen & Jason)*

Book 2: How Much I Care *(Maria & Austin)*

Book 3: How Much I Love *(Dee's story)*

Nochebuena, A Miami Nights Novella

Book 4: How Much I Want *(Nico & Sofia)*

Book 5: How Much I Need *(Milo and Gianna)*

The Gansett Island Series

Book 1: Maid for Love *(Mac & Maddie)*

Book 2: Fool for Love *(Joe & Janey)*

Book 3: Ready for Love *(Luke & Sydney)*

Book 4: Falling for Love *(Grant & Stephanie)*

Book 5: Hoping for Love *(Evan & Grace)*

Book 6: Season for Love *(Owen & Laura)*

Book 7: Longing for Love *(Blaine & Tiffany)*

Book 3: I Saw Her Standing There *(Colton & Lucy)*

Book 4: And I Love Her *(Hunter & Megan)*

Novella: You'll Be Mine *(Will & Cam's Wedding)*

Book 5: It's Only Love *(Gavin & Ella)*

Book 6: Ain't She Sweet *(Tyler & Charlotte)*

The Butler, Vermont Series

(Continuation of Green Mountain)

Book 1: Every Little Thing *(Grayson & Emma)*

Book 2: Can't Buy Me Love *(Mary & Patrick)*

Book 3: Here Comes the Sun (*Wade & Mia*)

Book 4: Till There Was You *(Lucas & Dani)*

Book 5: All My Loving *(Landon & Amanda)*

Book 6: Let It Be *(Lincoln & Molly)*

Book 7: Come Together *(Noah & Brianna)*

Book 8: Here, There & Everywhere *(Izzy & Cabot)*

Book 9: The Long and Winding Road *(Max & Lexi)*

The Quantum Series

Book 1: Virtuous *(Flynn & Natalie)*

Book 2: Valorous *(Flynn & Natalie)*

Book 3: Victorious *(Flynn & Natalie)*

Book 4: Rapturous *(Addie & Hayden)*

Book 5: Ravenous *(Jasper & Ellie)*

Book 6: Delirious *(Kristian & Aileen)*

Book 7: Outrageous *(Emmett & Leah)*

Book 8: Famous *(Marlowe & Sebastian)*

The Treading Water Series

Book 1: Treading Water

Book 2: Marking Time

Book 3: Starting Over

Book 4: Coming Home

Book 5: Finding Forever

Single Titles

Five Years Gone

One Year Home

Sex Machine

Sex God

Georgia on My Mind

True North

The Fall

The Wreck

Love at First Flight

Everyone Loves a Hero

Line of Scrimmage

Romantic Suspense Novels Available from Marie Force

The Fatal Series

One Night With You, *A Fatal Series Prequel Novella*

Book 1: Fatal Affair

Book 2: Fatal Justice

Book 3: Fatal Consequences

Book 3.5: Fatal Destiny, *the Wedding Novella*

Book 4: Fatal Flaw

Book 5: Fatal Deception

Book 6: Fatal Mistake

Book 7: Fatal Jeopardy

Book 8: Fatal Scandal

Book 9: Fatal Frenzy

Book 10: Fatal Identity

Book 11: Fatal Threat

Book 12: Fatal Chaos

Book 13: Fatal Invasion

Book 14: Fatal Reckoning

Book 15: Fatal Accusation

Book 16: Fatal Fraud

Sam and Nick's Story Continues....

Book 1: State of Affairs

Book 2: State of Grace

Book 3: State of the Union

Book 4: State of Shock

Book 6: State of Bliss (Dec. 2023)

Book 7: State of Suspense (Coming 2024)

Historical Romance Available from Marie Force

The Gilded Series

Book 1: Duchess by Deception

Book 2: Deceived by Desire

About the Author

Marie Force is the #1 *Wall Street Journal* bestselling author of more than 100 contemporary romance, romantic suspense and erotic romance novels. Her series include Fatal, First Family, Gansett Island, Butler Vermont, Quantum,  Treading Water, Miami Nights and Wild Widows.

Her books have sold more than 13 million copies world-wide, have been translated into more than a dozen languages and have appeared on the *New York Times* bestseller list more than 30 times. She is also a *USA Today* bestseller, as well as a Spiegel bestseller in Germany.

Her goals in life are simple—to spend as much time as she can with her "kids" who are now adults, to keep writing books for as long as she possibly can and to never be on a flight that makes the news.

Join Marie's mailing list on her website at *marieforce.com* for news about new books and upcoming appearances in your area. Follow her on Facebook at *www.Facebook.com/Marie-ForceAuthor*, Instagram at *www.instagram.com/marieforceauthor/* and TikTok at *https://www.tiktok.com/@marieforceauthor?*. Contact Marie at *marie@marieforce.com*.